The intruder [...] with a black [...] he saw Hellboy barreling toward him, he [...] man like she weighed nothing and tossed her right at the cloven-hoofed BPRD operative.

Hellboy tried to be gentle, cupping Liz's body against his own to cushion the impact as he caught her and fell backward. He laid her down gently, touching her neck, searching for a pulse. She gasped for breath, the pale skin of her throat already starting to bruise.

"Pal, you better hope your health insurance is all paid up," Hellboy snarled as he rose and spun toward the intruder.

Liz's assailant was no longer alone. There were six of them now, all dressed in the same long coats and hats, standing perfectly still as they watched Hellboy advance.

"You have friends," Hellboy growled, flexing the stone-like fingers of his right hand. "Good for you."

As if responding to some cue, four of them slipped off their coats and tugged off their hats, moving in unison. Hellboy froze where he was, staring at them, trying to figure out what the hell he was seeing.

"What the . . . ?" he managed.

They'd definitely been human once, three men and a woman. But they were long past their expiration date, the stink of death and rot coming off them in waves. They were each encased in some kind of crude exoskeleton constructed from wood and metal.

"It was a near-perfect day up till now. But zombie cyborgs . . ." Hellboy sighed. "I'm not sure I deserve this much fun."

Other HELLBOY titles available from Pocket Books

THE GOD MACHINE

THOMAS E. SNIEGOSKI

POCKET **STAR** BOOKS

New York   London   Toronto   Sydney

An *Original* Publication of POCKET BOOKS

A Pocket Star Book published by
POCKET BOOKS, a division of Simon & Schuster, Inc.
1230 Avenue of the Americas, New York, NY 10020

This book is a work of fiction. Names, characters, places and incidents are products of the author's imagination or are used fictiously. Any resemblance to actual events or locales or persons, living or dead, is entirely coincidental.

ISBN-13: 978-1-4165-0784-0
ISBN-10:   1-4165-0784-1

This Pocket Books paperback edition August 2006

10 9 8 7 6 5 4 3 2 1

POCKET STAR BOOKS and colophon are registered trademarks of Simon & Schuster, Inc.

Cover art by Mike Mignola

Manufactured in the United States of America

For information regarding special discounts for bulk purchases, please contact Simon & Schuster Special Sales at 1-800-456-6798 or business@simonandschuster.com.

For Jack Kirby . . . The King.

ACKNOWLEDGMENTS

As always, this book couldn't have been written without the support of my loving and beautiful wife, LeeAnne, and the unwavering loyalty of Mulder the Wonder Dog.

A very special thanks to Mike Mignola for allowing me to play with his awesome toys, and to Chris Golden for helping me to get it just right.

Thanks also to Jen Heddle, Dave Kraus, Greg Skopis, Don Kramer, Dave Carroll, Liesa Abrams, Mom and Dad Sniegoski, Mom and Dad Fogg, Eric Powell, Jon and Flo, Bob and Pat, Ken Curtis and Timothy Cole and his Graken Spriggin down at Cole's Comics.

Farewell and adieu.

PROLOGUE

Lynn, Massachusetts, July 1891

Ten-year-old Absolom was frightened, afraid that he wouldn't have enough time. But the boy stubbornly pushed his fear aside, repositioned himself upon the stool and continued to work. Time was running out.

He'd realized how close it would be the other day when he'd heard her coughing in the early hours of the morning. Coughing so furiously that it drew him from the protection of his bed and down the hall, where he'd found himself standing in the doorway of his parents' room. His mother had been sitting at the edge of the bed, his father close beside her, gently rubbing her back. She was coughing into one of her pretty lace handkerchiefs—but it wasn't pretty anymore. It was stained a deep red. Even in the early-morning gloom Absolom could see the color, bright as the beacon of a lighthouse.

Blood.

His gasp had been loud enough to catch his father's attention. There were tears on the man's face, and he became enraged, angry that his son had seen his weakness.

"Go to your room!" he had bellowed over the sounds of his wife's continued plight, and then he'd slammed the door closed in Absolom's face.

It was then that Absolom knew he had to do something—but what?

He waved away a fly that hovered above his work, remembering how he had wracked his brain that morning as he returned to his room—what could he do?

The voices of the dead had been especially loud that morning.

Boy, where am I?

Where's my baby? He was with me but a moment ago—help me find my child.

Normally Absolom would have listened to them, as he had most of his young life, but that morning had been different. He had tried to close them out. But there remained one voice—a single voice far off in the distance—that he couldn't ignore, for it claimed to have the answer to his question.

"Do you know how to make my momma well?" he had finally asked, sitting on the floor of his bedroom.

And he'd waited, holding his breath, for an answer from beyond.

Now Absolom wiped a trickle of sweat from his brow before it could rain down upon his work. Time was running out; he could practically hear it ticking away. His mother had gotten sicker—weaker in the few days since he'd first heard that faraway voice.

It had told him to open his mind. And though he was afraid, Absolom had done just that. How could he not? His mother was dying.

The voice had filled his mind with a wondrous idea, and now he was racing against time to use that strange knowledge to save his mother.

Last night at supper his father had mentioned taking her into Boston, to see a doctor familiar with her condition. But Absolom knew that he was just going through the motions. The pain of loss was already etched deeply upon his father's face. There was nothing more a doctor could do for her, there was no one who could save her.

Except him.

If this works, there is a way, he thought, eyes focused upon his work, staring into the opened chest of a dead bird splayed upon the wooden worktable.

He'd killed the sparrow by drowning it, the most painless and least damaging manner of death he could conceive. Then he had taken it back to his secret place—a fort that he had built with his own two hands—and began his work in earnest.

Using his mother's sewing needles, he had pinned its wings back on a makeshift table—a plank atop an old wooden barrel that had once contained salt. Very carefully, he cut open its chest, and slowly, systematically, began replacing the small organs with the mechanics he had found inside his father's prized pocket watch. If the bird came to life when he was finished, he knew that he could fashion larger parts to replace the ones that had gone bad inside his mother.

It had to work.

He'd asked the voice for guidance as he attempted to utilize the strange information that rattled around inside his head, but the voice had been oddly silent, leaving him to his own devices.

Absolom's eyes burned as he carefully placed the tiny metal wheel inside the sparrow's gaping chest cavity. He had slept not a wink since the evening before, sneaking out to his fort soon after supper. Though he worked by lanternlight, the first rays of the morning sun began to peek through the slats of the fort, providing him with additional illumination for his chores.

Again he thought of the time and how quickly it was slipping away.

He placed the last of the springs and miniscule cogs inside the body of the bird, just as he'd seen in the diagram in his head. But there was something missing. He could see it there, in his mind's eye, but he didn't know what it was or where he could find it.

Fingers stained with the blood of the tiny animal went to his mouth as he began to panic. They tasted of copper, but it barely registered.

"Please," he whispered to the pockets of shadow in the fort, his voice trembling. "Help me to succeed in this, and I promise shall serve you all the rest of my days."

The deafening silence continued, and he clasped his hands together, begging to be heard.

Then Absolom felt something move inside his mind, emerging like a tadpole from beneath the mud, and he was filled with a sense of power that he could not begin to understand—or survive. At that moment he knew he would die—that this strange power from somewhere beyond the realm of his understanding would fill him up so that he would be destroyed.

And just as suddenly it was gone, leaving him alone, his body tingling with but a reminder of what had just occurred, and the voice echoing inside his mind as it receded further and further away.

It is not yet time.

Absolom was filled with a nearly overpowering sense of loss. He had been close—so very close. The presence had been about to share the secret that would have helped him save his mother, and it had pulled away because he was not strong enough to know.

"Please!" he screamed aloud. "I have to know!"

Time was slipping; he could feel it with every beat of his frantic heart, and every frenzied gulp of breath.

Absolom looked down at what he had done—knowing how close he'd come and realizing he was still so far away.

No, it can't be, he thought frantically, sitting back down upon his stool, determined to finish what he had started. He used a needle and thread to connect the parts inside the sparrow, and then to close up the bird's chest. Completing the last stitch, he bent over the body of the bird to break the thread with his teeth, and he caught the first whiff of it, the smell of death—of decay.

Will Mother smell like this? he wondered.

Then his guard fell, and the spirits of the dead surged forward, all clamoring to be heard. Still, he refused to listen.

He removed the needles that secured the sparrow's wings to his worktable, noticing that its body had grown stiff. He gazed down at the tiny creature, wishing it back to life.

The dead continued their cries, but Absolom remained firm, all his attention upon the body of the bird resting in his hands.

"Absolom!" called a voice that he mistakenly confused with that of the dead. The door to his shelter swung open to reveal the silhouette of his father.

The boy tossed the dead bird into the air, willing it to live—willing it to fly. But it fell to the floor at his feet, the tiny mechanics spilling through the torn stitching in its chest.

"She's gone, boy," he heard his father say, the whisperings of the dead around him confirming the mournful message. "Your mother's passed in the night."

So close, the boy thought, the scalding tears of loss beginning to fill his eyes as he stared down at his failure. It was not yet time; the voice had told him so.

But soon.

Soon.

Two Months Ago. October, 1995

Things were looking up for Stan Thomas.

The tall, gangly man took in a deep lungful of sharp November air and surveyed what he hoped would soon be his home. He smiled faintly to himself, a king surveying his fabulous kingdom.

According to the real estate agent, Elijah Attwater, the dilapidated farmhouse had stood unoccupied for nearly fifty years. The elderly agent's father had supposedly purchased the property from the city of Lynn, Massachusetts, in the early 1900s, but for some reason could never find anyone other than an occasional renter who was willing to make the house a home.

Christ, somebody even tried to burn the place down ten years ago, Stan remembered Elijah saying. There were still scorch marks visible on the side of the foundation.

The house stood at the end of an unpaved dirt road that bordered the Lynn Woods Reservation. This was the third time Stan had brought his family here. The idea of buying the old place, with all its blemishes, filled his belly with a bizarre mixture of giddy excitement and overpowering dread. He wasn't fooling himself; he knew there had to be a reason why the house had never sold, but he hoped that his skills as a jack-of-all-trades would be enough to tackle the inevitable problems.

Stanley glanced at Bethany and wondered if she was feeling the same kind of trepidation. He thought he saw tears in his wife's eyes and abruptly his uncertainty was suffocated beneath the weight of his devotion to this woman who had stuck by him through thick and thin. Stan had been through serious depression, a layoff from his job, and financial ruin, and now he and Bethany were rebuilding their lives.

She had loved this place from the start, but she deserved so much more. He vowed to himself that this ramshackle farmhouse would be just the start of the perfect life he would make for her.

"I don't even have to ask what you think," he said, as Bethany gazed at the property. They'd looked at other places in nearby Saugus and Salem, but nothing had spoken to them like this run-down farmhouse with the sagging roof.

"It's going to be one headache after another, but—"

He pulled her closer, and she laid her head on his shoulder.

"It's so beautiful, Stan," she continued, and reached

up to wipe the moisture from the corners of her eyes before it could run down her ruddy cheeks.

Their seven-year-old daughter, Rebecca, came skipping around the side of the house. She bent down and picked up a stick, waving it in the air like a magic wand.

"Yeah, it is that," Stan agreed. "And it's going to be ours—if that's okay with you."

Bethany stared up at him, a momentary look of confusion on her face. "Do you mean . . . are you serious?"

He nodded, and she squealed in excitement, jumping up and throwing her arms and legs around him, holding on tight as she planted sloppy kisses all over his face.

"I love you," Bethany said, between frantic kisses and ecstatic laughter. "Love. Love. Love you. I really, really do."

He held her close, basking in her adulation, and made a silent promise that he would never again give her a reason not to love him. Then he kissed her passionately.

"Ewww, there they go again," he heard his daughter moan, and they both began to laugh, ending the kiss before things got out of hand.

Bethany made a move to tickle Rebecca, and the child squealed in mock terror, dropping her stick and running in the same direction her older brother had headed a few minutes earlier with the family dog.

"Be careful," Bethany called after her. "Find your brother. We have some really cool news for you guys."

Bethany returned to her husband's side, slipping her hand into the back pocket of his jeans. "I can't believe it," she cooed. "We're actually going to buy a house."

"Let's not get ahead of ourselves here," Stan replied, good-naturedly checking his hip into hers. "First our offer has to be accepted."

She threw her arms around him again. "It'll be accepted." She squeezed him tightly. "This is our dream house; we *have* to live here."

Stan glanced at the house, with its listing front porch and peeling red paint. "Yeah," he agreed, imagining the future—their future. "Yeah, I think you just might be right."

Bethany squealed again, jumping up and down, unable to contain her excitement, and planted another wet kiss on his cheek. Stan couldn't help but laugh.

He had discussed the price of the place with Attwater after their first visit and thought it was reasonable, but now after visits two and three, he was beginning to think it might be time for a little game of let's make a deal. The more he looked at the place, the more work he saw that needed to be done, and the more supplies he'd need to buy. Stanley Thomas saw lots of overtime in his future, and was glad that his new job for Costa Construction allowed him the option. *More work than hours in the day,* his foreman Greg Skopis always said, and amen to that.

"First thing we have to do . . ."

"After we make an offer and it's accepted and the house belongs to us free and clear, you mean," Bethany said, and started to laugh.

"Touché," he responded, bending down to kiss the top of her head. "After all that, the first thing we have to do is slap a new roof on the place before winter hits full force."

She agreed, pointing out specific areas where the ancient tar shingles had peeled and lifted and where the roof seemed to sag in on itself.

Their daughter's voice interrupted Bethany's observation, and the two of them turned to see Rebecca running toward them through the overgrowth that bordered the property.

"What is it, honey?" Bethany called, caution in her voice. Rebecca was often a drama queen, and her excited cries could be for something as simple as the fact that she'd found a quarter, or something worthy of genuine concern, like the time she'd needed twelve stitches in her palm.

"Jack said he found something really weird and wants you to come see!" the little girl bellowed, turning to head back the way she had come. "Follow me!"

Stan and Bethany followed close behind, keeping Rebecca in their sight. "Really weird, huh?" Stan said with a chuckle.

"Wonder what he's found this time," his wife said, as they continued down the winding path tromped down in the thick underbrush.

Even for November the weeds were pretty high. *Must look like a jungle at the height of summer,* Stan thought.

The three of them came to a clearing where it looked as though another structure had once stood, the remains of a stone foundation still visible, but little else. Stan remembered Attwater saying something about a barn.

Up ahead, Stan could see his son squatting in the square of the stone foundation with their dog, Sadie. The Labrador–German shepherd mix barked excitedly at the sight of them, bounding in their direction, then circling back to hover around his son. Whatever it was that Jack had found was interesting enough to hold not only the fascination of a ten-year-old, but also that of a dog.

"Probably some animal bones," he said to Bethany, who wrinkled her nose in distaste.

"Hey, Jack," Stan called out. "What'd ya find?"

Jack looked up and waved. He was holding a gnarled tree branch, and had been poking at something in the dirt.

"Come here!" the boy cried. "Ya gotta see this." His sister had joined him, picking up her own stick, but it was snatched away by the easily excited Sadie.

"I hope it isn't anything gross," Bethany said as she

stepped carefully around the stones and debris that littered the ground.

The couple moved beside the children and Jack looked up from where he was probing with his stick. "It's not gross," he assured his mother, a twinkle in his young eyes. "Just kinda weird."

"Weird," Rebecca echoed in agreement. She had managed to pull the stick away from Sadie and was holding it high so the dog couldn't take it back from her.

"I was looking around at stuff, and these things just pushed right up out of the ground."

"I saw 'em too," Rebecca exclaimed, waving her stick in the air. Sadie sat at attention by her side, eyes on the stick, tail wagging.

Stan crouched down for a closer look and saw five cylindrical objects sticking up out of the earth. They seemed to be made of metal—copper by the looks of them. They reminded him of the old-fashioned batteries he had seen in some of the older houses he'd worked in, but he'd never seen any quite like these before.

He was suddenly filled with an overpowering dread—the kind of feeling that would strike him when the phone rang in the predawn hours and he would be certain, deep down in his gut, that somebody had died.

"What are they, Dad?" Jack asked, extending the stick to tap one of the copper objects.

"Don't, Jack," he barked, somehow knowing that they shouldn't . . . *upset them*. "I don't know what they are, but we should get away from here and . . ."

Bethany moved closer, and Stan wanted to grab the children and run away as fast as he could. But his rational brain overruled his increasingly irrational emotions.

"Look, Mommy," Rebecca said, pointing at the cylindrical objects. "They're like funny plants growing out of the dirt."

Funny plants.

Normally Stan would have laughed at his daughter's ridiculous observation, but he could find nothing humorous about their current situation. The intense sense of apprehension continued to grow.

"They *are* funny," Bethany said, moving even closer herself.

Stan reached out, grabbed her arm and yanked her back.

"Ow," she said, pulling her arm away indignantly. "What'd you do that for?"

"Sorry," he said, his eyes fixed upon the cylinders.

"Mr. Attwater said there was a barn here a long time ago, and that the people who lived in the house got killed when the people in town set the barn on fire," Jack piped up.

"That's terrible," Bethany said, still rubbing her arm. "Why did they do that?"

Jack shrugged. "Mr. Attwater said that the people

in the town didn't like what they were doing in the barn. They had machines and stuff."

"What were they doing, Jack?" Rebecca asked. "In the barn."

"He didn't say," the boy said, then extended his stick and gave one of the cylinders another poke.

"Jack!" Stan snapped, and everyone jumped. "Don't touch them," he ordered as he pulled his son away. But that was all he could say. He couldn't tell them *why* the objects filled him with such anxiety, why they made him so afraid, for he didn't know himself.

The air grew heavy with the acrid stench of ozone, like being outside after a heavy thunder and lightning storm.

"What's that?" Rebecca asked, her tiny fingers pinching her nose shut. "It stinks!"

The stink became stronger, and the air seemed to hum with an electrical charge. Stan could see that the others were feeling it now as well, looking around curiously for some kind of explanation.

Rebecca began to laugh uproariously. "Look at my hair," she cried, pulling off her hood to allow her hair to stand on end. "It's electric."

Stan could feel a tingle in his own scalp, and the hair on his arms stood up, the skin prickling.

"What's going on, Stan?" Bethany asked, reaching out to pull their giggling daughter closer.

He was about to tell them that they had to get out

of there right then, when Sadie began to bark wildly, her hackles rising as she crept toward the cylinders.

The objects were glowing, the terminals on the exposed ends sending snaking arcs of white, electrical current up into the air. The exposed portions of the cylinders pulsed with an eerie light.

"I'm afraid," Bethany whimpered, and Stan found himself stepping between the objects and his family, yelling at the dog in his sternest voice to come. But Sadie seemed to be picking up on the same vibes as he, sensing a danger to her pack.

What happened next unfolded in a kind of slow motion. With a guttural whine, Sadie lunged, snapping at the pulsing cylinders, the loose skin around her muzzle pulling back to reveal glistening pink gums and sharp teeth. And as the tip of her black nose made contact with one of the objects, there was a flash, and a sound like the cracking of a bullwhip.

Sadie cried out.

Stanley stared in horror as a bolt of blue electrical energy shot up from the cylinder and lanced through the dog's left eye. It exploded out of the side of her neck in a puff of oily smoke and arced down to connect with the copper terminals of the cylinder beside it. That was followed by another and then another until all five of the batteries—if that indeed was what they were—were linked by cords of the crackling discharge.

Stan screamed as the bolt of electricity ripped

through his dog's flesh, setting her fur on fire. He knew he had to protect his wife and children, to scoop them all up in his arms, and carry them to safety . . . but everything was happening so fast—*and yet so slowly*—that there was nothing he could do.

Except scream.

The conjoined cylinders lashed out at him with a single bolt of electrical force, a hissing cobra strike that pierced his chest, turning his insides to liquid fire before exiting through the fingertips of his left hand.

The lightning current shot into his wife and from her into Jack, and then from the boy into little Rebecca. They were linked together now in a strange kind of circuit—the dog, his family, and the objects that had pushed up from the ground.

Stan wondered if they were going to die.

A voice like an angel's spoke in his mind, reassuring him that his sacrifice, and that of his family, would not be in vain, that they would be instrumental in bringing about a new and glorious age to mankind.

A god is coming to the world, the voice inside his head whispered. *And this time, there will be nothing to prevent it.*

Stanley Thomas wasn't there anymore.

Certainly, if one were to observe the tall man, dressed as he almost always was in his Levi's and heavy leather jacket, suspicion would never be aroused that everything that defined the man as an individual—his loves, likes and dislikes—had been locked away.

Replaced with another's.

The man who was no longer Stanley Thomas stood trembling in the midafternoon New England cold and gazed down at hands not his own. They were strong hands, hands that were used to a hard day's work.

His vessel had been chosen wisely, for there was much that needed to be done.

How good it is to be seeing through actual eyes again, he thought looking about. The land upon which he stood appeared vaguely familiar, but so much had changed since last he stood here.

There was a sound from behind him and he turned slowly, an expression of rapturous joy blossoming upon his new face as he recalled that he was not alone in this.

He looked upon them, dressed in their new vestments of flesh, blood and bone, and though he did not recognize them—the woman, two children and a dog—he knew them all.

"Brothers and sisters," he said, pleased with the strength that he heard in his new voice.

"It is good to be back."

CHAPTER 1

Now. December, 1995

*T*his guy seems kinda squirrelly, Hellboy thought, as he entered the home of Donald Kramer. Or maybe it was just the fact that a seven-foot-tall, red-skinned demon dressed in a trench coat and packing some serious heat was standing in the guy's foyer. *Nah, that's not it.* Kramer just seemed like one of those types.

The man's hands hadn't stopped moving; touching his face, running his fingers through his hair, as he explained why he'd called in the Bureau for Paranormal Research and Defense.

"One day it was there in the backyard like it always was," he said with a shrug and a twitch. "And then it was gone." Kramer gnawed at one of his fingernails like he hadn't eaten in a week.

Hellboy glanced at the clipboard in his hand. "We *are* talking about a rock, right?"

The man nodded eagerly. "Yes, a boulder. Been there forever. It separated my property from the woods behind it."

19

Alarm bells had gone off at the BPRD headquarters in Fairfield when some desk jockey at the Plymouth, Massachusetts, Police Department keyed Kramer's case into their computers. The Bureau had a deal with most of the police departments in the U.S., and hundreds of locations abroad; if anything out of the ordinary was reported, it raised a flag and a copy of the file was sent to the BPRD. Most of the stuff was junk, but every once in a while something piqued their curiosity. Lately, that had been happening more often than usual. The brain trust at the BPRD had noticed a pattern. Things were being reported missing—odd things.

The BPRD didn't like patterns.

"Was there anything unusual about this boulder?" Hellboy asked.

"No," Kramer answered sharply. "It was just a rock—a big rock. Why?"

Hellboy scratched the back of his head, unsure how to explain. This particular "big rock" had been cataloged in the Bureau's informational database as an object of religious significance, something worshipped by a primitive people long ago. The cheat sheet Hellboy had on his clipboard didn't give him much more information than that, but he knew that it was only the latest in a long list of similar items that had disappeared throughout the region over the past month or so.

"No reason." Hellboy shrugged his large shoulders.

"Just covering all the bases." He placed the clipboard under his arm. "Can I take a look at the scene of the crime?"

A twitch had developed at the corner of Kramer's right eye. "A crime? Do you think a crime's been committed?"

Hellboy sighed. "It's just an expression. So can I take a look?"

"Certainly," the man replied after breathing a sigh of relief. "It's through here." He turned toward a room behind him.

Yep, definitely squirrelly.

Kramer led Hellboy into a room filled with books, floor to ceiling, on shelves and in piles on the floor.

"Do a lot of reading, huh?" Hellboy was careful not to disturb any of the precariously balanced stacks.

The man stopped halfway across the room and turned. "Yes, yes I do. For my work. I'm a writer. This is my reference library."

From the corner of his eye, Hellboy saw something dart around one of the piles to disappear behind a heavy-looking, floor-to-ceiling bookcase. It was bigger than a mouse, maybe a rat, but he couldn't be sure.

"Do you read much, Mister . . . Boy?"

Hellboy looked quickly back at Kramer to find the man glaring at the bookcase. He had seen it as well.

"Not as much as I'd like. I read a little Louis L'Amour, some Spillane, and I really like that Mc-Murtry guy."

"Yes," Kramer nodded, obviously humoring him. "I hear he's quite good."

"Wish I had more time," Hellboy said. "But you know how it is, slave to minimum wage and all."

The man nodded—smile way too friendly for an ordinary suburban guy having a conversation with someone big and red, with hooves and a tail. Hellboy normally made ordinary citizens nervous at first, and as squirrelly as Kramer was, he didn't think he was the cause.

Kramer continued on across the room. "I know what you mean."

Hellboy followed, searching for anything else out of the ordinary. "So what kind of writing do you do?"

An arched doorway at the end of the room opened into another hall. A large, winding staircase on the right led up to the second level, and the hallway straight ahead would take them to the kitchen.

"Fantasy mostly," Kramer said, turning back to face Hellboy. "I have a best-selling series about a wandering knight who—"

"You got dragons in those books, Don?" Hellboy interrupted. "I can tell you some stuff about those babies that'll curl your toenails." He winked conspiratorially.

Kramer forced a smile. "That . . . that would be wonderful. Maybe after you find out who took my stone . . ."

Something crashed to the floor in the room above

them. Hellboy's gaze darted to the ceiling and then the stairs.

The writer laughed uneasily, moving to the staircase. "It's nothing," he said. "Probably just the cat getting into something he shouldn't."

"Yeah, they're like that," Hellboy said.

Kramer gestured down the hallway. "The back door is right down there."

There was another, louder crash, followed by the sound of breaking glass. The look on Kramer's face was one of absolute terror. He shrieked, frantically starting up the stairs on his hands and knees.

"Leave it alone," he screamed. "I told you I would make it right!"

There was more commotion from above, and Hellboy took a wild guess that it had nothing to do with a curious cat. He pulled his revolver from its leather holster. He didn't want to chance being caught with his pants down. A few months back he'd been chasing a Stullenwurm across the Alpine passes from France to Austria. He thought he'd had the cat-headed, lizard-bodied beastie cornered in an ice cave and barreled inside with a flamethrower, only to find a nest of pissed off Fire Drakes, eager to eat his weapon and fry his ass black.

Man, did he catch a ton of crap from the guys back at the Bureau for that.

Hellboy winced with the memory; patches on his body were still tender from the blunder. He had no idea what he would be facing today and hoped the gun would be enough.

"Let's find out," he grumbled, ascending the stairs two at a time.

As he reached the second floor he spotted Kramer standing in a doorway at the end of the hall.

"Stop it, please!" he cried over the din of destruction from inside the room. "I told you I'd get the stone back . . . please!"

Hellboy held the pistol tight in his grip as he strode toward the room.

Kramer turned to see him coming and held out his hands. "Don't go in there," he pleaded. "They're angry enough as it is."

"Don't worry." He pushed the writer out of the way with ease. "I'm Mr. Personality. Everybody loves me."

The room had more bookshelves, a desk and a computer, and Hellboy figured it was Kramer's office. The place was also full of Graken Spriggin, at least fifty of them.

Leprechauns, Goblins, Brownies, Faerie Folk: he'd take any of them in twice the number over Graken Spriggin. These little bastards were the worst.

They had tipped over multiple file cabinets, torn artwork from the walls and pushed the computer off the desk to the floor, where it lay in broken pieces. The two windows in the room had been shattered as well and large, black crows with tiny saddles upon their backs perched on the glass-covered sills. In the center of the room, several of the six-inch Graken Spriggin wielded wooden matchsticks like torches, preparing to set fire to a pile of shredded paperback books.

"Knock it off," Hellboy roared, watching in amusement as the leathery-skinned forest folk retreated from the sound of his voice. "What the hell do you think you're doing?"

The Graken stood unified beneath the broken windows. The tiny creatures glowered, brandishing weaponry created from rubbish—an ax made from a disposable razor, a sword fashioned from one-half of a pair of scissors. Some were even wearing armor that had been cut from soda and beer cans.

Hellboy let them get a good look at the gun he was carrying. One well-placed shot could easily kill ten of them. "So which one of you little freaks is gonna tell me what the problem is?"

"She's gone, ya red bastard!" one of the creatures screamed in a high-pitched brogue, crazy with emotion. "She's gone, and we've nary a clue as to where she was taken!"

The Graken shook a nasty-looking spork over his head, and Hellboy could have sworn he saw tears in the tiny warrior's eyes.

The others started to become agitated; their escalating emotion riled up the crows perched on the windowsills above them. The cawing of the birds was starting to give him a headache.

"All right, all right!" He holstered his weapon. "Let's start over. Why don't you start by telling me who's gone?"

"The blessed mother of us all!" the Graken cried in unison, and before he could respond, they swarmed at him, fury and grief etched on their ugly little faces.

"Aw, crap," Hellboy grumbled as they leaped onto his coat, scaling his duster. He tried to swat them away, watching in awe as they hit the floor hard, shook themselves off and started toward him again.

"Knock it off, ya little creeps!" he barked, shaking his leg and sending at least twelve of them flying. "Let's talk about this."

The Graken Spriggin weren't listening.

"He's likely the one what took her!" bellowed one, wearing an old knitted dog sweater and a helmet made from a bottle cap.

"I didn't take a damn thing!" Hellboy yelled, trying not to squash his pint-sized attackers. "And if you don't knock this crap off, I'm really gonna give you something to cry about!"

The crows sprang from their perches, squawking and making as much of a racket as the Graken themselves. They flew at Hellboy's eyes, wings flapping furiously, razor-sharp beaks seeking out the vulnerable orbs.

He raised his arms, swiping at the attacking birds. "You no good sons of . . ."

He was temporarily blinded as he tried to shield

his face, and could feel the weight of Graken as they continued to climb him like Everest. He stumbled, thrashing his body and whipping his tail around as he attempted to dislodge the diminutive assailants. He could hear Kramer out in the hallway, begging the Graken to stop, but they weren't too keen on listening to him either.

A Graken that had managed to reach Hellboy's neck, lashed out with one of its crude weapons. "Feel the bite of me ax, you filthy hellspawn," it cried, swinging the razor-sharp blade of its makeshift battle-ax into his throat.

Hellboy yelled, his massive, stonelike right hand instinctively slapping at his neck, crushing the tiny attacker like an annoying mosquito.

"Little bugger," he spit, swiping the crushed Graken from his neck. "Now this crap is just getting out of hand."

The crows renewed their assault on him with vigor. One of them came in beneath his flailing arms and jabbed its beak into the tender flesh at the corner of his left eye. Hellboy snarled, stumbling backward. More of the birds came at his face, driving him back across the room. One of his hooves landed on a piece of jagged glass from the window.

"Son of a—" Hellboy shouted, as his hoof slid out from under him, and he toppled out through one of the broken windows.

He crashed onto a small roof below the window

with a grunt, then tumbled off into space yet again before landing in Kramer's backyard with a thud that knocked the air from his lungs. He could hear the crows above him, and could have sworn they were laughing.

"That's it," he grumbled beneath his breath, pushing himself up from the frozen ground. He wiped stinging blood from the corner of his eye and groaned when he caught sight of more Graken Spriggin emerging from the woods that encircled the yard, dressed in aluminum can armor and brandishing makeshift weaponry. The Graken from the office scrambled out onto the roof, some hitching rides to the yard on the backs of the crows, others shinnying down the drainpipes.

"I've had about enough of you cockroaches," Hellboy said, drawing his gun again.

The circle of Graken drew tighter around him, their primitive features scowling. They were without a doubt the nastiest of the tiny folk that had emigrated from the Isle of Man, but they were also pretty private and seldom ventured out into the open. *This is nuts,* Hellboy thought. *What the hell's gotten them so riled up?*

He looked at the army that surrounded him, at the crows that cried above his head, and cocked his pistol with a loud *click*. "Last chance," he said. "Tell me what the problem is, or in the next couple'a seconds, things are going to get messy."

The tension in the air continued to build. The Graken said nothing, gripping their tiny weapons all the tighter.

"Wait!" cried a voice, and Hellboy looked to see Donald Kramer standing on the deck attached to his house, breath pluming white mist in the cold. "Stop this right now!"

Kramer wasn't wearing a coat, and he hugged himself against the frigid winter air.

"It is too late for that, human," said a small, yet surprisingly powerful voice, carried across the yard.

A rabbit had emerged from the underbrush, and an ancient Graken sat authoritatively in a saddle upon its back: the Graken King—a crown of small animal teeth around his head. The rabbit steed lowered its body for the king to dismount.

"She is gone, taken from where she has rested lo these many centuries." The king gestured toward an area at the back of the yard where several female Graken knelt, wailing and burying their faces in the overturned earth.

The king seemed to be talking to Kramer, and Hellboy decided to keep his mouth shut, to see what he could learn before stepping in.

"Good King Seamus," the writer said, descending the wooden steps to the yard. Twenty or so Graken soldiers swarmed to stand in front of their ruler, weapons pointed to defend. "I have no idea what has happened to your blessed mother," Kramer continued. "But I'm doing everything I can to see her returned."

Seamus pulled at the long, wispy hair on his chin. "And what of him?" He pointed at Hellboy. "Why has a crimson spawn from the fiery pits come to your domicile?"

Hellboy started to speak.

"Silence!" King Seamus bellowed as he raised a dismissive hand. "I have not given you permission to speak."

It was all Hellboy could do not to stomp the rodent-sized monarch into the ground. Diplomacy had never been his strong suit.

Kramer stepped closer. "This is Hellboy—of the BPRD, he's come to help."

The tiny king crossed his arms over his chest and studied Hellboy with an unwavering eye.

"Can I talk now?" Hellboy asked.

The Graken soldiers moved closer.

Hellboy squinted down the barrel of his pistol. "I'd step back if I were you," he warned. "Big gun, big bullets, big mess."

The soldiers scowled but stepped back.

"You may speak, Hellspawn," King Seamus pronounced.

"It's Hell*boy*," he said, holstering his weapon. "Appreciate it. Look, Skipper, what your boy Kramer here said is right. I've come about the stone, so maybe you could explain why it's so freakin' important?"

There was an uneasy silence in the backyard as the

king seemed to consider his response. He returned to his mount and climbed back into the saddle. Taking hold of the reins, and making an odd, clucking sound, he steered the rabbit toward the Graken women. "You will follow me."

Kramer at his side, Hellboy did, careful not to step on any of the little creatures swarming around his feet. "What's your connection to these guys?" he asked the writer.

Kramer vigorously rubbed at his arms, trying to warm them against the December chill. "Years ago, when my career had kind of stalled, I made a deal with them. In exchange for certain items—bread, alcohol, an occasional candy bar—they would *assist* me."

The wound near his eye had started to itch, and Hellboy rubbed at it as Kramer's words started to sink in. "These guys help you with your books?"

Kramer fixed him in an icy stare. "Would it be easier to accept if they were helping me make shoes?"

Hellboy shrugged. "Just never figured the little buggers as writers. See, even in my line of work I can still be surprised."

King Seamus had again climbed down from his bunny mount and was standing with the grief-stricken Graken Spriggin women. Hellboy could see where the stone had sat, the soil dark and rich, the area around it overturned by activity.

"And you didn't hear a thing?" Hellboy asked the man standing beside him.

Kramer shook his head. "Nothing. I woke up, and it was gone."

"This is where she rested," the king said, falling to his knees and reaching down to sink his tiny hands into the earth.

"You keep making reference to *she*," Hellboy commented. "No offense, I'm just saying, but, she's a rock."

Seamus rose, wiping the dirt from his hands. "She was our queen, the first of us all, Sheela-Na Gig, and from her blessed womb we sprang."

The female Graken began to wail again, throwing themselves in the earth and burying their faces. Most of the soldiers were crying now.

The king continued. "Those lesser races that came after us—the Gathan, the Goblin, the Fittletot and the Whoopity Stoorie—they was all jealous of our mother's love fer us, and us fer her, and joining their evil magicks together, they cursed her to stone."

"Bastards!" screeched one of the soldiers, inciting a fit of cursing among the gathered.

"But even as cold and lifeless stone, our mother's love was strong, and she continued to bless us, allowing our kind to grow in number over the centuries even as those who had turned her to rock dwindled and eventually were dust."

King Seamus reached over to gently stroke the brindle-colored fur of his rabbit mount as it nibbled on what remained of the late-fall grass. "But now she is gone, and already I see signs that our days are short."

A female Graken approached the king, hands upon her stomach. "A babe grew inside me, but now 'tis gone," she cried in a tiny, pathetic voice. One of the soldiers, the husband, Hellboy guessed, came to her then, taking her in his arms. They cried inconsolably.

"This is why we are enraged, Hellspawn," King Seamus said, voice rising in anger. "This is why we are moved to war, for without our Sheela-Na Gig, we will soon be no more, going the way of the Gathan, the Goblin . . ."

"Yeah, yeah, the Fittletot and the Whoopity Stoorie," Hellboy finished for him, moving closer to where the sacred stone had lain. "I get the picture. Without the rock, little Graken production goes belly-up."

He knelt in the dirt, after making sure that none of the Graken were beneath him, and began to check out the scene. *BPRD file said the rock was at least five hundred pounds,* Hellboy thought, stroking his chin. *Whoever took it needed some heavy machinery, or was pretty damn strong.*

He stood up, looking around for any signs that a machine had been driven across the yard, but found nothing. The lawn was intact.

Kramer stood shivering with the Graken legions.

"You heard nothing," Hellboy said to him again,

hoping to jar some memory that might give him something to work with.

The man shook his head as he blew hot breath into his cupped hands. "Not a sound."

Hellboy turned his attention to the Graken Spriggin. "And I suppose you guys didn't hear or see anything either?"

The creatures were silent, helplessness etched on their homely faces.

"Evil is afoot," King Seamus said, slowly nodding his large head. "'Tis dark magick that took our mother."

"Y'know what, Tiny," Hellboy said, gazing up into the gray winter sky, at the cawing crows circling above. "You just might be right."

Hellboy reached across the meeting table for a bagel. "Does this look like cinnamon raisin to you?"

Abe Sapien popped a piece of lox into his mouth and started to chew. "Either that or chocolate chip," he said after he'd swallowed. He brought a napkin to his mouth. No talking with his mouth full for Abe.

The amphibious BPRD agent had excellent manners.

"Whatever." Hellboy cut the bagel in half with a knife. Breakfast meetings with actual breakfast weren't the norm at the Bureau for Paranormal Research and Defense, but every once in a while the suits tossed a bone to the grunts—to keep morale up and all. Hellboy wasn't complaining; he was starved.

"Is there any cream cheese?"

Kate Corrigan, the assistant director of field operations, looked up from her notes long enough to pluck a small container of cream cheese from the tray in the table's center and slide it over to him.

"Hey, H.B.," Liz Sherman called from across the table, where she sat slumped in her chair, hands clasped in a death grip around a steaming mug of coffee. "Hear you kept us from going to war yesterday."

Hellboy thanked Kate and glanced at Liz, petite and pretty, dark circles under her eyes from too little sleep.

"Yeah, I guess," he said as he slathered his bagel with the cream cheese. "Had a tribe of Graken Spriggin up in arms over in Plymouth 'cause a statue of their mother got ripped off."

"Graken Spriggin," Abe repeated, pretending to shiver with revulsion as he helped himself to more of the raw salmon. "They are a nasty bunch."

"Yeah, real sweethearts," Hellboy agreed, around a mouthful of bagel.

"So what'd you do?" Liz asked, taking a sip from her coffee.

"Good question," Kate said, setting her pen down. "Considering that I don't have a report on the case yet."

"You look particularly stunning this morning, Kate," Hellboy said as he wiped cream cheese from the corner of his mouth. "That a new blouse you're wearing?"

She smirked. "Yeah, like you'd really notice. Keep this up, and I wouldn't be surprised to see Manning take you out of the field until your paperwork's caught up."

"Ouch!" Hellboy grimaced.

"So where *is* Tom this morning?" Abe asked, expertly diverting the subject.

Good one, Abe. I can always count on you.

"Yeah, where is he?" Hellboy joined in. It wasn't like the Director to be absent from a morning meeting. "Surprised not to see our fearless leader, especially with the grub and all."

"The Director's running a little late, I guess," Kate said, quickly glancing at her watch before picking up her pen and removing the cap. "So, who wants to start?"

Liz sat forward in her chair. "Now, hold on. I hate cliffhangers. Is Hellboy going to tell us how he kept the Graken from going on the warpath or not?"

She reached for the carafe of coffee and refreshed her cup.

Hellboy spread what remained of the cream cheese on the other half of his bagel. "I promised 'em I'd bring their boulder back, and then I had to swear on a sacred woodchuck."

Abe stared with dark, glistening eyes. "Sacred woodchuck?"

Hellboy shrugged, mouth full. "Could'a been a weasel, I guess."

Liz stared at him. "You're making that up."

"Would I do that? It'll be in the report."

"And if you can't bring this rock back, what then?" Liz asked.

He finished chewing and swallowed. "Then the Graken Spriggin will lay siege to the world."

Kate sighed, picking up her notepad and turning to a fresh page. "So what've we got, people? Should we be worried?" She looked around the table. "Abe, what did you find?"

Abe cleared his throat. "As you saw in *my* report . . ." He glanced briefly in Hellboy's direction.

Hellboy coughed suddenly into his hand, the barking hack sounding an awful lot like *kissass*.

Unfazed, Abe continued. "The missing item is a cup supposedly used by Elvis Presley before going on stage for what would be his last live performance in Indiana's Market Square Arena on June 26, 1977."

"You get to check out stolen Elvis memorabilia and I get Graken Spriggin? Where's the justice in that?" Hellboy asked, crumpling up his napkin and throwing it down onto his plate.

"The cup had been purchased for an undisclosed amount from an online auction, and was being transported by courier to its new owner in Massachusetts. The vehicle ended up at the bottom of the Merrimack River in Lowell. The driver was killed, and the Elvis cup was not recovered. The suspicion is that it was stolen right after the accident."

Kate gave Hellboy the evil eye as he started to hum "Don't Be Cruel." "What've you got, Liz?"

She set her coffee mug down and ran her fingers through her straggly, shoulder-length red hair. Hellboy guessed she hadn't bothered to shower this morning, catching every possible moment of sleep before the meeting. He was half-surprised she hadn't shown up in her pajamas.

"Nothing as cool as a missing Elvis cup," she assured them. "I've got a water stain that looks like the Virgin Mary. Evidently it was caused by a combination of renovations to an office building and heavy rains last spring. Word got out, and the faithful started flocking to the building. The guy who owned the place even started to charge admission."

Hellboy stood and rummaged through the bagels again. "So what happened," he asked, picking up a sesame-seed-covered bagel and sniffing it. "Somebody steal the water stain?"

"Not exactly," Liz said, running her finger along the rim of her mug, a mischievous grin spreading across her face. "They stole the wall."

Hellboy froze. "C'mon, a hunk of wall was stolen out of an office building? How is that done?"

"Same way a boulder is taken from a yard and a cup is stolen from a truck in transit," Kate answered. She set her pen down and looked up from the notepad. "So, we have a pattern. Anyone see any logic in it yet?" she asked, sounding like a teacher fishing for answers from her students.

"They're all items of adulation," Abe said, stroking his chin with a webbed hand. "Strange objects to be certain, but inspiring devotion nonetheless."

Kate tapped her pen on the tabletop. "And this is just the stuff we know about," she said. "Who knows how many other things may be missing."

"Couldn't it also be just some bizarre coincidence?" Liz asked. Hellboy noticed a faint glow coming from the palm of her hand as she gripped the side of her mug—using her pyrokinetic talent to reheat the contents of her cup.

"You've been with the BPRD for how long, and you still think there's such a thing as coincidence?" Abe asked.

"I'm just not sure we should be getting worked up over a missing Elvis cup," she added, carefully taking a sip of her now steaming coffee.

"What do you think, Kate?" Hellboy asked. He'd taken his seat and was digging into the second bagel.

The assistant field director shook her head slowly. "I'm not going to sound the alarm yet," she said, "but this is certainly something we should keep an eye on." She placed the cap back on her pen and stood. "That's it for me," she said, grabbing her notepad and heading for the door. "And I can expect your report on the Graken incident when?" Kate asked Hellboy as she passed.

"It's the next thing on my list," he told her in all seriousness.

Both Liz and Abe started to laugh, and he gave them a look.

"Keep it up, and you'll give me a complex," he said to his supposed friends as he stood and followed them from the conference room.

"So, H.B.," Liz asked, "what's on the agenda now?"

Hellboy shrugged, throwing his breakfast trash in a barrel beside the door. "Probably head back to my place, maybe watch a few videos, why?"

"I thought you were going to do your paperwork?" Abe said, holding open the door that would take him into the corridor that led to their living quarters.

"Right," Hellboy agreed. "Next thing on my list."

CHAPTER 2

Using the body of Stanley Thomas, Absolom Spearz smiled and waved from the porch of the old farmhouse. An annoying high-pitched peal filled the air as the truck from Advent Technology slowly backed down the rutted, unpaved road, delivering the supplies Spearz had ordered just days before.

What fascinating times these are, he thought, recalling how easy it had been to obtain the equipment he'd need for his holy tasks—a brief conversation on the telephone, and then reciting the number he'd found on a card in his host's wallet. So much had changed since he was last flesh and blood.

Spearz looked at the others standing on the porch with him, his faithful congregation. Geoffrey Wickham now inhabited the body of Mrs. Thomas, a fine-looking woman, and considering how homely Geoffrey had been in his time, it would seem he had made out quite well. Now if only Spearz could prevent him from constantly touching himself.

"Brother Wickham," Spearz said to the woman

standing beside him, her hand stuck within her coat, languidly massaging her left breast. "Restrain yourself."

"Sorry, Absolom," Wickham said in an unfamiliar voice, pulling her hand from within the coat, a spark of shame in her deep brown eyes. "I know it's been weeks, but I never realized how wonderful it would feel—to be of flesh again."

Spearz nodded with understanding. "All I ask is that you exhibit restraint when in public."

The sound of giggling caught his attention, and he turned to look at the Thomas children—the young boy hosting the mind and spirit of Tyler Arden, and the little girl, Annabel Standish.

"Did I say something amusing?" he asked them. He found it interesting that the youngest members of his congregation had found their way into the youngest bodies. Another example of the strange synchronicity affirming that the time of their return was correct.

The children bowed their heads in reverence.

"No, sir," Tyler said in a voice yet to feel the change of puberty. "It's just that we know how Brother Wickham feels."

"To have a body again," Annabel added, holding out her small hands and flexing her fingers. "It's glorious."

Spearz noticed that the girl's fingernails were painted a bright shade of red. *A harlot's shade.* Yes, these modern times filled him with wonder, but they also made his blood boil. No matter, if all went according to plan, it would not be long now before everything was finally set right.

He returned his attention to the truck that had come to a lurching stop before them. The incessant beeping ceased and the property around the farmhouse returned to blessed silence.

The dog that had been lying silently on the porch, face between its paws, climbed to its feet, tail wagging furiously as it growled and whined.

Spearz reached out to stroke its head. Not all of his flock had fared well. Poor Silas Udell had had nowhere else to go but into the vessel of the family pet.

The dog's dark eyes gazed into his imploringly.

"Patience, Silas," Absolom said, feeling a familiar tingle in his fingertips—the urge to design, to create, to build. He would help his friend as soon as he was able.

"I wonder how they will explain their sinful lives when they come face-to-face with God?" Annabel mused, young eyes on the delivery truck.

"That's not for us to worry about," Spearz said, as he stepped from the porch to greet the man climbing down from the vehicle, clipboard in hand. "Ours is to pave the way for his righteous arrival. What happens after that is none of our concern."

"Road's a bitch," the deliveryman said, vulgarity spewing from his mouth with ease.

Spearz wanted to slap the man's face, but restrained himself. "Yes," he agreed instead. "We've been meaning to do something about that."

The man grunted and plucked a pen from behind one of his protruding ears. "You Stanley Thomas?"

"Yes, yes, I am," Spearz replied. It had been mere weeks in this new body, but he felt as though it had always been his own. It had only taken him hours to sift through his host's thoughts, learning all he needed to know about these modern times.

"Got a delivery for you." The man handed Spearz the clipboard and pen. "Sign at the bottom."

A second man had climbed down from the passenger side of the truck and was opening the rear door, exposing the numerous boxes and pallets.

A cascade of images flooded Spearz's mind—the innumerable inventions that he and his followers would construct. He saw every nail, every piece of metal, every nut, bolt and screw required to build these fabulous machines.

"You all right?" the driver asked, startling him from his reverie.

"Yes, of course," Spearz replied, his mind aflame. "I'm fine." He reviewed the receipt on the clipboard before affixing his signature. Everything seemed to be in order. Now they could begin their work in earnest.

The man passed a cursory glance over the signature, then tore the yellow copy away from the clipboard and handed it back to Spearz. "Here ya go, Mr. Thomas."

Spearz smiled politely as he accepted the receipt.

The driver brought the clipboard back to the truck, then returned, pulling on a pair of work gloves he'd taken from his back pocket. "Where would you like us to put this stuff?"

"Right here is fine," Spearz answered, pointing to the ground at his feet. "My family and I will see to them after that."

The deliveryman glanced doubtfully at his followers, who still stood upon the porch in the bodies whose owners they had usurped. The man shrugged. Absolom knew there was no way he could even begin to suspect what had recently occurred on this property—but it didn't hurt to be cautious. There was so much at stake; the fate of the world, and the glory that was due it, was now in their hands.

The two men lugged multiple boxes from the truck and stacked them outside. Spearz watched, his mind filled to bursting with the work that awaited them; hard, grueling work, but all for the most magnificent prize.

"All this stuff," the driver asked, grunting with exertion as he hauled the last box from the truck. "You building a rocket ship or something?"

"Oh no." Spearz said as he closed his eyes. "It's more than that." He smiled broadly, imagining the future.

"Something that will change the world."

* * *

Tom Manning came awake with a gasp, his cheek resting on the rough weave of the small area rug around his desk. Immediately his thoughts went to those fears that men, as they grow older, often have.

Am I all right? Did I have a stroke? He was afraid to move, fearing that he'd be unable to, but gradually he came to realize that he was, indeed, fine.

But am I really?

He struggled to all fours, looking around his office, wondering how he'd come to be on the floor. He saw the time and felt a twinge of panic. He was late for work.

Using the corner of the desk, he climbed carefully to his feet. His body was shaking. Again he looked about the room, and everything appeared to be in order. Then he saw the notebook.

The Director of Field Operations for the Bureau for Paranormal Research and Defense, still wearing his bathrobe and pajamas, sat down heavily in his leather desk chair, staring at an open notebook on the desk before him, and felt long-established defenses beginning to crumble.

He read the words on the open page, and suddenly felt dirty. Defiled. His heart fluttered uneasily as he gazed at his hands—hands stained black. He picked up a Magic Marker that lay beside the notebook. The tip of the thick pen had been pressed nearly flat. He dropped it into the trash barrel beside his chair.

Something had happened to him, something worse than a heart attack or a stroke.

He'd always suspected that the world was a much stranger place than it seemed, even before he went to work for the BPRD, while he was still with the FBI. He remembered his first encounter with the Bureau, and its best field agent, Hellboy. It was a serial killer case out of Columbus, Ohio, and the primary suspect had proved to be something far less than human.

That was when everything had changed for him. Manning remembered how it had felt, the fearful realization, and found himself again reading the words scrawled in the notebook.

Working with Hellboy had confirmed his worst suspicions, testing the bonds of reality, driving home the fact that there really were things that went bump in the night, monsters under the bed, things that would eat you alive if given the chance. And with that knowledge confirmed, he had no choice but to adjust how he dealt with the world. It was either that or go completely insane.

Tom had established a kind of *bizarre-free zone* around his personal life. It was his way of not letting the job consume him. He would handle the strange and horrible things he saw with the FBI, and then with the BPRD, with full efficiency and professionalism. But when it came time to call it a day, he would raise the barrier and the weirdness of the world would be locked out until it was time to go back again.

This worked quite well for him—or at least it had.

Manning pulled his eyes from the notebook and looked around his office disdainfully, as if it had somehow betrayed him. He was supposed to be safe here. It was meant to be a place where he could trick himself into thinking that the paranormal was nothing more than rich fodder for popular entertainment. Here was where he could be blissfully ignorant. But not anymore.

It had broken through his defenses.

He allowed his gaze to fall back to the open book, where a message had been left in a handwriting not his own.

Manning had gone to bed shortly after Leno's monologue, checking the alarm clock settings, as he did every night before shutting off the light and falling asleep almost immediately. He'd never had any difficulty sleeping, thanks to his *free zone*. But now he had to wonder if sleep would ever come so easily again.

He had no recollection of leaving his bed, and certainly none of coming downstairs to the office, removing the notebook from the desk drawer and writing this strange message.

Not much time. King's cup . . . stone Queen . . . Virgin wall. All stolen. Medicine bag next. Stop them. Was right. DANGER! Go to Waldoboro. Stop them. Don't take any wooden nickels.

Manning felt an icy finger of dread run down the

length of his spine. There was something disturbingly familiar about the tone of the message, something that began to dredge up painful memories long buried by the passage of time.

The image of a sad old man restrained upon a hospital bed flashed before his mind's eye, and Tom gasped aloud, slamming closed the cover of the notebook.

Ghosts of the past, never laid to rest.

Franklin Massie held on to the sides of the embalming table, the painful arthritic throb of his old joints making him momentarily unsure he could continue with the task before him. He paused, gazing down at the elderly corpse laid out before him, and decided that he must.

Not much older than me, he thought, reaching down with hands sheathed in rubber gloves to pluck an unsightly hair from the corpse's nose. Franklin studied the man's features. It was obvious that his passing hadn't been pleasant, for there was a certain strained expression on his face. He took note of the ruptured capillaries in the nose, the distended belly and the yellowed skin. Alcohol abuse had claimed another one.

This was nothing new to the funeral director, especially when dealing with the more troubled populace of the old city. He had an agreement with City Hall to handle the arrangements for those who passed from life with no one to mourn them, nor funds to pay for the cost of burial. The City paid him a flat rate for his services, barely enough to cover expenses, but he didn't mind. It made him feel good that these poor souls were at last being shown some proper respect. He treated them as he treated all of his clients. To Franklin Massie, death was the ultimate equalizer.

Franklin imagined himself lying naked upon the cold metal table, a stranger's hands preparing him for his own final slumber. *It won't be long now,* he thought. The ache of his joints was growing steadily worse, and he was finding it increasingly difficult to handle his equipment. It had been the same with his father, Walter. When Father could no longer get up in the morning to open the doors of the Massie Funeral Parlor, he had simply surrendered his spirit. Franklin wondered if he would be as smart, or would he be found dead in the embalming room one day, an extra body on the floor, in addition to the one on the table.

He turned from the corpse, forcing the unpleasant thoughts out of his mind, and flicked the switch to start the embalming machine. He picked up the long, sharply pointed trocar and turned back to the deceased.

"I know this looks bad, but I guarantee, you won't feel a thing," the mortician said, preparing to plunge the pointed tip of the shaft into the corpse's belly.

A green light began to flash above the room's entry-way—someone was at the door upstairs.

"Wonderful." Franklin set the trocar down and switched off the machine. "Sorry about this," he said to the corpse. "But it looks like we'll have to finish up later."

The pain in his hip was sharp, and it made him wince as he turned, removing the rubber gloves and throwing them in a nearby trash receptacle. He hobbled to the sink, washed his hands dutifully with a powerful, antibacterial soap, then dried them well with paper towels.

The light above the door continued to flash.

Franklin lurched toward his cane propped against the wall near the door, then shuffled out of the room and over to the basement stairs. This was actually the hardest part of his job these days, he reflected, using both the wooden handrail and the cane to ascend slowly, step by painful step. He could hear the bell now, and prayed that, after all his effort, the person at the door wouldn't get fed up and go away. Not for the first time, he wished business was better and he could hire someone to help him, but he was barely keeping up with expenses as it was.

"Coming!" he called out in his loudest voice, just to be on the safe side.

Franklin reached the top of the stairs and exhaled loudly. It seemed to take a little more out of him every day. He glanced into the mirror on the wall of the foyer and ran his fingers through his head of thinning gray hair as the doorbell rang yet again.

He turned the crystal knob on the heavy oak door. Pulling it open, he found a tall, thin man standing on the stoop.

"Sorry about the wait," Franklin said as he opened the storm door and stepped back for the man to enter. "I was working downstairs." He held up his cane. "Not as quick as I used to be."

Franklin shut the door and turned back to the stranger. There was something vaguely familiar about him. "Have we met before?"

The man nodded. "But it was a long time ago—I barely look the same." He extended his hand. "You're Franklin Massie."

Franklin took the man's hand in his own, and they shook. "I'm afraid you have me at a disadvantage, sir."

"I am Absolom Spearz, Franklin," the man replied, a strange twinkle in his eyes. "Do you remember me?"

The funeral director rolled the name around in his mind for a few seconds. "The name's familiar, but I can't . . ."

"Your father and I were close for a time."

Franklin chuckled. "My father passed away a long time ago, I doubt you were even born then."

The stranger smiled again, and Franklin felt a sick sensation in the pit of his stomach.

"Do you remember the Band of Electricizers?" he asked.

Franklin blinked, the name dragging long-forgotten memories to the forefront of his mind. He had

been young—no more than five or six. There had
been a man who used to visit his father, a preacher of
some kind. Absolom Spearz and his so-called congregation had been called the Electricizers. Yes, he
remembered. He had thought it was a funny name,
even when he was five.

"I *do* remember them," the old man said, shaking
his head, a bit bemused. "But that was seventy years
ago."

Absolom clasped his hands in front of him, tilting
his head strangely to one side. "My how the years have
flown," he said. "It seems like only yesterday that I
watched you sitting on the floor of this very hallway
playing with your tin soldiers."

Franklin smiled uneasily. "You remember me playing in the hall, do you? There must be some really
good genes in your family."

The man calling himself Absolom Spearz looked
around the foyer of the funeral home. "It really hasn't
changed much," he said casually. "Your father would
be pleased. The business was very important to him."

"What exactly can I do for you, Mr. Spearz?"
Franklin asked, a hint of annoyance in his voice. He
leaned heavily on his cane. His hips had begun to
throb even more painfully than before, and he wanted
nothing more than to sit down.

"The last time I was here I made a proposition to
your father," Absolom said, checking his reflection in
the hall mirror before turning his gaze back to

Franklin. "It was refused, quite vehemently I might add."

Franklin's stomach roiled, and the agony in his hips pulsed with the beat of his heart. He remembered his father's voice now, screaming in anger, yelling at Spearz to get out and never return. He'd asked his father about it later that evening, but his inquiries were met with a beating and bed without supper. Spearz was never mentioned again, nor thought of—until now.

"Look, Mr. Spearz . . . or whoever you are, I have a pretty busy day ahead of me. I'd appreciate it if you would get to the point of this visit."

The man smiled. "The apple didn't fall far from the tree, did it, Franklin? Will you evict me from this place as your father did?"

The mortician blinked.

"Yes, Franklin, the vessel in which my spirit resided then was different, but I *am* the same Absolom Spearz." He took a step toward the funeral director, and Franklin tried to back away, but his hips balked sharply, and he fell backward to the floor. "And now I come to you, adorned in new, healthy trappings of flesh, blood, muscle and bone."

"You're crazy!" Franklin rasped, shaking his cane to keep Spearz away. "Get out, get out of here right now!"

Spearz stepped back, allowing Franklin to struggle to his knees.

"Look at you, you're dying by inches," he said quietly. "I can help, you know. I can free you from the rheumatism-wracked carcass you are burdened with."

Franklin forced himself to his feet, the bones in his hips grinding painfully. The man approached, but he held his ground.

"You are an old man in body, but your spirit is young, Franklin Massie," Spearz continued. "I can imagine how that feels, to be the prisoner of your infirmity."

And suddenly Franklin could not help but agree. How he resented his body, with all its aches and pains. "My . . . my spirit *is* young," he murmured.

Spearz nodded. "Of course it is, and that spirit deserves so much more than to pass from life when that withered husk you're wearing finally breaks down."

The man's words were mesmerizing, seductive, and so powerful in their truth. *Who is he, really?* The mortician's mind raced with an insane notion. *Can he actually be who he claims to be?*

"I . . . I want you to leave," he said halfheartedly.

Spearz nodded, heading for the door. Gripping the crystal knob, he turned. "Does your spirit not deserve more, Franklin?" he asked. "If you truly believe it doesn't, I will leave at once, and you'll never hear of me again."

Franklin wanted to send the madman away, but a tiny, pathetic voice at the back of his mind whispered,

I don't want to die. "It does," he said, feeling his eyes well with tears. "It does, it does . . . but there's nothing . . ."

"Oh but there is, Franklin," Spearz said, moving back to his side. "As I have done for myself, and those who listen to my good words—I can do for you."

Spearz threw his arm around Franklin's shoulders, and the mortician's body pulsed with a strength he hadn't felt in years. And then he realized that his pain was gone. The man's touch had taken away his suffering.

"Think of it, a vitality you have not felt since adolescence," Spearz whispered in his ear. "Do you remember those days, Franklin?"

He nodded fiercely. "I . . . I used to run," he said, squeezing his eyes closed, remembering how good the wind felt upon his face as he sprinted home from school.

"And you will run again," Spearz said reassuringly, squeezing him closer. "Give me what I ask, and it will be as if time has been reversed, the hands of the clock forced to give back what they have taken away."

Tears streamed down Franklin Massie's face. He wanted to believe. He wanted to feel alive again, and he knew he was willing to pay the price. "What do you want? What could I possibly have that you . . ."

Still gripping his shoulders, Spearz slowly turned him, pointing him toward the doorway that led downstairs.

"I ask of you what I asked of your father," Spearz said, as they shuffled toward the stairway. "I must have certain raw materials in order to create the tools by which I may best serve my God."

"Raw materials?" Franklin asked, allowing himself to be guided down the steps to the embalming room below.

"The dead, Franklin. I have need of the dead."

CHAPTER 3

"Look at this friggin' mess," Hellboy grumbled as he stood amid the rubble that was his videotape collection. Two shelves on the plastic unit that held the multiple tapes had collapsed, spilling the contents all over the floor. "Must be a million tapes here," he said, shaking his head with exasperation.

"At least," Abe replied, keeping his distance. "Want some help?"

Hellboy dropped to his knees. "Naw, that's all right. I had them in a specific order. Maybe if I'm lucky, they won't be too messed up." He reached for a tape, picked it up, frowned and tossed it back where he'd found it. "But then again."

Abe sat on the overstuffed sofa. "I'm surprised how many tapes you have." He plucked a magazine from the end table and started to flip through it. "Have you heard about this new thing? DVD, they call it."

"Smart-ass." Hellboy began piling the tapes behind him. "Nope, they're not gonna get me this time."

"Who?" Abe asked, looking up from last month's copy of *Bon Appétit*.

"The tech monkeys—you know, the guys who decide what's going to be the next big thing to replace the thing that we already got that works perfectly fine? Well, I ain't fallin' for it this time."

Hellboy leaned across the pile, reaching for a particular tape. He nearly lost his balance and as he recovered, his tail swished to one side and knocked over the pile he'd started behind him.

"Damn."

Abe closed the magazine and studied its cover. "So you think DVD is just a way for big business to separate you from your money."

"Exactly," he said. "It's just like what happened with eight tracks. Remember eight tracks?"

Abe tilted his head to one side. "Certainly, they were eventually replaced with cassette tapes."

"Bingo!" Hellboy jabbed the air with his finger. "That's what I'm talking about." He paused. "You know, I really loved that eight track player. I think I might still have it around here someplace."

Abe nodded. "I'm sure you do."

Hellboy leaned back on his haunches. "Let's say I buckle and convert to this DVD business. You know they're only going to come up with some new technology—an even smaller doohickey that they screw directly into your brain or somethin'—and then I've got to start all over again."

"Sounds exhausting. I think I'll stick with books," Abe said, putting the magazine back where he had found it.

Hellboy climbed to his feet, the pile of tapes in front of him looking no smaller. "Think I might have to tackle this later, maybe after some lunch. You in?"

Abe stood. "I'm not all that hungry from breakfast, but I could eat a salad."

"I think they're having Sloppy Joes in the cafeteria today. Put down a few of them babies, and I'll be rarin' to get back to work . . . or a nap. A nap might be good."

They both headed for the door.

"Remember, you promised Kate that you'd . . ."

"Yeah, it's the next thing on my list." Hellboy reached for the doorknob just as a knock sounded from the other side. He shot a dark look at Abe. "Crap, you jinxed me."

He knew who was on the other side even before he pulled the door open. "What's going on, Kate?"

"How'd you know it was me?" she asked.

"I know your knock. Abe and I were just leaving to grab . . ."

"What happened here?" she interrupted, pushing past him, attracted to the mess in the corner of the room.

"Shelves gave way. Like I was saying, we're going to get lunch. You want to come?" He didn't want her messing up his stuff any more than it already was.

Kate squatted down and began looking through the tapes. "Man, you certainly have a lot of crap here," she said with a chuckle. "Why would you even want to keep most of this stuff?"

"Look, my tastes are more on the . . ." He couldn't think of the word he wanted, and looked to Abe for help.

"Esoteric?"

"Yeah, esoteric side."

"Esoteric?" she said with a laugh. "I guess *Caltiki the Immortal Monster* certainly fits that bill." She held up the plastic case with its garish cover art depicting a giant, bloblike creature battling tanks.

Hellboy snatched it away from her. "Look, are you coming to lunch or not?"

"Nope, and you're not going, either," Kate told him. "Manning wants to see you and Liz in his office pronto."

"I thought he wasn't coming in until later. Can't he wait until—?"

"Nope, he wants you now." Kate walked back to the open door. "Oh yeah, and I need your report on the Graken Spriggin by tomorrow morning. Talk to you guys later," she said, and disappeared out the door with a backhanded wave.

"Sometimes she can be a real pain in the neck," Hellboy muttered, then noticed Abe staring at him. "What?"

"*Caltiki the Immortal Monster?*"

Hellboy looked down at the cassette case still in his hand.

"It's a classic."

Baltimore, Maryland, 1898

Peter Donaldson had come to Absolom Spearz so that the medium could help him communicate with his dear, departed mother, but instead, he appeared to be dying before Absolom's eyes.

Absolom tried to break the man's grip upon him with little success. They had clasped hands at the beginning of the séance, and now it seemed that the fates had turned the tables on poor Mr. Donaldson, triggering a seizure of some kind. No spirits had manifested themselves or inhabited Absolom's body to speak through his mouth. Instead, Mr. Donaldson had begun to shake uncontrollably. Now a thick trickle of froth dripped from the side of his grimacing lips.

"Mr. Donaldson, can you hear me?" Absolom asked, hoping to break the spell. "I want you to try and relax."

He'd heard of such things happening to other mediums, but had never experienced it for himself. Evidently, it had something to do with the spiritual energies amassed within the room triggering fits in the overly sensitive.

Absolom stood and was about to call for his wife. There were only five rooms in the apartment they rented in this working-class neighborhood on Durant

Street, and she would surely hear him and go to fetch a doctor.

But then Mr. Donaldson spoke. Or, rather, something spoke through Donaldson, as if the grief-stricken man himself was the medium, rather than Absolom.

"I can feel you there, Absolom Spearz," said a voice that sounded nothing like the kindly old man. His mouth did not move, remaining agape, as if frozen in a scream, but the voice issued from between his lips. "I can see you, out in the light. Listen now, and well. I am the god, Qemu'el, harbinger of a new age, and you have been chosen."

All Absolom could do was stare, held in a grip equal parts terror and wonder. He had heard this voice before, as a child. But it had gone strangely silent after the death of his mother, perhaps sensing the anger and bitterness young Absolom felt toward it for failing to provide the last piece of information that would have allowed the boy to save her life.

Donaldson's body trembled, as if attempting to contain some powerful force. The old man's skin had taken on a sickly pallor, an unhealthy yellow made all the more unappealing by the muted light of the gas lamps hanging from gold sconces on the wall.

"It has been too long, Absolom Spearz," the voice continued. "But at last, the time has come."

He knew exactly what the voice was talking about and felt his brain begin to tingle in anticipation. He still yearned for what had been denied to him so long ago.

"I have called to you—and four others of your ilk," the god explained, "you, who have the abilities and fortitude to help humanity achieve its highest aspirations."

Donaldson's body had started to wither, as if the moisture was somehow being drawn from his body. Absolom gasped as he watched the old man's yellowing flesh grow tighter to the bone, giving him a cadaverous appearance.

"My time is short, for this poor soul is already nearly expended. The others will become your new family, and together, you will be the priests of a new faith, able to achieve the greatest of things."

Absolom wanted to look away from the nightmarish visage before him, but couldn't.

"The world will soon be as this body—old, and tired, withering away until it is nothing more than a pale shadow of what it once was, never realizing what it could have been."

The flesh of the man was now like ancient parchment, cracking and falling from the bone to reveal the skeleton beneath.

"What would you have us do?" Absolom whispered, filled with anticipation. "What can we, mere mortals, do to stop the world's decline?"

Donaldson's eyes shrank beneath paper-thin lids, and fell back into the skull, leaving two holes filled with darkness.

"Open your mind to me," the god demanded, and Absolom Spearz obeyed.

Once again he felt the presence of something totally alien blossom within his mind, and then he knew what had to be done. At long last, he'd been given the answer.

"It's wonderful," he whispered. His body trembled with a new sense of purpose as he began to understand the ways in which he would bring the world that much closer to Heaven.

"For these wonders to occur, I must be more than just a voice speaking from the beyond," Qemu'el continued from within its withered conduit. "My divinity must be made corporeal—I must be born into the world that I will deliver unto greatness."

Absolom nodded furiously. "We will do this, oh god. With the knowledge you have given me, I and these others shall bring you from the beyond so that you may heal this ailing world."

"Yes," the god hissed. The old man's skin had withered away, leaving behind the blanched remains of a skeleton in a threadbare suit—but that too was starting to disintegrate. "Only one power will be able to tear asunder the ebony veil that separates me from the world that craves my touch—the power of belief."

Absolom felt warm tears fill his eyes. "*I* believe," he told the deity, his lips trembling with an adoration he'd never felt before. It was almost more than he could bear.

"That is not enough," the god replied, Peter Donaldson's skull slowly shaking from side to side upon
the segmented spinal column. "No matter how true
your faith, one man's belief is not enough. It will take
the passionate faith of dozens. Hundreds. Thousands.
The beliefs of others must be collected, harnessed as
the source of strength that will enable me to walk in
your world."

The spiritualist searched his newly invigorated
mind for the means with which to collect this power,
but found nothing that would allow him to do as his
god was asking.

"How will we achieve this?" he asked the skeletal
remains, whose dry, bony hands were still clasped in
his. "What will we use to gather and to contain this
power?"

"I shall give to you and to the others with whom I
have communicated a precious gift," the god explained,
"a vessel in which to store the energies needed to transform the world."

Donaldson's cadaver pitched forward. Absolom
recoiled, pulling back his hands as the skull struck the
middle of the circular table and exploded into dust.
The bone cloud filled his lungs and he gagged, coughing wildly as he leaped up from his seat, stumbling
away from the choking cloud.

A precious gift, the final words of a god echoed in
his ears. *A vessel in which to store the energies needed to
transform the world.*

As the bone dust settled, Absolom cautiously approached the table. In its center, among the powdery remains, was a single object, a strange cylinder.

The clock upon the wall chimed the hour as the medium reached down into the chalky mess and removed the cylinder. It was no more than six inches long, perhaps an inch and a half wide, and appeared to be composed of some kind of opaque glass. He studied the object, wiping away the white dust that covered it. He could feel it feeding, drawing upon his strength—his belief in this most holy of missions. The vessel came to life, pulsing with a faint, eerie inner glow.

But more energy would be needed, so much more.

There came a gentle knock upon the study door, and Sally stepped into the room. "Absolom," she said cheerfully, a smile upon her attractive features. "Mr. Donaldson's time is over, and we must prepare for . . ."

She stopped in midsentence, staring first at her husband and the glowing object he held in his hand, then at the mess of chalky white powder that covered the tabletop, the chair, and the rug beneath them.

"What on earth has happened?" she asked.

He wasn't sure how much he should tell her, and decided that he would wait to explain how dramatically their lives were about to change.

"Nothing to trouble yourself with, dearest," he told her, slipping the glowing cylinder into the pocket of his vest, close to his heart. "Something wonderful has occurred and that's all you really need to know right now."

"But where's Mr. Donaldson?" She looked around. "I was sitting outside the door and would have seen him leave if—"

"Mr. Donaldson has served his purpose." He walked across the thick dust to slip his arm about her shoulder. "We won't be seeing him anymore."

"Oh, how sad," she said, allowing him to lead her from the room. "I quite liked him."

"Yes, he was a kind soul," Absolom agreed. "But there are still so many others in need of my help, desperate for my talents to communicate with the world beyond ours."

So many others hungry *to believe.*

He felt the god Qemu'el's gift to him vibrate against his chest in anticipation.

"You're a kind man, Absolom Spearz," his wife said, as she gave him a loving peck upon the cheek. "Always concerned with the needs of others."

"Yes," he agreed. "Now, let's find a broom and clean up that mess before our next appointment arrives."

Tom Manning sat at his desk and took the crumpled piece of notepaper from his briefcase, a sickly feeling of foreboding churning in the pit of his stomach. He'd thought about staying home, but it just didn't seem like a place he really wanted to be. Now here he was in the neatly appointed office he'd had ever since becoming Director of Field Operations for the BPRD. The view outside the window revealed a gorgeous Connecticut landscape, but inside all was drab and practical.

He felt cold and alone, and wondered if he was going a bit crazy. It ran in the family, after all.

The minutes from the morning's staff meeting had been left on his desk, and he placed the mysterious note down beside them. When he'd come awake earlier that morning, lying upon the floor of his office at home, he'd felt disturbed—violated—but now he was beginning to entertain a creeping suspicion that there could be much more at stake here than just the intrusion on his bizarre-free zone.

He glanced at Kate's notes—reviewing the unique items that had been reported missing, then compared those to what had been written in his note.

. . . King's cup . . . stone Queen . . . Virgin wall.

Manning felt the uncomfortable prickle of perspiration upon his balding scalp and lifted a hand to wipe it away.

It was clearly a warning. Something—*or is it someone*—was attempting to alert him to some kind of threat involving these thefts.

Don't take any wooden nickels.

He read the odd phrase again. All morning, memories buried deeply by the passage of time had slowly forced their way to the surface. In his mind's eye he could still see the man, healthy, vibrant, full of life, a sly smile upon his face as if he were the keeper of a secret that could rock the world to its very foundation.

Manning found himself smiling, warmed by the recollection, but the image was instantly replaced by another; the same man—older, frailer, restrained in a hospital bed, begging to go home.

"Are you okay?"

Kate Corrigan stood in the doorway to his office, frowning at him in concern. From the position of her hand, he presumed she'd knocked on the doorframe, but he hadn't heard her until she'd spoken aloud.

He welcomed the intrusion. Kate had chased away painful memories with things of a more immediate nature.

"Sure," he said, covering the note on his desk with his hands. "I'm fine."

"Hellboy and Liz should be up shortly," she informed him. "Do you want me to sit in on this one or . . . ?"

"No, no, that's all right. I can handle it."

She nodded and started to leave, but paused. "Are you sure everything's all right?"

Tom felt a sudden urge to share what had happened to him earlier in the morning, but it wasn't time. There was still too much he didn't know.

"I'm fine," he said again, forcing a smile.

She left then, and Manning was alone with the nagging remnants of his past. *Wouldn't it be just like him?*

Hellboy and Liz arrived soon after and took seats at his small conference table while he gathered his materials for the briefing. He didn't yet have his answers, but it did not change the fact that *something* had used him as a conduit to get across a message—a warning of some impending threat.

Stop them. Was right. DANGER! Go to Waldoboro. Stop them.

He had no choice but to listen.

Absolom Spearz slid limply from the stool in front of a cluttered workstation and slumped to the floor of the farmhouse subbasement. He twitched and shuddered, and his head snapped back.

Hundreds of snaking, multicolored wires clipped to the skin of his face and arms connected him to a device of his own construction. A strange hum came from the device, which was composed mainly of exposed circuit boards and glowing vacuum tubes. The soldering iron he had been using to attach the last of the wire connections to the machine slipped from the table and struck the back of his hand, searing the delicate skin with its red-hot tip and filling the vast subterranean room with the stench of burning flesh.

Absolom felt nothing.

He lay in the dirt, curled into a tight, trembling ball, exhausted by his attempts to communicate with Qemu'el. Since his return to the physical world, he had been desperate to reestablish contact with his almighty, but his importunings remained unanswered.

Where are you, lord? he thought, trying not to panic. He and his followers had been restored—given another chance to complete their sacred chore—but without their god, they had no purpose. *Have we offended you? Did our failure taint your love?*

"Absolom?"

He opened his eyes to find his congregation standing around him, their eyes glistening expectantly. It was still odd for him to look upon these unfamiliar faces, for his mind held on to the memory of how they had appeared long ago, before their bodies were destroyed by the deeds of the ignorant.

Geoffrey Wickham was first to speak. In his mind's eye, Absolom pictured a white-haired gentleman, spine twisted from scoliosis, not the attractive features of a middle-aged woman.

"What did he say?" Geoffrey asked in a soft, female voice that Absolom doubted he would ever grow entirely used to. "What message did he have for us?"

They all moved closer. The children, Annabel and Tyler, reached down with their small hands to help him up from the floor.

"Tell us, Absolom, please," Tyler demanded.

"Is the god well? Has he heard our prayers?" Annabel asked breathlessly.

"Our god is still silent," Absolom replied gravely.

With a burst of anger and frustration, he tore at the wires still connected to his body, pulling away swatches of his skin with the clips.

The band gasped in unison. They clasped their hands together and bowed their heads, as if their sudden attempts at prayer would somehow reach the absent deity.

"But why?" Tyler pleaded. He fell to his knees, the others quickly following suit. "Tell us, Absolom, what has happened to our savior?"

They all raised their new faces to him, pleading, and even though they did not appear as he remembered, Absolom could still gaze deeply into their eyes and see the men and woman who had become his beloved flock. He could see their souls.

A thought occurred to him. A realization.

"Perhaps it is a test," Absolom replied, drifting toward his newest creation, the machine that had enabled him to project himself even deeper into the beyond. He reached out and cut off the power to the humming device, the subbasement falling eerily quiet.

Quiet as a church.

"It *must* be a test. We failed in our initial attempt to bring his blessing to the world, and he has not forgotten."

Silas Udell whined, his ears flattening against his head, tail tucked fearfully between his legs.

"What can we do?" Wickham asked, his hands nervously drifting over his female form. "Certainly he

knows that was beyond our control—that the attack
upon us was . . ."

Absolom silenced his friend with a look. "Of
course he knows," he scolded, rubbing at the angry
burn left by the kiss of the soldering iron on the back
of his hand. "He is god—but it does not change the
fact that we disappointed him. Look at the time that
has been wasted—time that could have been used to
bring about change, time in which each and every one
of god's creatures could have been lifted up to a new
level of greatness. But we failed, and our god was
forced to wait. The world was forced to wait."

His disciples hung their heads in shame, and
Absolom could feel the pain of knowing that they had
displeased their lord and master.

"But all is not lost, brothers and sisters, for even
though he does not speak, he *has* given us a second
chance," Absolom said, a slow, euphoric smile creeping across his face.

He began to walk around the basement, feeling the
desperate eyes of his flock upon him. "Secreted away
from the eyes of the infidels, in our deep, dark hole
beneath the ground, we shall continue to perform our
sacred tasks. Faith, my brothers and sisters, is what we
need if we are to achieve our goals. Faith from our
hearts, faith from the hearts of others."

He directed their attention to the corner of the
room, where a wooden pallet held the first of their
prizes: a large rock that resembled a woman lying

tightly curled in the fetal position, a paper drinking cup, one side of the rim chewed as if by rats, and, leaning against the dirt wall of the chamber, a piece of plasterboard, a brown water mark in the shape of a veiled female, head bowed in prayer, staining its center. How to collect the residual power of veneration from these objects had been but the first hurdle Absolom was forced to confront upon his return.

"These are but the start," he continued. "In time . . ."

"But when will it be enough?" Annabel Standish interrupted, wringing her tiny hands. "When will there be enough that he will no longer be angry?"

Absolom smiled. He was as much in the dark about their god's whereabouts as they, but he would not show it. In order for them to achieve their goal, they had to believe that all would turn out as planned, that it was only a matter of time before they were to be reunited with Qemu'el, and the world changed forever.

"Soon," he whispered, opening his arms to them.

"Very, very soon."

CHAPTER 4

They had been at the Museum of Native American Culture in Waldoboro, Maine, for just over three hours, and Hellboy was starting to get itchy.

"I don't know about this," he said to Liz, as he rummaged through a brown paper bag.

The museum had closed for the winter and wasn't scheduled to open again until Memorial Day, but it still employed a full-time security guard to patrol the grounds and the adjoining gift shop and visitors center. George, a full-blooded Micmac, had been waiting for them when they'd first arrived, and since Hellboy and Liz weren't sure what the night would offer, they had sent him home. The man was so grateful for an evening off that he left them his bag lunch to share.

"Cut the guy some slack," Liz said from her seat on a folding chair in the middle of the exhibit hall. "What did you want, a five-course meal?"

Hellboy looked up. "I'm not talking about George's lunch, Liz. I'm talking about this." He waved his hand in the air. "About being here. I think we're wasting our time."

"Oh," she said, crossing her arms and slouching in her chair. "Well, Manning said he had a source."

Inside the paper sack, Hellboy found a cheese sandwich, cookies and an apple. His stomach grumbled. Some of that cheese sandwich would hit the spot. He pulled off the plastic wrap and took a bite.

"Yeah, and what's up with that? Since when does Manning have *sources*?" he asked through a mouthful of bread and cheese.

Liz shrugged. "I don't know. He has sources, so what?"

Hellboy carefully sat down in the chair beside her and handed her the other half of the sandwich. "He seemed kind of off. A little antsy. Especially when he got to the part about the sources. I think he was holding out on us."

"Why would he do that?" she asked, taking a bite.

"Haven't got a clue." He glanced into the lunch bag again. "Apple or cookies?"

"Cookies," she replied, wiping the corners of her mouth before taking another bite.

Hellboy removed the apple and tossed the bag to Liz. "He just seemed more close-mouthed than usual. More uptight, if that's possible." He polished the apple on the arm of his coat. "I don't know, maybe I'm just being paranoid."

"You?" Her tone dripped with sarcasm despite a mouthful of cookie.

"Bite me," he growled, getting up to stroll around the main exhibit hall.

George had taken them on a brief tour of the building before heading out for the night, but Hellboy hadn't looked at the displays all that closely. Since they probably had a few hours to kill, it seemed as good a time as any. The museum was small, but the room was filled to the brim with all kinds of Native American cultural artifacts, representing not only the Micmac, but also the Malaseet and Penobscot tribes.

Hellboy stopped in front of a particular case, leaning in for a closer look while taking a bite from his apple. "So you think this is what we're supposed to be protecting?" he asked, eyeing a pouch.

It was quite old, about the size of a woman's handbag, and appeared to be made from tanned animal hide, most likely deer, or maybe elk. There was an interesting zigzag pattern painted on the front of the pouch in red and white, the colors barely faded even after all these years. GLOOSCAP'S MEDICINE BAG read a small plaque just below the glass cube that contained the artifact.

"It's the only thing here that vaguely matches Manning's description," Liz said, joining him. She was still munching on the sugar cookies from George's lunch.

They had asked George if he knew anything about medicine bags, and he had brought them to this case almost at once. He told them about Glooscap, a demigod and the subject of many Micmac folktales. Glooscap was the earthly embodiment of the great deity, Kitche Manitou, and had taught the Micmacs how to hunt, fish, and make tools and weapons. He prophesied the coming of the white man and Christianity, but eventually he left the world, leaving behind his powerful medicine bag as proof that he would return to his people in times of war and hardship. According to the security guard, it was the crown jewel of medicine bags.

"Kind of small, don't ya think?" Hellboy commented, taking another chunk from the apple. "Wallet, a pack of gum, car keys, and that baby's pretty much full. How much medicine could this Glooscap keep in there?"

"It's magic," Liz replied, her reflection in the glass case dwarfed by her partner's. "Sort of like Felix's bag of tricks."

Hellboy looked at her confused. "Felix who?"

"The Cat," she answered. "Felix the Cat? Don't *even* tell me you don't remember. I know Felix, and you're way older than I am."

"Oh yeah," he nodded. "Thanks for the reminder."

"Do you remember the name of his arch nemesis who always tried to steal his bag of tricks?" Liz asked. She went back to her chair, where she'd left her coat, and started digging through the pockets until she found her cigarettes.

Hellboy threw the core of his apple into a nearby

trash barrel. "I can see him in my head, had a crazy white mustache, didn't he?"

She plucked a cigarette from the box. "He was called the Professor. I don't think we ever got the rest of his name." She started toward the door, far across the exhibition hall. "I need a smoke."

"Aren't you going to wear your coat?" he called after her. "It's freezing out there."

"Warm-blooded." She smiled and held up her index finger. An orange flame flickered to life on her fingertip, and she lit the tip of her cigarette.

Hellboy shook his head and turned away, focusing his attention on a totem pole in the corner, its carved faces alternating between animals and gruesome fright masks.

He heard Liz open the door. "Be right—"

She didn't finish her sentence. Hellboy frowned and tore his attention away from the totem pole, wondering what had stopped her.

Liz stood in the doorway—and she wasn't alone.

"Hey, who's that?" Hellboy called, starting toward them. Whoever had come in was half in shadow, and he couldn't make out the face. He hoped the security guard had come back and brought them some coffee. "Is it George?"

But even as he asked, he knew it wasn't George. Something made the hair at the back of his neck stand up. The wind outside was blowing, and gusts of frigid air laced with snow invaded the relative warmth of the museum.

"Liz?"

She turned ever so slightly and he could see the look of wide-eyed shock on her reddening face—and the hand locked firmly around her throat.

"Jeezus!" he bellowed, bolting across the exhibit room.

The guy in the doorway was dressed in a long coat with a black cap pulled down tightly on his head. When he saw Hellboy barreling toward him, he lifted Liz like she weighed nothing and tossed her right at him.

Hellboy tried to be gentle, cupping her body against his own to cushion the impact as he caught her and fell backward. He collided with the folding chairs, sending them flying, and crashed to the floor.

He laid her down gently, touching her neck, searching for a pulse. She gasped for breath, the pale skin of her throat already starting to bruise.

"Pal, you better hope your health insurance is all paid up," Hellboy snarled as he rose and spun toward the intruder.

Liz's assailant was no longer alone. There were six of them now, all dressed in the same long coats and hats, standing perfectly still as they watched Hellboy advance.

"You have friends," Hellboy growled, flexing the stonelike fingers of his right hand. "Good for you."

As if responding to some cue, four of them slipped off their coats and tugged off their hats, moving in unison. Hellboy froze where he was, staring at them, trying to figure out what the hell he was seeing.

"What the . . . ?" he managed.

They'd definitely been human once, three men and a woman. But they were long past their expiration date, the stink of death and rot coming off them in waves. They were each encased in some kind of crude exoskeleton constructed from wood and metal.

"It was a near-perfect day up till now. But zombie cyborgs . . ." He sighed. "I'm not sure I deserve this much fun."

The one that had attacked Liz sprang first. The thing moved crazily, its long-fingered hands, adorned with nasty-looking serrated blades, slashing at Hellboy. He blocked the attack with his right hand and drove a punch into the creature's chest.

It grunted as his fist connected, stumbling back, belching a foul-smelling gas. Then it bent over and vomited a viscous stream of murky fluid filled with springs, cogs, screws and wire.

"Now that's just gross," Hellboy sneered, stepping back so as not to be splashed.

The others came at him. They were stronger than they looked, and disturbingly silent as they grabbed at him. Only muffled whirring, like the mechanics of a windup toy, could be heard coming from somewhere inside each of them. Hellboy swatted one of the creatures aside with his right hand and punched another, his fist sinking into the soft decay of its belly.

"Yarrrrgggh!" Hellboy recoiled in disgust, yanking his hand back. As he did so, the creature's innards spilled out onto the wooden floor; again, nothing more than springs and wires, gears and cogs. Then something else that momentarily caught his eye, a glowing canister. It dangled from a thick cord attached somewhere inside the hollow man and pulsed with an eerie, rhythmic light.

"Like clockwork," Hellboy grumbled, pulling his gun from its holster and firing into another attacker's face. It flipped backward onto the floor, arms and legs thrashing wildly.

"Hellboy!" Liz croaked, voice rasping from the whole nearly getting strangled thing.

He spun around to see the zombie robot he'd discarded seconds before coming at him, brandishing the totem pole he'd been admiring earlier like a Louisville Slugger. He tried to get out of the way, but his foot slipped in some of the oily spew. The totem pole caught him across the chest, sending him flying through the museum. The sound of shattering glass and splintering wood was all he could hear, as he at last came to rest in the remains of an exhibit of Native American blankets.

He rose from the wreckage just as the Babe Ruth zombie was heading in for a second turn at bat. Hellboy reached down and grabbed up one of the colorful blankets. "Here, cover up. You'll catch your death," he said, tossing it over the creature's head.

The zombie robot stopped short, the totem pole falling heavily from its grasp. It clawed at the blanket with long, skeletal fingers adorned with what looked like steak knives.

Hellboy pummeled the creature to its knees.

A clanging alarm filled the museum, and, with a hiss, drenching artificial rain began to fall from the sprinklers in the ceiling. For just a second, Hellboy wondered what had set off the sprinklers, then chided himself for such a stupid thought.

Liz was back in the fight.

He glanced over and saw her standing, legs apart and hands out in front of her. Fire blazed from her fists and engulfed the two remaining zombie cyborgs. It was never a good idea to make a firestarter angry.

Liz had them backed into a corner, the stench of roasting meat replacing the odor of rot in the air. The metal and wooden parts of the framework that encased their bodies had started to burn, the exposed flesh charred to black—but they were still alive, or what passed for life with these things.

"Liz!" Hellboy shouted, stepping over the crumpled, blanket-covered thing he'd just pummeled into oblivion. "You want to dial it down a bit?"

She looked over her shoulder, sparks leaping from her eyes.

Man, she's pissed.

"What the hell are these things?"

"Haven't a clue," Hellboy replied. He could feel the

heat coming off her as he drew closer. "But keep this up, and you're gonna burn the place down, buy the BPRD a whole political incident."

She looked at him again. There was still anger in her gaze, but he could see from the softening at the corners of her eyes that she was starting to calm down. He felt the heat in the room diminish immediately as she bent her head, ever so slightly, and drew the power back within herself.

"Now I'm getting wet," she said, as he stepped up beside her.

"Join the club," he responded. "How's the throat?"

She touched her neck. "Sore, but it'll heal."

He couldn't take his eyes from the twisted things smoldering in a pile against a section of wall burned black by the intensity of Liz Sherman's anger. The creatures writhed, some of their metal parts fused together—connecting them as one grotesque thing that had no reason to still be moving.

"So do you think this is what's been stealing that stuff?" Liz asked with a shiver, wrapping her arms around herself as the artificial rain continued to fall.

"Sort of makes sense. They're pretty strong for corpses filled with wires and junk . . ." he trailed off.

Over the din of the still-clanging alarm, he caught the sound of an engine revving up outside and went over to look through the window set into the door. "Must be the Waldoboro Fire Department," he said, swiping away a swath of thick condensation. "This oughta be good."

He was getting ready to pull open the door when he realized the engine was growing louder and the headlights closer.

"Crap!" he managed, scrambling to get himself and Liz out of the way as the front of a vehicle came crashing through the doors into the museum.

Both front doors came open and two more of the watch-capped, coat-wearing zombies spilled out into the museum to stand beside the vehicle, watching them with milky white eyes—dead eyes.

"They drive a minivan," Hellboy growled in disgust, climbing to his feet. "It just keeps gettin' worse."

Liz came to stand beside him.

"Ready for round two?" he asked.

"They don't seem all that interested in attacking," she said.

One of the pair turned and reached inside the van, and Hellboy wished that he could have found his gun. Stepping in front of Liz, he watched as the creature pulled out a large burlap sack tied with a length of rope.

"What, they bring their laundry?" he muttered as the mechanical man cut the rope with one of his knifelike fingers and pulled open the sack.

With a buzz, the air filled with a swirling maelstrom of tiny bodies, high-pitched calls, and the flapping of metallic wings.

Birds, Hellboy thought.

Freakin' mechanical birds.

It's like being in the middle of a tornado. Hellboy raised his hands to shield his face. Hundreds of screaming, mechanical sparrows with razor-sharp beaks and wings swirled around him. He reached out for Liz.

"Get over here," he growled, pulling her toward him.

She was a mess, her shirt in tatters. Blood spattered her face and arms where she had been cut by the frenzied birds. His skin was tough, but even he was beginning to feel the razor-thin gashes in his leathery hide.

Hellboy pulled open his coat and shoved her inside. It wasn't much, but at least it offered some protection.

"What are they doing?" Liz screamed over the deafening sounds of the birds and the fire alarm, her face pressed close to his chest.

He held his massive right hand in front of his eyes, attempting to see through the maelstrom of birds and into the museum. He could just about make out the shapes of their latest attackers skulking back to the van.

"I think they got the medicine bag," he bellowed. "Walk with me."

He started toward the vehicle. Liz stayed close, moving as he did.

"Damn it," he cursed, as he heard the van's engine

grinding to life over the museum clamor. "They're getting away."

Hellboy tried to move faster, swinging his stonelike hand, plucking the fragile mechanical birds from the air and dashing them to the floor. Tiny springs and cogs exploded from their bodies as they hit the ground.

"This is going to take you forever," Liz said, and pulled away from him.

"No!" he yelled, trying to drag her back to the relative shelter of his coat, but she fought him.

"It's my turn," she said, and he felt the air around them grow stiflingly warm, then suddenly so hot he could barely breathe.

A blast of intense heat drove the birds back, shattering them against the wall as their dead flesh and feathers burst into flames. With the storm of birds diminished, Hellboy could see again, just as the minivan began to back out of the hole it had smashed in the front of the building.

"Oh, no you don't," he shouted, springing at the vehicle and grabbing hold of the bumper. He tried to get his footing as he was dragged from the museum, but it had been snowing, and a good two inches of the powdery stuff coated the ground.

Holding on tightly with his left hand, Hellboy drew back the oversize fist of his right, preparing to punch his way through the van's radiator and into the engine block. The windshield of the vehicle suddenly exploded outward, showering him with a rain of safety glass. A clockwork zombie slid down the short expanse of hood toward him, grabbing hold of him, razor fingers slashing as the van came to a sudden stop and skidded on the slick surface of the parking lot.

Hellboy heard the squeal of screws and the snap of heavy-duty plastic as the bumper tore away from the vehicle, sending him and his attacker across the lot in a tumbling heap.

"Get off me!" Hellboy yelled, trying to throw his attacker from him, but the zombie hung on tight. Its knifelike fingers jabbed for his eyes, and he barely had time to move his head as the blades descended.

"That's it," Hellboy roared, grabbing hold of one of the zombie's wood-and-metal-splinted arms and wrenching it from the socket. "Bet you didn't see this comin'," he yelled, using the arm as a weapon to thrash his attacker. He managed to kick the zombie robot away, just in time to see the van picking up speed and heading for the exit.

He started to run, wildly hoping he could catch it, but an explosion of pain in his leg stopped him. He looked down to see the one he'd just torn apart holding tight to his leg with its remaining arm, sinking its teeth into his thigh.

"You've gotta be kidding me!" He hammered his fist down at the thing, breaking its neck and driving it to the ground. "Thanks, freak. Now I'm probably gonna need a tetanus shot."

He examined the wound, rubbing at his thigh where the skin had been broken.

"Hey, Red," Liz called, and he looked up to see her coming across the lot. She was still giving off a lot of heat, leaving a clear path through the snow as she made her way toward him.

Hellboy gazed down at the horrific thing writhing in the snow: an arm torn off, its head flopping unnaturally upon a broken neck. In their struggle, its stomach had been torn open and a faint glow of something green radiated from inside.

"The van got away, huh?" Liz stood beside him, clothes in tatters, face and arms covered with lacerations.

He nodded. "Mr. Twisty here kept me from stopping it."

In the distance, a ghostly wail filled the air. The Waldoboro Fire Department was near.

"So, what now?" Liz asked, hugging herself, starting to shiver.

Hellboy removed his tattered coat and threw it over her shoulders, then prodded the wreckage of the mechanical monstrosity with a hoof.

"We take them home and see what makes 'em tick."

CHAPTER 5

Lynn, Massachusetts, Spring 1901

Sally Spearz carefully made her way through the kitchen of a house she had yet to accept as her home. She carried a serving tray, upon which rested a crystal pitcher of freshly squeezed lemonade and six of her finest glasses. Only two weeks had passed since Sally and her husband, Absolom, had settled here upon their arrival from Baltimore, and she had not yet developed a level of comfort in the new farmhouse.

She used her hip to push open the swinging kitchen door and went through the dining room to the parlor, where her husband entertained his guests. He paced about the room in front of his captivated audience of five, who were seated in chairs taken from the dining room.

Sally was still in awe of how much her husband had changed over the last two years. Gone was the man who used his unique talents sparingly, replaced by another who seemed almost driven to share his gift. He'd begun to develop quite a name for himself, and with that celebrity came some financial security. Without his sudden transformation, they would never have been able to afford to buy this land—land his own family had once lived on—or build this farmhouse, or any of the other wondrous inventions Absolom had started to tinker with in the months since the Donaldson reading. Sally recalled the sad old man, his image replaced with the memory of a thick, chalky dust that had taken her weeks to clean away properly. Absolom had never fully explained what happened to the old gentleman, and she had come to believe that was probably for the best.

Her husband fell silent as she entered the parlor, turning to give her his most charming smile, a smile very much like the one he had used to ensnare her in a bookshop on North Avenue back in Baltimore.

"Ah, some refreshment," Absolom said to his audience. "And just in time. I do have a tendency to drone on, as my darling wife can attest."

They all laughed politely.

"Quite the contrary, Absolom," said a heavyset, older gentleman, his back twisted with some unknown malady. "I find your assertions absolutely fascinating."

Sally felt momentarily sorry for the man. At his size
he must have been quite uncomfortable. They'd not
had enough funds remaining from their move to buy
the parlor furniture she'd wanted, and were forced to
make do with the chairs from the dining room set her
parents had given them for a wedding present.

"Lemonade, Mr. Wickham?" she offered the man
with a polite smile.

He fixed her in his gaze with a leer snaking across
his jowly features. "Call me Geoffrey, my dear, and
yes, I would love some."

This was the first time Sally was actually meeting
her husband's . . . she really had no idea what to call
them. They were business associates, she imagined,
sharing the same esoteric profession and spiritual
beliefs, having begun their correspondence around the
time of Mr. Donaldson's disappearance.

Sally handed Wickham his glass, and he caressed
her hand as it passed from hers to his. Suddenly she
wasn't quite as sorry for the uncomfortable furniture.
Quickly, she moved on to the next two guests. They
were obviously a couple, their chairs pushed scan-
dalously close together. The woman's name was
Annabel Standish, and the handsome young man was
Tyler Arden.

Annabel poured two glasses of the lemonade herself, handing the first to Tyler, then taking her own
with a polite thank-you. Sally had to admit that the
two made quite a fetching pair.

"I wonder if you might have something with a bit more of kick?" inquired a thin gentleman with slicked jet-black hair and a handlebar mustache that he constantly played with.

Sally raised her eyebrows disapprovingly but kept her tone polite. "I'm sorry, Mr. Udell, but we do not partake of spirits in this house."

Silas Udell laughed and stood to take one of the crystal glasses of lemonade. "Kind of ironic, isn't it?" he asked, looking around the room. "A gathering of mediums, and not a spirit to be found."

He returned to his seat, a swagger in his walk. According to Absolom, Mr. Udell fancied himself quite the ladies' man, and these lecherous urgings had been his downfall in a number of cities.

Serves him right, Sally thought, and turned toward Absolom and their final guest. The two were standing across the room in the midst of a whispered conver-sation. She did not care for Mary Hudnell, and hadn't since first meeting the woman on their arrival in Lynn. She had found Miss Hudnell to be arrogant and brash, thinking herself superior because of her father's great wealth. The Hudnells owned one of Massachusetts's larger shipping enterprises, and Mary was their only child.

She was not a spiritualist like the others, but was instead a true believer of Absolom's theories of a higher plane of existence. And at the moment, Sally was convinced that Miss Hudnell was interested in something more than just her husband's teachings.

Clearing her throat loudly, she approached them with the tray of refreshment. "Lemonade, darling?" she asked her husband, then offered the same to their guest. "Miss Hudnell?"

"No, thank you, dear," Mary snapped, clearly annoyed by the interruption.

Her husband helped himself, leaning in to give his wife a peck on the cheek before taking a sip from his glass. "Thank you so much, my love," he said, and she could practically feel the daggers shooting from Mary Hudnell's eyes. Sally smiled sweetly and headed back to the kitchen.

She set the tray carefully upon a small, makeshift kitchen table. It had been an enormous risk leaving Baltimore, abandoning paying clients who depended on her husband's ability to communicate with the spirit world to guide them through life. But something of a higher nature had called him here, and it was a request that Absolom could not ignore. Sally didn't understand it exactly, but something had reached out to her husband—to all of them gathered in her parlor.

Her reverie was interrupted as she heard Absolom call her name. She left the kitchen and found the small group seated around the dining room table. "Join us, my dear," Absolom said, standing behind a chair at the head of the table.

Normally she would have declined, but at once she noticed that Mary Hudnell had taken the chair directly across from Absolom and thought better. Instead, Sally took a seat in the only available chair, between Mr. Wickham and Miss Standish. Almost immediately she felt the hunched old man's leg brush suggestively against hers.

"And now the reason we are all here," Absolom began, leaving his chair momentarily to retrieve something he had placed upon the windowsill.

It was covered with a sheet, but Sally already knew what was about to be revealed. He'd said that its design had come to him in a dream. She wasn't entirely sure why it required that they travel to Massachusetts, but he had said that it had something to do with the lines of communication being more apt to flow in this region.

Absolom gently placed the object down in the center of the table. He pulled the covering away with a flourish, and Sally watched the expressions on the faces of those gathered. They weren't too far removed from the look she'd given him when it was first revealed to her. He had always been good with his hands, but she had never known him to become so obsessed with the building of anything, forgoing meals and sleep in order to tinker with the strange contraption. It was a bizarre box with three sides, its mechanical innards exposed for all to see.

"What is it?" Geoffrey Wickham asked, reaching out a liver-spotted hand to touch it.

Her husband reached across the table to swat away

the old man's hand. "This, my brothers and sisters, will enable us to communicate more easily with our otherworldly benefactor."

Sally remembered Absolom telling her that there were others like him, chosen to represent the power that could very well change the world. It was all very thrilling, and she had allowed herself to be caught up in the wave of her husband's excitement. She looked about the table. These were the chosen ones—the *Electricizers* as he liked to call them.

"This is all so exciting," Mary Hudnell said breathlessly, her eyes riveted upon the machine.

Sally scowled. She knew why Miss Hudnell had been invited to the gathering, her copious funds being partially responsible for the new inventions Absolom was presently toiling over. Mary Hudnell had once paid a visit to her husband's place of business while visiting relatives in Baltimore and had become smitten with his talents, starting a correspondence that had lasted until their arrival in Lynn two weeks ago.

"Each of us has been touched by this power, and promised a part in its plans to reshape the world," Absolom said in a compelling voice.

The others nodded, their eyes glassy as they stared at him, hanging upon his every word.

"This will be a momentous occasion, my brothers and sisters, as our minds and hearts are opened to the ideas of a being beyond our comprehension. A god

that plans to entrust us with the sacred duty of helping him change the world as we know it."

Sally grew uneasy as she listened to her husband
and started to stand. Wickham's hand dropped firmly
upon her thigh, holding her in place.

"Isn't it exciting?" he whispered, his foul breath
nearly making her gag.

"Yes, of course," Sally replied, quickly removing his
hand and rising to her feet. "But if you'll excuse
me"—she looked directly at her husband—"I'll leave
you all to matters of a spiritual nature while I attend
to things in the kitchen that better suit my talents."

"Wait," Absolom protested, raising his hand. "You
must partake of the ceremony as well."

She smiled, hands fluttering to play with the lace
collar that suddenly seemed too tight about her
throat. "Surely I can add nothing to this gathering . . ."

Absolom's face grew very serious.

"Please, my love," he said, in a voice flat and
strangely devoid of emotion. "We have need of you."

She started to protest, but stopped as she found
herself slowly sitting back down. Something didn't feel
right. The atmosphere in the room seemed suddenly
cloying, as if all air circulation had suddenly come to a
stop.

Absolom swayed upon his feet and reached out to
grip the front of his chair. His eyes were closed now,
and his brow furrowed as if deep in concentration—*or*

is it pain? Sally had seen this happen to him before, when a particularly overzealous spirit was eager to establish communication.

The room grew deathly quiet, and all eyes were upon him when he suddenly gasped, his body falling limp. If he hadn't been gripping his chair, Sally was certain that he would have collapsed to the floor.

She stood again, making a move toward him, but he raised his hand, stopping her in her tracks.

"No," he said firmly. "Return to your seat. It is time."

He looked at her, and for a moment, she did not recognize him. Gone was the perpetual twinkle in his eyes, which was present even in the most depressing of times. It had been replaced with something altogether different, something that seemed visibly to weigh upon him. In that brief instant, even though it seemed mad to her, Absolom was suddenly much older.

"I'm fine," he responded to the question that was just about to leave her lips.

She sat back down, watching the man she loved with growing concern. He had been pushing himself for quite some time, and she worried that the strain was becoming too much for him.

"Was it the spirit—the one from our dreams?" Mary asked breathlessly, and Absolom nodded, pulling out his chair and sitting down.

"The god is aware of our gathering, eager for us to hear what he has to say."

Sally tried to catch his eye, but he refused to look at her. His strange aloofness wasn't doing anything to ease her growing fear.

"I ask you each to present your gift from our master," Absolom said, reaching into the pocket of his waistcoat and removing the crystalline cylinder he had been carrying since the day Mr. Donaldson disappeared.

The other mediums—Wickham, Arden, Standish, and Udell—followed suit, producing similar objects and placing them on the table before them.

"What are those?" Mary Hudnell asked. "Where can I get one?"

Ignoring her, Absolom rose from his seat and carefully collected the glass cylinders. A strange light burned in the center of each, as if something alive was trapped within the murky, colored crystals. And as her husband gathered them together, Sally could see them glow all the brighter, throbbing with an eerie luminescence.

He inserted the five crystals into the machine, in a compartment specifically designed, it appeared, to contain the cylindrical objects, and as the last of the crystals fell into place, the device began to hum, the mechanical innards to move, suddenly brought to life.

Sally watched as Absolom grinned, obviously proud of his accomplishment. Whatever it was that he had built, it appeared to be working as planned.

"Now take the hand of the one beside you," he instructed. "We must form a complete circuit if the machine is to function as intended."

"What . . . what does it do?" Tyler Arden asked, taking first the hand of his lover, then that of Silas Udell.

The young man appeared nervous, and Sally couldn't help but share his feelings. Even with her disgust at the feeling of Mr. Wickham's sweaty hand in hers, she knew that there was something else that didn't feel right.

"It will open a door," Absolom said, staring at the contraption in the center of the dining room table. "Now close your eyes and clear your thoughts."

Almost immediately Sally felt a change in the temperature of the room. Not only was it incredibly stuffy, it was now uncomfortably cold, as if the season had changed in the wink of an eye, and they were now in the midst of winter. She opened her eyes a crack to peer at the others. They seemed to be in the grip of a trance, similar to ones she had witnessed her husband experience on numerous occasions while communicating with the afterlife.

The machine grew louder, a low, vibrating hum that made it seem the machine was moving across the table of its own accord.

"It's not enough," Absolom gasped, his face twisted in deep concentration, beads of sweat dappling his brow. His voice was louder, more frantic. "It needs more . . . more if we are to breach the veil."

The machine continued to dance about the table-top, the sound of its internal emanations making the hair on the back of Sally's neck stand on end. The expressions upon the faces of the others were pained as well, and for a moment she felt a slight twinge of jealousy not to be part of the bigger picture. Even Mary Hudnell seemed somehow connected to what was happening at the table.

And then Sally seemed to be punished for her moment of envy. A sudden, searing pain, the likes of which she had never known before, tore through her body. She gasped aloud, the agony seeming to enter through her hands, gripped painfully tight by Wickham on one side, and Standish on the other. It traveled up her arms and into her chest, where it nestled, pulsing with the beat of her heart, every throb more excruciating than the last. She fought to pull her hands away, but it was impossible. The pain continued to grow, flowing through her body, filling her stomach and branching to her legs. Within seconds her entire body was in the grip of unbearable torture, and she cried out, rallying her strength, pushing past the paralyzing sensation to find her voice, to call her husband's name; he would know what to do, he would help her.

But her screams did not break the spell, and the torment churning inside her continued to grow unabated. Like a wild animal, she thrashed, but they wouldn't wake up, they wouldn't let go.

And when Sally believed it wasn't possible to hurt any worse, she saw that her husband's eyes, all of their eyes, were open. They were watching her pain, and they did nothing to stop it.

It was becoming more and more difficult to breathe. She tried to speak, to beg for help, but they just continued to stare.

"It's not enough," Absolom repeated, looking directly into her pain-moistened eyes.

Why won't he help me? Her frenzied mind wanted to know. *Why won't the man I love help me?*

"To show our commitment, there must be more," he bellowed over the sounds of the machine, which had grown steadily louder since her agony had begun.

There was a plaintive sound to his voice, as if Absolom was trying to explain something to her. But she didn't want his explanations; all she wanted was for the pain to stop. And then it became terrifyingly clear as her flesh began to bubble and smoke, the inner fire that she could feel seething inside her, was eating its way out.

"There must be sacrifice," he said, his eyes riveted to hers. "You are the one he chose."

Her nostrils filled with the sickening smell of roasting meat, and her sight began to dim as the fluid within her eyes started to boil.

"I'm so sorry," she heard her husband say, just as the inner fire erupted from her body with a ferocious

roar, the last of the pale, delicate flesh that Absolom
had once so loved to caress, charred black.

"The sacrifice is you."

Tom Manning stood at the window of his office, lost
somewhere in the corridors of the past. It had been
snowing since early morning and a good three or
four inches had already accumulated in the parking
lot and on the cars below. But it really didn't register.

He hadn't gone home last night, choosing instead
to stay in his office at BPRD headquarters, and
though he'd tried to distract himself with work, he'd
found his thoughts drifting on more than one occasion.

It was amazing how much he still remembered. He
could almost hear the sounds of the nurses' rubber-
soled shoes as they squeaked upon the waxed linoleum floors of the institution, smell the overwhelming
odor of antiseptic that filled the air in an attempt to
cover the reek of sickness, that hint of something gone
sour beneath the stink of industrial-strength cleaning
products.

I'm going home soon, right, Tommy?

Tom shuddered and pulled himself from the past.
He was actually startled to see how much more snow
had fallen while he'd been lost in thought. His phone
rang, and he picked up the receiver, placing it to his
ear with a quiet sigh of relief.

"Yes."

"Hellboy and Liz are back," Kate said. "They're waiting for you in R and D."

The two agents had called in a report on their way back from Waldoboro, and Tom was anxious to see the specimens they had gathered.

"Good, I'll be along shortly," he replied, and hung up the phone.

But memories again forced their way into the forefront of his thoughts.

"Are you two close?" a pretty nurse had asked as he'd completed the paperwork to commit the old man to the institution.

"Excuse me?" he'd responded, flustered.

"You and your uncle, are you close?"

The image of the old man—his uncle, lying restrained on a hospital bed, withered and frail—imposed itself upon his mind's eye, and no matter what he did, Tom could not make it go away.

Uncle Steve.

Manning drifted back to the window, the knowledge of what he had done tender, a wound that refused to heal.

He died alone.

Hellboy dumped the Indian blanket filled with the remains of zombie robots onto the steel examination table with a loud clatter.

"Take a look at this, guys," he said, stepping back so that the three techs could inspect the remains.

He called them the Stooges: Curly, Larry and Moe. He had no idea what their real names were, although he was sure that they had told him at least a dozen times over the years. It was just easier to call them by their Stooges' monikers. They said nothing, slipping on rubber gloves and protective eye gear as they converged on the table.

"Pardon the stink," he said, waving a hand in front of his face. "There are real corpses at their chewy centers."

Abe rolled his shiny dark eyes and shook his head. "So these things actually attacked you?" he asked, craning his neck to see between the bustling bodies of the techs. The three were muttering among themselves now, excited by their findings.

"Yep, this one and a whole bunch of others," he said. "But one got away with the bag."

Abe looked at him, head tilted to one side. "Bag?"

"Medicine bag of some powerful Indian mystic dude," Hellboy explained. "Another pilfered item of worship to add to the list."

The amphibious man had to sidestep quickly to avoid a collision with Curly as the tech moved around the table to approach his investigation from another angle. "And how's Liz?" he asked.

"She's at the infirmary now. Got a little cut up by the mechanical zombie birds."

"Mechanical zombie birds," Abe repeated, voice a bit hollow.

Hellboy moved toward the table, reaching down to pluck one of the broken, mechanical sparrows from the remains. The Stooges let out a strange, hissing sound as he took the object away.

"Don't get your tighty-whities in a twist, I'll bring it right back," he assured them. "Man, it's like they've never seen reanimated corpses before."

He showed the mechanical bird to Abe.

"Would you look at that," Abe said, reaching out a long, delicate finger to touch the edge of one of its wings and drew it back quickly. "It's sharp!"

"No kidding," Hellboy said, tossing the sparrow back onto the tabletop. "You should try dealing with a whole flock of these things." He opened his arms to show off the hundreds of tiny gashes that had been made in his red flesh. "It's a good thing I don't scar easy."

Moe stepped away from the table, as if looking at the remains of the robotic monstrosity from a distance would give him some new perspective; the others followed suit.

"So what's the verdict, guys?" Hellboy asked them.

"Nope," Moe said with a shake of his head. "There isn't any conceivable way that this device functioned on any level."

"Never mind engaging you and Miss Sherman in combat," added Larry. He too was shaking is head in disbelief.

"Look at it," Curly chimed in, pointing to specific

areas on the automaton. "It's just a corpse with pieces of wood and metal bolted to it." He removed one of his rubber gloves. "Its belly is stuffed with wire, for God's sake. There's no way this thing would have been able to walk around."

Hellboy sighed, slowly nodding, as if finally understanding. "Yeah, you guys are totally right," he said. "I musta just imagined getting attacked by an army of these things. Thanks for setting me straight. Hey, Abe, would you mind going down to the infirmary and telling Liz that she doesn't have to worry about getting those cuts looked at. After all, they were only made by figments of our friggin' imaginations."

Moe looked flustered. "We're not saying you weren't attacked," he attempted to explain.

"It's just that we can't imagine how and . . ." Larry seemed suddenly at a loss for words.

Moe was at the pile again, poking around inside the corpse's stomach cavity. "Well, well, what do we have here?" he muttered as he snatched a funky-looking tool from a stainless-steel tray nearby and spread the creature's stomach wider. His hands disappeared inside the corpse and withdrew a cylindrical object. "Come to poppa," he said, his protective eye gear reflecting the glow from the object.

"What'd you find?" Hellboy asked, craning his neck for a look. He'd always felt a bit left out around these science guys.

"Looks like some kind of crude storage cell," Larry said, adjusting his safety glasses.

"But for what kind of energy?" Curly asked, reaching out to tap at the thick glass body of the cylinder. "I've never seen anything like it."

The energy inside the battery moved around like something alive—like a puppy in a pet store window, responding to the lab technicians' attentions.

Wires dripping with moisture trailed from the bottom of the cylinder, leading back into the body. Moe reached behind him, feeling the tray for another tool. "I'll disconnect these wires and we can begin our analysis on . . ."

The body bolted upright upon the table.

"Yaaggh!" Hellboy yelled, jumping back.

The Stooges stared in awe, watching as the reanimated corpse turned its dead eyes upon them. It lashed out at the technicians with one of its razor-fingered hands. All but Moe managed to get away. The creature slashed his face, and he stumbled, letting the glowing cylinder fall from his grasp.

Hellboy grimaced as he grabbed the dead thing, restraining it. "Sorry about that, guys. I thought they were pretty much dead."

The creature bucked Hellboy off and pushed away, falling from the table, scattering various pieces of zombie robot in its wake.

"It's getting away!" Moe screamed, a towel pressed to the wounds on his face.

"Hey, get back here!" Hellboy snapped, moving around the table in pursuit.

Missing its left arm and right leg, the creature skittered across the linoleum floor, heading toward the open door.

"Oh no you don't," Abe said. He ran forward and threw his body against the door, slamming it shut.

The mechanized corpse reared back like a cobra ready to strike, looking frantically around the basement lab for another means of escape.

"Got anything I can use to kill this thing for good?" Hellboy shouted at the lab techs.

Larry and Curly rummaged through drawers and open cabinets.

The zombie robot fixed its gaze upon an upper window. In a flash, the creature crawled across the floor and scaled the cinder-block wall like some sort of twisted insect.

"Anytime now," Hellboy said, running to the wall.

The creature was pulling on the black metal screen that covered the window, removing the bottom screws from the frame with its razor claws.

"Here!" Curly called, and Hellboy turned.

He caught the glinting metal object and gazed down into his hand with disbelief. "What the hell am I supposed to do with this?" he asked, waving a scalpel around in the air. It looked ridiculously small in his large hand.

The third screw broke free from the window frame,

and the zombie robot lashed out, smashing the window behind it. It started to wiggle its body through the opening.

Tossing the scalpel aside, Hellboy leaped and grabbed hold of the automaton's ankle, giving it a good yank.

"Where do you think you're going?"

The creature tumbled from its perch, and he threw it violently to the floor.

The zombie robot lay there, its power source pulsing at the end of a braid of multicolored wires, almost convincing Hellboy that this time it was down for the count.

But then the animated corpse sprang up from the floor, propelled by its one good leg, its mouth open in a silent scream of rage as it attached itself to him. Hellboy stumbled backward, almost knocked off his feet, and crashed into a desk in the corner of the room.

"God damn it!" he growled, peeling the thrashing creature away, its clawed hand raking ineffectually down his chest.

Abe stood over by the Stooges, checking the lacerations on Moe's face. "Need some help with that?" he called to Hellboy.

"I got it," Hellboy snapped, again throwing the zombie to the floor. It tried to get away again, but he brought his hoof down upon its ankle, pinning it. "Not so fast, Stinky."

It clawed at the ground with its single hand. Hellboy grabbed an office chair out from beneath the desk and used it like a club, bringing it down upon the thrashing corpse, once, twice. When he hit the struggling creature for the third time a flash of emerald radiance temporarily blinded him. Hellboy stumbled away from the clockwork zombie, letting the chair fall from his grasp.

"What the hell did you do?" Larry asked, as they all rubbed at their eyes.

"Guess I broke him," Hellboy replied, shielding his eyes from the steadily increasing flow of energy from within the corpse. "Actually, I think I broke the battery."

Strange, almost human shapes began to form in the crackling discharge, many of them dissipating like so much smoke, while others seemed to look around, examining their surroundings before suddenly departing in a blink, as if drawn away by some silent siren call.

Abe came to stand beside him, a clinical spectator. "Ghosts?"

"Yeah," Hellboy replied. "I guess our robot zombies run on spook power. Didn't see that one coming."

Most of the ghosts simply vanished, sucked off into the ether. But the last of the spectral residue lingered, hanging in the air above the corpse. It expanded and began to take on shape.

"Come on! What now?" Hellboy muttered, and grabbed for his chair again.

Like an amoeba, the ghostly energy divided, splitting into two separate forms, each of them gradually becoming more and more defined. One of the shapes became a woman clothed in a pretty, high-collared dress from an earlier era. Her flesh was charred and blackened, making the cause of her death obvious. The second of the amorphous energies coalesced into an older man with thick, black-framed glasses and a balding head. Strands of ghostly hair wafted in the air where they had been placed in a pathetic attempt at a comb-over. The ghost wore a button-down shirt, oversize cardigan sweater, and sagging wool trousers.

The ghostly old man brought a hand up, adjusted the glasses on his face and smiled.

"Hey, Sally, look who it is," he said to the horribly burned woman floating by his side. "It's Hellboy."

The ghost rubbed his hands together as if in anticipation.

"I always wanted to meet this guy."

CHAPTER 6

Absolom Spearz was not happy.

Eight of his mechanical agents had been sent to Maine to retrieve the latest item from his list, but only one had returned. It stood before him now, swaying on its reinforced legs of metal and wood, the ornate Indian medicine bag clutched tightly in one of its spindly hands.

"Give it to me," he ordered, and the drone held the bag out to him.

Absolom carefully pried the Indian artifact from its rigid fingers, and brought it to his workstation. He felt his followers' eyes upon him. They were a nervous lot, and could he blame them? The last time they had attempted this task the result had been the demise of their corporeal forms. Now that they were once again flesh and blood, they did not want to risk losing their coveted physical shapes.

He took the bag and placed it inside the framework of a pyramid-shaped device constructed from strips of copper. A bank of machines nearby immediately began to click and chatter. Colored lights flashed wildly as a black needle on a gauge gradually began to move from right to left, measuring the degree of residual power stored within the medicine bag.

"Excellent," he stated, anger abating as he watched the needle fluctuate very close to the maximum level.

Absolom then took the medicine bag from within the pyramid, walking across the subterranean room to store it with the other items they had obtained over the last few days. The pallet was overflowing with objects collected by his clockwork drones—religious statuary, rare limited-edition books, children's toys— all items loved, and in turn, saturated with an energy created from adoration, an energy that would eventually be put to a far greater purpose.

He set their latest prize down beside an urn filled with the ashes of a writer who, if what Absolom understood was true, had established his own religion, setting himself up as some kind of earthly deity receiving messages from a being that lived amid the stars.

Blasphemy.

It took all of his self-control not to smash the man's remains to the ground for formulating such sacrilege, but he held his anger in check, for the faith-instilled power stored in the funeral urn was far too valuable to waste on a fleeting display of anger.

He turned away from the items to see that his followers had returned to their appointed chores. There was much still to be completed to set the stage for their god's arrival, and he was overjoyed to see that they had embraced these tasks with great determination. There were other things that required his own attention, Absolom knew, and he headed back to the clockwork drone still standing at attention where he had left it.

"What of your brethren? Who prevented their return?" Absolom reached out to his silent servant, cupping its cold, pale cheek. The corpse was that of a young man, its face gaunt from sickness. "If only I'd given you the gift of speech, eh?"

He removed a penknife from the pocket of his jeans and used the blade to slice open the decaying flesh of the drone's stomach. He reached into the cavity, feeling around for its power source. Recognizing its shape, he withdrew the battery for inspection. The spirit-energies were nearly depleted, he saw, and disconnected the power cell so that it could be recharged.

Absolom heard the sound of someone approaching and turned to see the dog gingerly padding toward him. "What is it, Silas?"

The mechanical voice box bolted to the shaved flesh of the dog's throat crackled to life. "Only one returned," Silas stated in a hollow, metallic-sounding voice.

Absolom started to feel the first twinge of regret for having constructed the device that allowed the canine Electricizer the ability to communicate.

"Shouldn't you be outside, patrolling the property like I asked?" he said, using a cloth to wipe the foul-smelling fluids of rot from the surface of the battery.

"What could have done this?" Silas prodded. "What could have prevented the others from returning to us?"

"It is not your concern." Absolom approached the dog and patted his large, blocky head. "Go back to your assignment."

"But what if there are forces that have learned of our return?" Silas asked, moving his head away from the man's comforting touch. "What if, like before, they are gathering to stop us from completing our sacred task?"

Absolom sighed. The thought had crossed his own mind, but he had not wished to give it credence.

"If only we could see what it saw," Silas's voice crackled. "Then we would know for certain if our plans are in danger."

The sudden pain inside Absolom's head was sharp, causing his eyes to water. It wasn't the first time he had felt such agony, like having steel needles driven through his skull. He called them his spells, and they signaled the beginning of some new, wondrous idea, when his mind would be filled with the designs and the knowledge to build the most incredible of machines. They were a gift from his god, the means by which to guarantee Qemuel's eventual arrival to the world of man.

"Absolom?" he heard the dog-Silas call to him, his electronic voice box the result of a spell very much like this one just two days ago. But Absolom was already in the grip of his vision, and his hands twitched eagerly to create that which was now burning in his mind.

He moved like a man possessed, snatching up pieces of metal, circuitry, and wire at a fevered pace. In a matter of minutes, the image inside his head had become a reality, and the pain inside his skull began to fade as he attached the last of the wire connections to a power source. Absolom gazed down at his hands to find them smeared with blood, tiny razor cuts in the tips of his fingers weeping crimson as the device neared completion.

The dog's tail wagged happily as he approached. "Was it something I said?"

"The eyes," Absolom said. "We'll see what it saw through its eyes."

He took out his penknife again and extended the blade as he approached the drone. There was little time for subtlety. He simply shoved the blade into the corner of the clockwork man's eye and popped the gelatinous orb from its socket. He repeated the process with the other eye, leaving just enough of the optic nerve dangling from each.

As he had suddenly known how to build the bizarre device, Absolom knew how to operate it as well. He brought the eyes to his workstation and carefully inserted two long, needlelike sensors into the ends of the dangling nerves.

His creative spell had caught the attention of the others, and they had wandered over to see what new invention their god had bestowed upon him. He didn't mind, for what they were about to see would help them in their task, showing the potential threat to their mission.

"As you're all aware," he said, flicking switches and turning dials on the front of the virgin device, "eight of our agents were sent out to recover yet another object of worship, but for some reason, only one returned.

"With this machine, we will see what our servant saw." A twenty-two-inch monitor, one of many scattered about the subbasement, came to life, the image upon it starting out barely visible, but slowly coming into view.

Absolom stepped closer, squinting, trying to discern the blurred images. "Who are you?" he asked, as two shapes slowly began to take form.

He reached down to the eyes resting upon the surface of his worktable, making sure that the connection to the optic nerves was solid. He gave one of the attachments the slightest jiggle, and the image appeared as clear as day—as if they were looking through a window.

And his disciples gasped, Annabel Standish letting out a tiny, frightened scream.

A woman, flames blazing from the tips of her fingers, and even more disturbing, a red-skinned monster, had appeared upon the monitor.

"Brothers and sisters," Absolom said, unable to tear his eyes from the nightmarish visage. "We knew that our attempts to bring our god into this world, to purify the evils here, would draw the attention of those who would stand against us. Our worst fears have been realized."

He reached out, tentatively touching the image of the crimson beast upon the screen.

"It appears that the Devil himself attempts to thwart our plans."

The first thing Tom Manning noticed as he opened the door into the lab was the extreme drop in temperature. He could actually see his breath.

"Why is it so cold in here?" Liz asked, entering behind him.

He had met up with the agent as she left the infirmary and been a bit startled to see the extent of her injuries. She wore a loose-fitting tank top, and the exposed areas of her face and arms were covered with small bandages. After he'd confirmed that her injuries were mostly superficial, they had headed for R and D together, while Liz briefed him on the mission that had earned her those wounds.

Now Manning stopped short and Liz stumbled against him. His eyes fell upon the mangled body lying on the floor, then he stared at the two ghostly apparitions floating in the air above Hellboy, Abe, and three of the Bureau's top science geeks.

"Can't let these guys out of your sight for a minute," Liz muttered.

"Join the party, boss," Hellboy said as he caught sight of Manning. "I was duking it out with one of those robot zombie things and when I busted open its power source . . . well, we got ghosts. Call the exterminators."

Manning stared at the floating specters, jaw hanging open in astonishment.

"Oh, God," Liz gasped.

It took Manning a second to realize that she wasn't reacting to the ghosts—it was hardly the first time she'd seen one—but to the charred appearance of the female phantom, who had obviously burned to death. Manning figured the burned woman stirred up disturbing memories from Liz's past, of the day that she'd lost control of her unique ability and killed her entire family in a flash fire.

But Manning's astonishment was reserved for the other ghost, the male specter who floated beside her.

"Uncle Steve," he said softly. He moved toward the apparition as if pulled by some powerful force, not really wanting to believe in the sight before him, but suddenly realizing that everything that had happened to him of late now made a twisted kind of sense.

"Hiya, Tommy," the spirit said cheerfully.

"Uncle Steve?" Hellboy said. "You're related to this spook?"

Manning nodded, unable to take his eyes from the ghost. "He is . . . he *was* my uncle."

"Freakin' small world," Hellboy muttered, crossing his arms and shaking his head in amazement.

Like a balloon caught in a current of air, the ghost of Manning's uncle drifted across the room to hover before him.

"It's been a long time, Tommy," Uncle Steve said, his voice sounding exactly as Manning remembered.

He didn't quite know how to describe what he was feeling; a bizarre mixture of surprise, sadness and a little bit of fear thrown in for good measure. Slowly, he nodded; it *had* been a long time. Manning thought back to his childhood, when he'd spent two weeks of every summer vacation in Lynn with his eccentric Uncle Steve.

Steve was an oddball, an unapologetic bachelor with eccentric qualities and even more bizarre interests. Everyone in the family thought he was weird, which was probably one of the reasons Tom had gravitated to him. He'd never tired of hearing his uncle's countless stories about his travels around the globe with the merchant marine, and his uncle never tired of telling them.

A floodgate of memories from his youth burst open. His first drink of beer, fishing in the Saugus River, learning how to play poker: All of those memories involved Uncle Steve. Even his perspective on the world was partially thanks to this man.

Unc had always believed that the world was much more than it let on, that it was a place of hidden mysteries. At first, Tom hadn't really understood what the man was talking about, but gradually, as the summers passed, he began to believe that his uncle just might have been a little crazy. Books and magazines on UFOs, lost civilizations, the Bermuda Triangle, Bigfoot, and Atlantis littered his apartment; no theory was too wild for his uncle. In the beginning, it had been sort of cool being lectured about the secrets of the world, but as Tom grew older, his feelings began to change.

He remembered his uncle's phone calls every June, how excited he'd been, wondering when Tom would be coming to stay with him. But after a while, Tom hadn't wanted to go anymore. He'd had more friends around his home, and was starting to notice girls, and the fact that his uncle was becoming increasingly eccentric did not help matters. Tom was growing up and really didn't have time for crazy relatives.

If Uncle Steve had been disappointed, he really hadn't shown it, telling him that he understood, and that maybe they could get together sometime later in the year or even the following summer, and then would launch into some story about cattle mutilations in Montana, and how he'd like to take a trip out there to investigate. But as far as Tom knew, Steve never did take those trips, instead remaining in Massachusetts, reading his books and magazines, uncovering new secrets about the world from the safety of his La-Z-Boy.

Darker memories from the last time he'd seen the man pushed their way past the pleasant remembrances, forcing Manning to recall the bad along with the good.

Tom had lost touch with his uncle over the years. In fact, Steve hadn't even bothered to show up for the funeral of his own sister, Tom's mother. But Tom continued to think of his weird uncle from time to time, wondering where he was and what he was doing. There was even a part of him that wondered if the old-timer had passed away without anyone being the wiser. And then he'd received the phone call from a social worker—Uncle Steve had been arrested for attempted arson and been sent to Mount Pleasant for psychiatric evaluation.

Tom had tried to ignore the phone call, but he felt a certain responsibility not only to his uncle, but also to his mother's memory. She'd always felt bad for Steve, even though he had pretty much rejected all of her attempts to maintain a relationship.

Manning studied the apparition hovering before him. The ghost of his uncle appeared precisely as Tom remembered him from those summers so long ago.

By contrast, the man he had gone to see at the Mount Pleasant Rehabilitation Center had been a pale reflection of the uncle he had known. He'd found a scrawny scarecrow of man, not the merchant marine who had supposedly dined with headhunters in the Philippines. A sick-looking old man, tied to his bed with soft restraints, had somehow replaced him. It was heartbreaking, but there was really nothing anybody could do. His uncle was suffering from severe dementia, and was a danger not only to himself, but potentially to others as evidenced by his attempts to set fire to a house. It was only pure luck that the home was unoccupied and that there had recently been heavy rains that kept the structure from burning to the ground.

At first his uncle hadn't known Tom, but gradually he had seen the spark of recognition come into the old man's red, watery eyes.

"Can I go home now, Tommy?" Steve had asked him, the man's once-booming voice reduced to a croaking whisper.

He'd tried to explain to the old man that he was sick, and that he needed to stay in the hospital until he was well again, but Steve would hear nothing of it, demanding to be allowed to go back to his apartment at once.

It shamed Manning to recall how he had lost his temper, worn down by having the responsibility for his uncle's care thrust upon him so abruptly. In a condescending tone, he had explained to the old man that the reason he couldn't go home was that they were all afraid that he might hurt somebody.

Through tear-drenched eyes, Steve had tried to tell him why he had tried to burn down the farmhouse, some nonsense about how something bad had been attempted there a long time ago, when he was just a little boy. It had been stopped, Uncle Steve had told him, but with the house still standing, there was nothing to prevent it from happening again. By burning it down, Steve said he was making sure that the evil didn't have something to return to.

Manning had realized then that nothing had changed. His uncle's stories had simply become crazier. In the end he'd told his uncle that he understood, and that he would talk to the doctors about letting him go home, and that had seemed to calm him. He'd sat with Steve until the old man finally drifted off into a fitful sleep, then Manning had quietly left the room and signed the papers to have his uncle involuntarily committed. He'd had Steve's best interests in mind, for the man was obviously sick and would require professionals to care for him.

Steve had passed not too long after Manning had left the FBI and gone to work for the BPRD. The old man had died in his sleep. A decent way to go if you had to choose, Manning imagined, but it didn't change the fact that Uncle Steve had died alone.

Manning had always intended to visit, to spend more time with the old man in the last of his days. He'd wanted to share some of what he'd seen with the BPRD, wanted to tell his uncle that he finally understood some of those crazy stories he'd told during those early summer vacations, that they really did have some basis in fact. But he never quite seemed to be able to find the time.

The guilt Manning felt over what he had done—what he *hadn't* done—was as painful now as it was then.

"Why . . . ?" he began, not sure really what to say to the specter from his past.

"Why am I here?" the ghost of Uncle Steve said, the words seeming to drift from his mouth, just as much phantoms as the man himself. "That's the million-dollar question, isn't it? There's something bad coming, Tommy."

There was an expression on his ethereal features that Manning could only guess was fear. *But what can ghosts possibly be afraid of?*

"The Band of Electricizers," his uncle's ghost said. "They're back."

CHAPTER 7

Lynn, Massachusetts, Winter 1901

Tonight was the night.
Everything had happened so quickly.

The god Qemu'el had spoken to them, each and every one of his Band of Electricizers, and in his words they heard a promise of paradise.

Absolom hurried across the frozen yard and down the winding path to the barn, barely able to contain his excitement.

He turned up the collar of his woolen coat and held it tight around his throat against the biting winter wind. His Sally had loved the winter, and had looked forward to spending her first in New England. An image rose in Absolom's mind of Sally as he'd seen her last. She'd been nothing more than a horribly burned husk, and yet, her clothing had remained untouched from the heat. Sally had burned from within. Their god had ignited her inner fire, using her life force, feeding on her life spark so that he could speak to them of his plans for humanity. It saddened him that Sally had been taken, but he was also certain that if she had known the importance of the message that the god had wanted to share with them, she would have given her life up willingly.

He missed his Sally dearly, but what was being offered to them—offered to the world—was so much bigger than one man's love.

At the end of the path stood his barn, a sturdy structure of unfinished oak with a stone foundation. As their work flourished, the subbasement below the house had grown too cramped, forcing them to relocate to the barn. When the house was being constructed, Sally had worried about the additional expense of a barn, but somehow, he had always known that it would one day become necessary.

Absolom rapped on the barn door, a quick pattern to the knock that was a secret signal the Band of Electricizers shared. One could never be too careful. As Absolom and his followers had gone about gathering and purchasing the supplies they needed to fulfill the god's wishes, they had drawn the curiosity of the citizens of Lynn. He could not confide in them—their primitive minds were not prepared to comprehend something of this magnitude—so he'd assuaged their curiosity by telling them that he had decided to add on to his home. That had seemed to satisfy them for a time, but just the other day, he had chased away several young boys he'd found snooping about the barn.

Waiting for a response to his knock, he could not help but smile. Out of all the souls that toiled upon the world, *he* had picked them to be *his* ushers, guiding *him* into the world. The thought warmed Absolom against the frigid New England wind.

Geoffrey Wickham, his drooping, hound-dog face showing signs of stress, opened the barn door, his cheeks flushed pink and dappled with sweat. The old man was wearing the special armor that Absolom had designed, made from burnished strips of copper attached to a heavy suit of woven mail. *What a sight he is,* Absolom thought, *a knight of a glorious new order.*

"Come in, come in," the old man said with urgency, his armor rattling. "We've been waiting for you—we think the time is near."

Absolom nodded, for the same feeling of imminence had touched him as well. He had been meditating at the house, opening himself to the ether in case the god should need to communicate any final instructions before his arrival. While deep in the grip of his trance he had once more been shown images of the world as it would be afterward, and how they could assist this messiah of a new age with its transcendence.

What a world it will be, Absolom thought, enrap-

tured by the vision still fresh in his mind. He saw
great cities dwarfed by towering spires, crackling
energy harnessed from the spirits of the dead connecting one tower to the next, filling the world with a
power it had never known. And he saw people, no
longer afraid, hands clasped and filled with the glory
of the god, awaiting their transformation, faces turned
to the heavens.

And it was all to start here, now.

"Yes. The time is near. And it shall be glorious,"
Absolom said as he entered.

He made a quick circuit of the barn, inspecting the
machinery that had been assembled there, fabulous
contraptions designed by the god but built by the
human hands of the Band of Electricizers. He called
them his god machines, for with them, he would
deliver his savior unto the world.

Absolom watched Tyler, Annabel, and Silas as they
went about their duties, each assigned vital tasks. In
the armor he'd designed, they moved heavily from one
device to the next, each of them checking and then
rechecking the work of the other. Everything had to
be perfect, or all of their work would be for naught.

"And the vessel?" he asked, removing his heavy
woolen coat and letting it drop to the floor. He too
wore the armor he had designed.

"Waiting to be filled," Wickham answered, hobbling over to join Absolom at a table in the center of
the room.

This was the most important of their creations, and Absolom felt his heart flutter as he reached down to pull away the sheet that covered the object upon the table. It was built in the shape of a man. Made of metal and wood, this vessel would contain the spiritual essence of their savior, giving their god a mighty form in which to lead them.

Absolom ran his fingers over the rough surface of the mechanical body. He pricked his finger upon a jagged edge of steel, smearing the metal that composed its broad rib cage with blood.

"Do you think he'll like it?" Absolom asked Wickham, suddenly concerned with the crudity of the armature. He brought his bloody finger to his mouth, sucking upon the weeping gash.

"I have no doubt that he will," Wickham said. "Our messiah will leave all who look upon him breathless."

Absolom closed his eyes and imagined his god adorned in the body he and his band had made, preaching to the masses. They would sit at his right hand, of course, high priests of a new world order.

"It cannot come soon enough," Absolom said dreamily, opening his eyes. "And where is the Madonna?"

Wickham pointed with his cane to the far end of the barn, where a door stood slightly ajar. "It was becoming too warm for her in here. She said she had to step outside before she burned up like poor Sally."

Absolom flinched at the memory of his wife's demise. "I see," he said, proceeding toward the open door.

"I think she knows that the time draws near," the old man said, reaching beneath one of the copper plates of armor draped upon his chest and producing a handkerchief, "and is a tad . . . anxious."

"Mary Hudnell will do just fine," Absolom responded. "Remember, it was god who chose her to deliver him into this world."

"Let us hope that your assumptions are correct," he said. "I'd hate for the birth of god to be tainted somehow by the tirades of a spoiled heiress." Wickham turned, hobbling away to join the others in their preparations.

The draft that crept in from the open, rear door of the barn was wonderfully invigorating. Absolom stepped quietly outside, not wanting to startle the mother-to-be. The winter sun had faded quickly, and the only illumination came from the starlit patches of snow still clinging to the forest floor.

"Mary?" he called softly, his eyes searching the shadows.

He found her leaning against a birch tree, staring out into the woods. She was clothed in a heavy wool dress, a shawl draped over her head, and he wondered if she was purposefully adopting the look of the mother of god.

"Absolom," she said, picking her way toward him

through what remained of the snow. From the way she waddled, he thought her belly might have grown even larger since he had seen her earlier that afternoon.

Mary threw her arms around him and held him in a tender embrace. He hugged her back, feeling the push of her hard, pregnant stomach against him.

Only days had passed since the first attempt to communicate with their god had resulted in the sacrifice of his wife—and *this*. From that moment of conception, Mary's belly had swollen by the hour. Using Sally's death as a source of power, the god had transferred his divine essence across the void to take root in Mary's womb.

A miracle—the first of many to come.

"How are we feeling?" Absolom asked, continuing to hold her close.

Mary was trembling, and he had to wonder how much of it was due to cold.

"I . . . I can feel him . . . growing inside me." She shivered, wrapping her arms tighter around him.

"As he should be," Absolom said, gently pushing her away to look into her eyes. He gave her his most reassuring smile. "He'll need to be strong to make the transition."

Absolom placed his hand gently upon her protruding belly, gasping aloud as his mind became filled with the god's presence.

"*It is time,*" Qemu'el whispered in his mind, and

Absolom was nearly driven to his knees by the intensity of the proclamation. He pulled his hand away, breaking the connection, his head still swimming from the sensory assault.

"Did he speak to you?" Mary asked. "What did he say? Is everything all right? Is he all right?"

Absolom gulped at the cold, winter air, desperate to catch his breath. "He seems to be fine. Eager to be born."

Mary placed her hands upon her bulbous stomach. "Is it time?" she asked, her voice little more than a whisper.

He nodded, reaching out to take one of her hands in his. "It is."

Her fingers were like ice and he gave them a gentle squeeze. "And are you ready?"

Mary began to cry, fat tears running down her pretty face. "Will he know me as his mother?" she asked, her voice trembling with emotion. "Will he love me?"

Absolom pulled her to him again in a tender embrace. "He will love us all. But I would not be surprised if he reserved a very special love just for you." And he began to lead her toward the door, the final steps toward a new destiny for the world.

"I would do anything to keep him safe," Mary said, as they entered through the doorway. "Does he know that?"

"I'm sure he does," Absolom reassured her, his

mind already beginning to review the process that would transfer the divine spirit currently growing within the womb of Mary Hudnell to the body that had been constructed to contain it.

He closed the rear door of the barn behind them, cutting off the breeze. Absolom led Mary to a special chair, built to assist her in the process of birth, and helped her to lie upon it. He placed a red velvet pillow beneath her head and, seeing that she was comfortable, turned to his disciples. They all stood together now, the twinkle of anticipation showing in their eyes.

"It's time, brothers and sisters," he said, barely able to contain his own enthusiasm.

From beneath their robes they each withdrew the god's gift to them. The crystal cylinders contained the power to run the machines that would allow their holy savior to make the transition from spirit to corporeal. The energy within the cylinders churned and pulsed with the power of conviction, of belief, collected over these last years. Those who had contributed had been blissfully unaware that they were helping to change the world. It was a powerful gift from a god that loved them so.

On a makeshift altar covered with scarlet cloth they placed their gifts, the keys that unlocked the doorway to man's ascension. Silas and Tyler went together to fetch the final piece of the mechanism that would make it all happen. It was little more than a wooden box, its four sides inscribed with strange symbols provided to Absolom by his savior. Sigils of transition, the god had explained. The two men, clad in their ceremonial armor, wheeled the unassuming apparatus toward him.

Absolom instructed them to position the machine between Mary and the hollow body they had constructed to be the god's receptacle. He undid a copper clasp on the front of the box and exposed the contraption's innards—tubing and wires, gears and pistons, copper and rubber, and beneath it all a separate compartment left open for the power source—the crystal cylinders. He barely recollected its construction but knew that he had been responsible. In the grip of divine inspiration, he had toiled for seven days and seven nights to bring it forth from his fevered mind.

"The gifts!" Absolom said.

The Electricizers returned to the makeshift altar, retrieving their faith-engorged crystals. One after another, they fed the cylinders to the machine.

Absolom was the last to place his holy offering within the belly of the device. He held his breath as he experienced a moment of self-doubt over whether the machine would function, but function it did, the internal workings coming to life as soon as the last component was secured within it. Silently he thanked his lord and master for giving him the knowledge to build such a miraculous instrument.

Mary screamed, writhing upon her birth chair. He went to her, taking her hand in his.

"What is it, dear one?" he asked.

Her eyes were wide and glassy, her breathing coming in short gulps. "It hurts," she gasped. "As . . . as if there's a fire growing inside me." She squeezed his hand nearly crushing the bones within it. "Please don't let me burn."

Panic was setting in, and Absolom knew that it was time. Tearing his hand away from hers, he returned to the machine. Coiled beneath the throbbing mechanism were two sets of thick cables, and at the end of each was a needle, precisely twelve inches in length.

"Take these to the subjects," he instructed as Geoffrey and Annabel rushed forward to embrace their designated chore.

The disciples moved toward the subjects, Geoffrey toward the Madonna and Annabel the vessel.

"Insert the needles," Absolom ordered, closely monitoring the function of the transference apparatus.

Annabel carefully slid the long piece of metal through the rib cage and into the metal body of the vessel. "Done," she said, stepping away from the table, a triumphant smile upon her face.

Absolom waited to hear the same from Wickham, but it didn't come. Annoyed that the old man was keeping them waiting, keeping their god waiting, he looked up to see Geoffrey standing beside the panting Mary Hudnell, her eyes clamped tightly closed so as not to see the needle bearing toward her.

"Geoffrey—insert the needle!" Absolom commanded.

But the man continued to stare somewhere beyond Absolom, toward the entrance of the barn.

"Geoffrey!" Absolom screamed again, leaving his station, reaching for the cable. "Give it to me."

"We're not alone," Geoffrey said, and at first Absolom did not understand, but then the old man pointed.

Absolom noticed the child first; a little boy no older than five, his eyes like saucers as he stared at them from across the barn. There were others as well, men and women, people that he recognized from his visits to town. Some were carrying torches, and others rifles.

"What is the meaning of this?" he bellowed authoritatively, crossing the barn, feeling his anger on the rise.

A man standing behind the boy slowly raised his weapon, pointing the shotgun directly at Absolom. He stopped short, gazing into the unblinking eye of the barrel.

"See here," he started again. "You do not have the right to come here and—"

"Walter Massie says you've been asking some weird questions about dead bodies," the man replied, speaking for the mob. "Says you asked him how to keep them from rotting." He looked about him with disgust.

Absolom cursed himself for not having been more selective with the people he talked to, but he had needed to plan for the future. Qemu'el had given him a way to create tireless drones from corpses powered by the raw spiritual energies of the deceased, slaves to do the bidding of the god and his high priests.

"Just a bit of research," Absolom explained.

"Then this boy says you folks're doing something funny out here," the man continued. "Inside the barn."

Absolom remembered the boy as one that he had chased away the other day. The child must have seen them at work, building the vessel.

"We thought it might be in our best interests to come on over and check it out," the man said, as his eyes passed over each of the machines the group had built over the last two weeks. "And from the looks of things, I'm glad we did."

Absolom smiled congenially, and spread his hands in front of himself. "We don't mean anybody any harm. We are simply in the process of completing some experiments that . . ."

"Is that part of your experiments?" the man asked, pointing with his gun.

Absolom turned and was startled to see that the birthing chair was empty. Mary Hudnell was gone. The man was referring to the metal body lying upon the table.

"Yes it is," Absolom said, turning away from the

mob to go to the vessel. His eyes darted about the barn, searching for signs of Mary, but she was nowhere to be found. He tried to catch the eyes of the others, but their attentions were riveted on the mob before them.

There was no further purpose to dissembling. Absolom smiled. "You see, using these machines, we're going to attempt to bring our creation to life."

A disquieted murmur went through the crowd.

Absolom stood beside the table, looking down at the vessel. "I know how this must sound to you all. Not much different from when primitive man told his brethren that he was going to create fire, I'd imagine. We're going to bring it to life, and nothing in the world will ever be the same again."

A figure clad all in black, whom Absolom recognized as the church pastor, forced his way through the gathering, a Bible clutched in his hand.

"Blasphemy!" the holy man screamed, raising the black leather book in the air. "Did you hear him, brothers and sisters? They're attempting to create life! It's the Devil's work they do here!"

The crowd began to murmur all the louder, growing agitated by what they did not understand.

"You have nothing to fear from us," Absolom said. He could feel their eyes upon him, and knew that the fact that he was dressed so strangely in preparation for the ritual of transference was not lending credence to his case. "What we do here tonight will benefit all of humanity," he tried to explain, slowly making his way toward them. "Please, listen to me."

He wasn't sure where the shot originated. There was a boom like sudden thunder as the shotgun fired, and an explosion of shrieking pain as he was propelled backward to the floor of the barn.

Then all was chaos.

Absolom heard more gunfire and screams. He watched helplessly as shots tore into the transference machine, shattering the crystal cylinders in a searing flash as the precious energy contained within them was released.

He fought to stand, the pain in his shoulder excruciating, his arm dangling uselessly at his side. The thick, noxious stench of what could only have been kerosene suddenly filled his lungs, followed by the smell of wood burning. The mob had set fire to the place, and a thick black smoke was beginning to fill the confines of the barn. It was as he had feared, those who did not understand their cause, seeking to destroy them.

How could it have gone so wrong so quickly? he thought as he stumbled through the smoke, hearing the screams of his disciples and trying to find them in the din. *Why has god allowed this to happen?*

Squinting through the billowing haze, he could barely make out members of the mob fleeing their handiwork, slamming closed the door of the barn as they escaped into the night. Then he nearly fell over Silas Udell, curled into a tight ball upon the ground.

"Where are the others?" Absolom screamed, reaching down to pull the man to his feet. There was a bleeding gash on his forehead.

"I . . . I don't know," he stammered, shaking his head from side to side. "When they started shooting . . . we ran. They're here." He coughed and gasped for breath. "Somewhere in the fire."

Absolom let Silas fall back to the ground and forged ahead through the blinding smoke. He noticed that some of the machines, even though damaged, were still working. He could almost feel the unearthly hum inside the barn, like a hive of bees preparing to swarm.

"Geoffrey!" he croaked, his voice scorched hoarse from the intense heat. "Annabel! Tyler! Where are you?"

Then he saw them through the conflagration, faint shapes upon the ground. He called their names again, but they remained motionless, and he couldn't be sure if they were alive or dead.

Over the hum of the machines and the roar of the fire, he heard what he thought to be his god's voice. "I'm so sorry," he cried, falling to his knees. But the god would have none of it, forcing him to his feet—compelling him onward through the smoke and flames.

The structure of the barn was beginning to give way, the moans and shrieking creaks of the failing beams adding to the symphony of destruction around him. Through eyes filled with tears, Absolom saw an unearthly glow. At first he believed it to be more fire and tried to back away, but the hissing voice of his god ordered him forward.

Absolom found himself standing in front of one of the most intricate of the god machines. It had been built to extract the spirit energies from the ether and store them in the cylindrical power cells. He ought to have fled, but the god compelled him.

A section of roof came down nearby in shower of cinders and burning timber, and the god ordered him closer to the machine. Time was of the essence, the messiah hissed from somewhere inside his skull, but Absolom knew that his god was very far away from them now.

He almost surrendered to despair and pain, then, almost gave in to his body's agony. Absolom pictured Mary Hudnell, her stomach swollen with a life that would have brought much needed change to the world, lying dead somewhere amid the rubble of the burning barn. It was almost more than he could stand, but his god would hear none of it, compelling him to take hold of the batteries—to remove them from inside the machine.

His hands burned as he took hold of the heated canisters. The god told him that if any part of their great plan was to be salvaged, five of the batteries would be a necessity.

Absolom had so many questions, wished for reassurance, but there wasn't any time. In a matter of seconds the barn would be totally consumed in fire. He put all his trust in Qemu'el, carrying the throbbing storage cells away from the machine and into the center of the barn.

There was a shriek of splintering wood, and Absolom looked up to see a charred section of the ceiling plummeting toward him through the smoke. The wooden support struck his head and drove him to the ground, the batteries spilling from his arms and rolling across the floor.

His body had gone completely numb; the only sensation he could feel was the tickle of blood as it ran down his face from his scalp. Absolom tried to stand but found that he was pinned beneath the piece of burning oak.

"So . . . sorry," he wheezed, the air in the barn so hot that it caused his lungs to shrivel. Absolom Spearz could do nothing more, finally giving in to the pain, succumbing to the blistering heat, and as he lay there, pinned beneath the burning rubble, dying by inches, he could not help but be mesmerized by the sight of the containment cells. They continued to glow, brighter and brighter still, pulsing with an eerie thrum that seemed to match the beat of his dying heart.

Then there was only the light; all the pain had left him, and he floated in a sea of nothingness.

After a time, he asked the void, *"Am I dead?"*

His god answered. "It is not yet your time to die."
Absolom Spearz had faith.
All he needed now was patience.

Steve looked about the conference room in awe. If he
hadn't already been dead, he would have dropped
and gone to Heaven.

I'm at a meeting of the BPRD, can ya stand it?

Besides Hellboy and the hot tomato named Liz,
there was a green-skinned fish man who went by the
name of Abe and reminded Steve of the deep-sea creatures described in the books he'd read about Atlantis.
Then there was his nephew, Tom, and Tom's assistant,
Kate Corrigan, as well as some other, less colorful
members of the field operations team. It was like a
dream come true, and all he'd had to do was die to get
here.

Hellboy shifted, gesturing at the ghost. "Hey,
Steve, you with us, pal?"

"Sorry, drifted off for a minute, no pun intended."
He tried to recall the question they'd just asked him.
"I'm not really sure what the Band of Electricizers was
up to in that barn. Remember, I was only five at the
time, and when things got bad with the shooting and
the fire, my mother got me the hell out of there. All I
can say is, whatever they were up to, it freaked everybody out big-time."

Hellboy leaned back in his chair, causing it to creak
loudly in protest, and placed his hands behind his

head. "But you remember seeing some kind of mechanical man on a table. Was it like the one you and Sally were trapped in?"

Steve glanced toward the horribly burned woman. He'd grown quite fond of Sally Spearz since their imprisonment within the spirit battery. He reached out to her, mingling his noncorporeal hand with hers. She smiled, the charred edges of her mouth turning upward.

"Sort of, but there were no corpses involved. It was bigger—fancier, like they took their time to make this one look really special."

"And you think these Electricians . . ."

"Electricizers," Steve corrected. "The Band of Electricizers."

Hellboy shrugged. "Yeah. Got it. You think they're back, and responsible for the thefts of all these sacred doodads?"

"And the robot zombies," Abe added. "Don't forget them."

"Right, and the robot zombies," Hellboy echoed.

"Yeah, I do think it's them, and so does Sally."

Steve drifted up out of his seat, floating above the table. The ghost wanted to be sure they were paying attention. He didn't want them to think that his story was simply the ramblings of some crazy person. He'd had enough of that when he was still breathing.

"Since that incident when I was five, I was fascinated with the freaky stuff, always the one flipping over the rocks to see what's under them. A lot of weird shit happens in the world every day, as I'm sure you guys know, and when I was alive, I wanted to know about every bit of it."

"After I passed," he continued, "I didn't go on. There was still so much I hadn't seen—hadn't figured out yet. I found myself sort of hanging around, haunting my hometown, visiting friends from time to time, and particularly the farmhouse where the Electricizers bought it. There was just something about that place."

Tommy crossed his legs at the head of the table, looking all official. Steve was so proud of his nephew, of what he had achieved. He remembered those summer vacations they'd spent together and liked to think he'd had a part in the kid's success.

"Was that where you became trapped?" Tommy asked.

"Not at first," Steve explained. "There was some activity going on around the farmhouse, a new family moving in and stuff. Personally I thought it would be good for the place, it could make a family a real nice home, but something had happened to them since the first time I'd seen them—something was off. Even the friggin' dog was off. Different."

The ghost shuddered, remembering how the animal moved strangely about the house, as if unaccustomed to its body.

"They spent a lot of time in the basement, building

stuff. At first I really didn't give it much thought, but then the local funeral home started delivering corpses, and needless to say, my curiosity was piqued."

"If the Electroluxes were all burned in the barn fire, then who are these freaks?" Hellboy asked, shifting uncomfortably in his chair.

"I think it *is* them," Steve replied. "I think somehow the Electricizers have come back. They've been reincarnated or possessed this family or something. If you want my two cents I think they're aiming to finish what they started ninety-four years ago—which isn't good, I guarantee you."

The ghost shook his head. "That family, they never stopped. Twenty-four hours a day they were working. I haven't a clue what they were making, crazy-looking machines right out of *Weird Tales*. It's when I seen them putting up this funky map of the region that I got really concerned."

They were all listening to him, even as the story got stranger they were listening. It was a little disconcerting. Most would have called the cops by now. Of course, he was a ghost, and they were all hanging out just shooting the breeze with him. Didn't get much stranger than that. But these weren't your average Joes, this was the BPRD for Pete's sake. They ate weird for breakfast.

"The father of the family, he looked to be the leader, started talking about acquiring items of . . . imbued power, I think it was."

He guessed he said the magic words, because everyone around the table started looking at one another and writing stuff down.

"And there were these marks on certain areas of the map. I wasn't sure what they were up to until I saw them robot things being sent out on missions and coming back with all kinds of bizarre stuff: big rocks, sections of wall, even a Styrofoam cup for Christ's sake. And as all of this crap was brought in, the marks on the map were removed."

Hellboy nudged one of the three technicians who sat beside him. "Be a peach and go and get us a map."

The tech nodded, getting up from his seat and leaving the room.

"And that was when you decided that you'd better get in contact with me?" Tommy asked.

"Yep, I knew they were up to no good. They just kept on building them freaky corpse things, using these batteries to make 'em go. I didn't realize what kind of power was being stored inside 'em until it was almost too late."

"Spook power," Hellboy said, reaching for the pitcher in front of him and pouring himself a glass of water.

"Right on the nose," the ghost responded. "Suddenly I was feeling this kind of tug from one of the freaky machines in the basement, and I realized that they were pulling me in with the other wandering spirits nearby. I knew I couldn't fight it for long, which is why I took you over, Tommy, and wrote the note. I had to make you aware of what was going on."

Steve paused, remembering the horror of it.

"It was like being ripped in half. I didn't think you could be hurt when you were a ghost. Hurt like hell though, but I managed to take a good look at their map to see where they were going to strike next and made you write it down; thought it might be useful."

His nephew gestured to another one of the science technicians. And just like show-and-tell, the man pulled up the broken containment battery and placed it on the table.

"And you became trapped within that until Hellboy freed you earlier this morning?" Tommy asked him.

Steve nodded, floating backward away from the thermos-shaped object. The ghost didn't even want to be near it. "Yeah, the machine kinda vacuumed me up, stuck me inside the battery with some of the other spooks that were floatin' around."

Steve looked around the table. "And now I'm here with you."

Everyone remained silent, ruminating on the information he had given them.

"Well, what do you think?" the ghost finally asked. "We got enough to be concerned or what?"

His nephew was the first to speak. "Kate, what have you found out about this Band of Electricizers, anything on record we could use?"

The woman tapped her pen against her temple. "Nope, nothing. I searched every database I have, and even a ton of hard copy, but I couldn't find even a mention of them. Whoever they were, they kept what they were up to pretty secret."

Steve glanced at Sally, hoping to make eye contact with the other ghost, this woman who had become so special to him in such a short time.

"So the million-dollar question is, what were they doin' then, and what are they up to now," Hellboy said, taking a sip of water. "We need some answers so we can figure out what we should be doing next."

Sally turned her attention to Steve. As their gazes met, something passed between the ghosts, and he hoped that she wouldn't be too upset with him for what he was about to suggest.

"I think Sally might be able to shed some light on that," he said, and they all looked at the spectral woman. She shook her head violently from side to side, her image beginning to soften like drifting smoke.

Disappearing.

"Sally, no," Steve called, drifting over to her. "Don't go, we need you. I know it's tough for you to remember, but I think you can help us out."

She was nearly gone, her image barely an outline, when it began to return—to solidify.

"That's a girl," he said, smiling. Steve reached out his ghostly hand to touch her charred cheek. "Anything you can share with us about your husband would be swell."

"Husband?" Hellboy asked, surprise in his voice. "Who's that?"

Everyone stared curiously at the specter of the burned woman—all except for Liz Sherman. She seemed to prefer to look anyplace other than at Sally.

The ghost of the woman raised a charred hand slowly to her throat—her mouth moved, but no sound came out.

"It's too much for her to speak," Steve said, "but if one of you wouldn't mind giving up your body for a minute, she could use your voice to speak with us."

There were no volunteers at first, but then the red-head—Liz—slowly raised her hand to volunteer, looking as though she'd just agreed to take a bullet.

"I'll do it," Liz said, her voice low and raspy. She wasn't sure exactly why, just that it seemed to be the right thing to do.

Maybe it had something to do with guilt over her reaction when she'd seen the ghost of the burned woman for the first time. Liz had been revolted, and she'd seen the look of hurt in the poor woman's dark, soulful eyes.

"You sure about this, kid?" Hellboy asked, shifting in his seat. He seemed almost as uncomfortable with the situation as she was.

Almost.

"I'm sure," she said, her gaze fully connecting with Sally's ghost for the first time. "What do I have to do?"

"Nothing," the ghost of Manning's uncle said, escorting Sally through the air above the table, toward her. "Just relax and let Sally do the drivin'."

This was it; there was no turning back now. Liz closed her eyes, took a deep breath, and tilted her head back slightly in preparation.

"Go ahead, honey," she heard Steve urge his friend. "Tell us what you know."

Liz opened her eyes in time to see the ghost of the burned woman flow toward her, her horribly burned visage moving closer. She fought the urge to move away, the hammering of her heart urging her to escape.

She had no idea what to expect, feeling the air around her becoming ridiculously cold as the ghost flowed around her, attempting to merge with her body. *It's like being immersed in a cloud of freezing vapor,* she thought. Liz gasped, feeling her body grow suddenly rigid, as she slowly accepted the ghost into her.

"Is she all right?" Hellboy asked, but he sounded so very far away.

"No problem," Steve explained, also from a great distance. "That's just Sally getting used to the driver's seat."

Where there had first been intense cold, Liz now felt only warmth. It was strangely comforting, as if the spirit of the woman who was taking control of her body was somehow attempting to reassure her that everything was going to be just fine.

And Liz Sherman believed her, stepping aside so that Sally could have her voice.

Liz wasn't exactly sure how much time had passed, but suddenly she found herself back in control of her body, not feeling much different than she had on the numerous times she'd dozed off during a debriefing or staff meeting. She felt kind of groggy and could have used a strong cup of coffee and a cigarette.

Sally's ghost had returned to float beside Manning's uncle across the table.

"Is that it?" Liz asked aloud, rubbing her hands across her face. Her cheeks felt numb.

"Yes, Liz, that's fine," Tom Manning said. "Thank you."

Everyone sitting around the table looked strangely apprehensive, and she was about to ask what had been said, when she realized it wouldn't be necessary.

She already knew.

Her head was filled with recollections not her own, but detailed nonetheless. Liz steadied herself in her chair as the rush of images cascaded through her mind.

She saw—*experienced*—it all, feeling the poor woman's emotions as she was sacrificed to an other-worldly power. Liz gasped aloud as she felt what it was like to burn from within. To be on fire. Despite her power, the fire within her, she had never *burned* like this.

"Oh my God," she cried, her body starting to tremble.

Hellboy was suddenly at her side, a comforting arm around her shoulder as he handed her a cup of water.

"Here, drink this."

Liz took the plastic cup from him, the images continuing to bombard her.

"The bastard," she said, before taking a sip from the cup. "He allowed her to die . . . to burn up." Liz drank in gulps, realizing how thirsty she was from her ordeal.

Everyone at the table was watching her, already aware of Sally's ordeal.

"Take it easy, kid," Hellboy said, his arm still tightly around her.

She remembered the darkness that followed Sally's death, recalling its every detail as if it were her own memory. In the darkness, something was waiting, and it all became horribly clear.

Sally had been the sacrifice, taken as payment so that her husband and his twisted friends could communicate with whatever it was that was supposed to be sleeping in the void.

Then she saw them, in the shadows of death, three shapes—three sleeping giants—but one was awake, and it was horrible. She felt its thoughts, its hunger to be free.

Its designs upon the world.

"I think we might be in trouble," Liz said, the realization of what they were dealing with finally hitting home.

Her words were met with an uneasy silence in the room.

Inside the farmhouse, in a room that he had claimed as his personal space over ninety years ago, Absolom Spearz, in Stan Thomas's body, sat before the computer monitor, his fingers flying over the surface of the keyboard.

What technological marvels this era has achieved, he thought, dazzled by what could be accomplished with this wondrous device.

He had imagined a device similar to the computer before his untimely demise, although his design had required a human brain suspended in embryonic fluid. He'd never had the opportunity to make his plan a reality, and he wasn't quite sure which of the devices would have been more effective. But at the moment, Absolom was more than satisfied with what he had to work with.

The Electricizers were in complete control of the bodies they currently inhabited but were still able to access the memories of their hosts, making it that much easier for them to acclimate to modern times. Absolom imagined how lost they would have been without the ability to understand the world to which they had been returned—a world full of cell phones, the Internet and automatic transmissions.

Using a search engine, he was able to call up information on the red-skinned abomination that had been recorded in the eyes of his mechanical agent. Relief flooded him when he learned that it wasn't actually Satan that had attempted to foul his plans, but the world's foremost paranormal investigator. The creature was known as Hellboy, and he worked for an organization called the Bureau for Paranormal Research and Defense.

"Fascinating," Absolom whispered, finding multiple references for the group.

The BPRD existed to combat threats of an unearthly nature. He wondered briefly if he and his band would be perceived as such—as the enemy. Of course they would be. There would be little difference between this Bureau and the rabble that had set his barn afire.

They wouldn't understand.

The images from that day so many years ago filled his mind, and his heart began to hammer inside his chest.

"Never again," he hissed, remembering how they had died, only to be reborn in the here and now—all except for one.

Absolom pushed back from the computer, the memory of Mary Hudnell's absence still painful. "Why isn't she with us?" he wondered aloud, though he doubted that his savior was listening. "Why wasn't she given the same chance as the rest of us—to carry out your wishes?"

He thought of her belly, full of life, full of promise, and nearly broke down into tears. With that memory still searing his brain, his fingers returned to the keyboard, typing in the name of his missing disciple. The woman intended to be the Madonna of their god.

There were multiple historical sources of information about the Hudnell family and their shipping empire, with nary a mention of Mary and her fate, but then something caught his attention.

It was an article from the *Evening Item,* Lynn's daily periodical. The story had been published on September 16 of the previous year and concerned a special birthday celebration for Mary Elizabeth Burchett, last surviving relative of the great Hudnell shipping family. He called up the article and his breathing stopped.

Is it possible? Can it actually be? he thought, quickly scanning the words on the screen.

Mary Elizabeth Burchett was the last of the Hudnells, one of the founding families of Lynn . . . married late in life . . . the two had no children . . . Mrs. Burchett had turned one hundred years old that day.

The age isn't right; she would have been well past one hundred years, but . . .

He scrolled down farther to find there was a picture of the old woman. Black-and-white, and quite grainy, sitting in front of an enormous cake, its surface covered in burning candles. Absolom leaned in close to the monitor just to be sure. The photo showed that she was bedridden, surrounded by what appeared to be medical staff. The old woman's ancient face was illuminated in the light from the candles.

A sound from behind him interrupted his search, and Absolom turned to see Annabel Standish standing in the doorway. The slightest hint of displeasure was ignited in him as he noticed the heavy red makeup applied to her young cheeks, her thin, child's lips painted to appear wet and full. She looked like a whore, but at that moment nothing could suffocate his growing excitement over what he had uncovered.

He was about to speak, to tell her his news, when she beat him to the punch.

"We can't . . . I can't deal with it anymore, Absolom," she stamped her tiny foot upon the floor. "Qemu'el has abandoned us, and you say that we're going to complete our mission, but you give us no explanation of how. We're down in that filthy, dirty basement all day and night working on projects that you say will help us to change the world but . . ."

He had already sensed the beginning of unrest in his disciples and knew that it was only a matter of time before they chose to confront him. Absolom was surprised that they had chosen Annabel. He would have imagined they'd pick the dog.

"Calm yourself, sister," he interrupted, the forcefulness of his words stopping her in midsentence. "Your concerns are justified, but you need worry no longer. Our mission is on track; it will only be a matter of time before we bask in the heavenly light of our lord and savior."

He watched as Annabel's expression became confused. She didn't understand how close they were. Absolom himself had had no idea until a moment ago.

He laughed at her confusion, pushing his chair back and gesturing toward the computer monitor.

"She's alive," he said, feeling a joy the likes of which he had not experienced since he first heard the voice of his god.

The little girl moved closer to see what it was that filled him with such excitement.

"The Madonna," he said to her, pointing to the computer screen. "She still lives."

CHAPTER 8

The angel of destruction stirred.

From within the womb of darkness Qemu'el sensed that its time was again drawing nigh.

Qemu'el and his brethren, Duma and Za'apiel, a host of three, had been created by the Almighty as a fail-safe. The fearsome Archons' sole purpose was to eradicate God's failures, to wipe away the Creator's mistakes so that creation could begin anew. In each of them was the power to wipe away entire civilizations, whole planets . . . galaxies. Combined, they could return everything to nothingness.

Return it all to the darkness.

They were God's destroyers, and yet their might had never been tested. Deemed no longer necessary by a loving Creator, Qemu'el and his brothers had been placed within a prison of shadow, devoid of life or substance, meant to sleep in peace until such a time when their unique talents might be needed.

But Qemu'el refused sleep.

From within the confines of his entrapment, the

162

Archon seethed. Za'apiel and Duma accepted their fate, succumbing to the pull of somnolence, but Qemu'el defied the Creator. He managed to tear a hole—just the tiniest of rips—in the fabric of time and space, so that he could watch the development of the Creator's prized puppets.

Accursed humanity.

The more he saw, the more his anger grew. Here was a species that did not deserve the wonders their Lord had bestowed upon them. Murder, poverty and war, the befouling of the planet itself; these were not the faithful creatures that the Almighty believed them to be. They were a blight, a pestilence, defying His wishes at every turn.

The Creator was blind to this, smitten by humanity's supposed charms. With every passing millennium the angel watched, anticipating the call. He expected to hear the voice of his God, ordering the Destroyers forth from their murky prison and unleashing them upon His failure. How Qemu'el longed to see their cities crumble, the tortured faces of the human race turned up to the heavens in desperate prayer as the skies were turned to fire, and they were expunged from the world—a horrible mistake erased, never to be heard from again.

But the Creator's voice was silent, and humanity continued on with its desecration of His holy gifts as Qemu'el watched and waited patiently for a time when he would be given the chance to wipe it all away.

Now that time was drawing near.

Qemu'el forced himself to contain his excitement, for he did not wish to disturb his brothers' sleep. If they had any idea as to the machinations that he had set in motion, they would surely rouse themselves from their slumber and attempt to stop him. And the Destroyer could not allow that to happen. He had waited too long for this moment.

Visions of what he would do to the world again filled his thoughts, and for just a moment, the angel dwelled upon the repercussions of his actions. How would the Almighty react? The Destroyer wondered, but the imagined cries of the hurtful creatures as they suffered their end filled him with such great antici-pation that he did not dwell upon the Creator's response. After all, this was why He had made the Archons.

This was the Lord's work.

She should have died that night.

The dream—the nightmare—of what had hap-pened was upon her again, and she saw the killers as clear as day; men, women and children, bearing weapons and fire.

The fools. If only they'd taken the time to fully understand what the band was attempting. Their god was ready to be born, to take humanity by the hand and escort it to a special place at his side. But they did not understand that all the world would benefit. They had been blind to the wondrous gift that the Electricizers were preparing for them.

She remembered the quiet moment before the violence. Every time she dreamed it the silence grew longer and sometimes, in the dream, she actually believed that this time the horror would not come, and that the man that she loved would convince the rabble that what was about to happen was a gift from Heaven.

But it came. It always came. The sound of gunfire, the choking smell of the barn ablaze.

She didn't even recall climbing from the birthing chair—as if some primitive survival instinct had kicked in, overriding her desire to stand by the side of the man she loved. The next thing she knew, she was in the cold, dark woods, the sounds of violence chasing her away, urging her to escape.

The future of the world growing inside her.

Mary Hudnell should have died that night, but her god had had other plans.

Alarm bells rent the air.

Rosalyn's eyes went to the monitors set up before her, checking her patient's heart rate and respiration. They were both elevated, but this wasn't unusual. The old woman was probably dreaming again.

Rosalyn Tillis had been with the Burchett family since graduating from nursing school, acting as the personal nurse to Mrs. Mary Burchett in her declining years.

She rose from her seat at the workstation in the grand hallway of the Burchett estate, her rubber-soled nursing shoes muffling her footsteps as she walked the long corridor down to her patient's room. *How many times have I made this trip in the last month alone?* The outcome was usually the same; the old girl having just awakened from a dream, her vital signs soon returning to normal. Well, as normal as they were going to get.

Rosalyn reached for the doorknob and felt that odd tingle of apprehension as she always did. She wondered if there would ever come a time when that would pass. *When the old girl is finally dead and gone,* a flippant voice answered in the back of her mind, and she quickly silenced it. She felt bad for the woman, she really did. Alone in this big old house, the only company her personal secretary and a nurse, the only big excitement coming when the doctor made his monthly visit. It just proved that no matter how much wealth one obtained, it could never buy happiness or health.

She turned the brass knob, watching her distorted reflection in its polished surface as she entered the room. The machines were chiming in here as well, and the nurse quickly went to them, again checking the readings before silencing their warning alarms.

From the looks of her bed it had been the dream, for the woman always kicked away her blankets and exposed herself in the throes of her nightmare.

Even after all these years, Rosalyn still found herself staring.

The old woman's body was skeletally thin, her arms and legs little more than flesh-covered sticks, but her stomach was round and protruding, as if bulging with life.

She'd had dozens of tests ordered by several different physicians over the years, and the doctors had all concluded one thing—hysterical pregnancy. There was nothing physically wrong with Mary Burchett, nothing growing inside her to make her abdomen bulge so. Odd as it might sound, her body believed that she was pregnant, had been pregnant, for the last seventy years or so.

Rosalyn had heard all kinds of stories about long-lost lovers old Mary had had before Mr. Burchett came along, and how it was but one love that caused her body to react in such a bizarre way.

Mary Burchett's eyes fluttered slowly open, her gaunt face turning toward the nurse as she readjusted the controls on one of the monitoring machines.

"Another bad dream, dear?" Rosalyn asked the ancient woman in her kindest tone. She really did feel bad for the old girl.

Mary swallowed dryly, a click in her throat sounding as loud as the snap of bony fingers. Rosalyn picked up a pitcher of ice water and poured some into a glass. Lifting Mary's head slightly, she helped her to drink.

Her nightgown had risen up over her stomach, and Rosalyn found herself staring at the old woman's abnormally distended belly. *It really does look as though she's pregnant.*

And then she watched it move, the flesh writhing as if something was actually alive beneath it. Rosalyn blinked in disbelief. *It's gotta be a trick of the light.*

Mary muttered something, and Rosalyn tore her eyes from the old woman's swollen stomach.

"Mrs. Burchett, I . . ." she began.

"That's quite all right, Rosalyn." Mary Burchett smiled wearily at her nurse, spidery hands reaching to pull her nightgown down over the taut, swollen flesh. "You can go now, I'm fine."

And so Rosalyn did, politely smiling at her employer as she turned away. Her gaze went to the woman's distended belly one last time, searching for signs of movement before she moved hurriedly toward the door.

Mary Hudnell moaned as she lay in her bed, the multiple machines attached to her frail body registering her life signs and the effects of her discomfort.

The presence inside her was stirring; showing more signs of life now than it had exhibited in over eighty years. Her hand went to her belly, caressing the swollen expanse of her stomach through the cotton of her nightgown. The stretched flesh was warm to the touch and growing increasingly warmer.

"What is it?" she asked, moving skeletal hands blotched with age over the bulbous surface. "After all these years, what has excited you so now?"

The essence within her roiled, as if in response, and she gasped aloud. Mary looked down at her belly, both horrified and delighted by the sight of her stomach, the flesh moving as something within writhed.

"Is everything all right, Mrs. Burchett?" Rosalyn's voice crackled over the intercom beside her bed.

Mrs. Burchett. She'd never really gotten used to bearing his name. Even though they had been married for well over thirty-five years, she was never comfortable with it. Robert Burchett had been a good man, a good husband, but he had been forced to exist in the shadow of the one true love that had been taken from her.

"Just a little discomfort, Rosalyn," Mary answered, spindly fingers upon the intercom device hanging from her bedside. "Nothing to concern yourself with."

Her mind was filled with terrifying imagery from that night so long ago, the people of Lynn attacking the barn where the Electricizers were about to advance mankind to its next evolutionary step. She would have died with them, but the presence inside her would not allow it. She had prayed to the god inside her—oh how she had prayed—for her love to be unharmed. Mary closed her eyes, remembering his handsome face. How long did she hold out hope that he would come back to her, to begin again, and this time, complete the ritual that would change the world? Many a night she had dreamed of his return, even going so far as to begin preparations for his arrival, but it wasn't to be.

A brisk knock at the door interrupted her thoughts, and Mary called out with permission to enter. A heavyset man wearing a blue blazer and gray dress slacks stepped gingerly into her room.

"Yes, Stewart?" The man had been her personal assistant for the last ten years.

"I hate to bother you, ma'am," he said from the doorway, as if afraid to come closer.

She waved his apologies away. It had been days since she'd last seen the man. As her condition continued to deteriorate, he came around less and less. *Probably eager for me to hurry up and die,* she thought.

"There are people downstairs, a family that wants to meet with you. I told them you weren't well, and that—"

"A family?" she asked, painfully lifting her head from the pillow. "Why in hell would a family want to see me? Probably looking for a handout," she suggested with disgust. "Send them away, and if they won't go, call the police."

The feeling inside her was suddenly excruciating. The machines around her bed beeped and chimed in response to her pain, and Rosalyn was suddenly there, pushing Stewart aside to get to her.

"Stewart, wait!" she called weakly, and the man returned to the doorway.

"Yes, Mrs. Burchett," he asked attentively.

"This family," she wheezed.

The nurse tried to slip an oxygen mask over her face, but Mary swatted it away.

"Did they tell you their name?"

The pain started to subside, but she suspected it could very easily return.

"Yes, yes they did. The father said for me to tell you that Absolom Spearz was here. He seemed to think that his name would have some meaning for you."

The machines went wild again as Mary felt her ancient body surge with vitality. She tore away the wires and tubes, ripping an intravenous from her arm amid furious protests from Rosalyn.

"Mrs. Burchett, please!" the nurse cried.

But Mary did not listen, hearing only the name of the one man she had ever truly loved reverberating in her ears, a man who was now waiting to see her. A man who had at last returned, as she always dreamed he would.

At last.

Absolom heard the screech of his name and turned toward the study. He and his brood had been ordered to wait within the dark room, its walls covered with floor-to-ceiling bookshelves, while Mrs. Burchett's assistant went to see if the woman was feeling well enough to speak with him.

At first it didn't even appear that they would be

allowed through the front door of the expansive
dwelling, but he had an especially persuasive way
about him that came in quite handy at times such as
this. *You could charm the birds from the sky,* his Sally
used to say, but he had to wonder if this talent was yet
another gift of being touched by god.

He heard his name called again, only this time
closer. There was a commotion, the sound of somebody quickly approaching, and he strolled toward the
door. His disciples were now standing as well, awaiting the arrival of the one who cried their leader's
name.

An ancient woman, clad only in a nightgown,
appeared from around the corner, her bulging stomach protruding from a nearly skeletal frame.

"Absolom?" she croaked, swaying upon bare feet.
Her milky eyes touched upon each and every one of
them within the parlor, before connecting with his.

He was both repulsed and overjoyed by what stood
before him.

"Mary?" he said to her, watching the expression of
bewilderment change upon her gaunt features. "Yes,
it's me."

Here was a mere shadow of the beauty that had
been Mary Hudnell, a withered crone who appeared
more dead than alive, but her stomach—

She is still swollen with life.

Mary lurched toward him, tubes still dangling
from her bony arms.

"Mrs. Burchett, please be careful," cried a nurse who followed her, reaching out to take hold of her arm. The old woman's assistant was there as well, trying to keep her from injury.

"Take your hands off me!" she spit, turning to glare at the two.

The nurse pulled away, an expression of shock and concern spreading across her face.

Mary turned back to Absolom, her snarling features immediately softening as she spread her arms to take him in her embrace. He wrapped his arms around her, careful with her delicate frame. She looked as though she just might shatter if one was too rough.

"I knew you would come back to me," she said, her body shuddering with what he hoped was joy. There was a medicinal smell about the woman, and something else.

A smell of decay.

Holding her in his arms, feeling the fragility of the woman's body against his, he knew that there was no reason for her to still be alive other than to provide refuge for the godly presence nestling within her. Absolom slowly brought down his hand from the crook of Mary's bony back, placing the flat of it against the side of her belly.

And his mind was suddenly filled with the ire of an angry god, bombarding him with images that nearly sent him to the brink of madness.

He quickly pulled his hand away, stumbling back-ward and falling into a nearby wing chair. Absolom's entire body tingled, his brain feeling as though it were swollen, pressing against the inside of his skull.

So angry, he thought, tears of joy and pain stream-ing down his face. *So impatient to be born.*

The god was aware of all that had transpired, aware even of the threat posed to his birth by the BPRD and its attack dog, Hellboy. The threat was real, and time was of the essence.

His followers came to him to see if he was all right. Silas Udell's warm tongue licked affectionately at his hand. Absolom pushed them all away as he climbed from the chair. Mary still stood there, a visage of death, yet radiating life. He had felt the god's panic; there was only so much that could be done to keep the body of the ancient woman alive. If Mary was to die, than Qemu'el would most assuredly die with her, and that could not be allowed.

"Are you ready, Mary?" he asked, holding out his hand to her. "Are you ready to change the world?"

The nurse produced a cell phone, placing it to her ear. "I'm calling the police," she said, and proceeded to dial the phone.

"You'll do no such thing," Mary Hudnell cried, spinning deftly around on spindly legs, reaching out to snatch the phone from the caregiver's grasp and smashing it to the hardwood floor.

"As of today I'll no longer be needing your services,

Rosalyn," she said to the woman, turning then to look at her assistant. "Nor yours, Stewart. I want you both to leave at once. You are both dismissed."

The two appeared stunned, speechless.

"My family will take care of me now," she said, turning to gaze lovingly at Absolom.

The nurse and secretary did not move, seemingly rooted in place, unsure how to react. Silas Udell began to growl, baring his fangs as he slowly padded toward the pair. Wide-eyed, they began to back from the room.

"Get out of my home this instant," Mary Hudnell commanded. "Before *I'm* forced to call the police."

Absolom stood watching as the two at last departed. His Electricizers gathered around him. They were all together now—their number complete. At last he had been able to communicate with his god. He knew what had to be done, but they needed to move quickly.

It wasn't at all good manners to keep a god waiting.

Chapter 9

Liz had no idea why she had volunteered to be a temporary puppet for the hideously burned spirit.

Guilt, maybe. A kind of twisted penance for all the lives incinerated when she'd lost control so many years ago. *It's as good an answer as any,* she thought. She wasn't quite sure what she'd expected, but it had been rather gentle, like sharing a seat built only for one, but if you squeezed over . . .

"Liz? You sure you're all right?"

She smiled, unable to put the real answer to that question into words.

Sally's dark, haunted gaze fell on her, and something passed between them. Where before she felt a kind of revulsion toward the woman's ghost, perhaps even fear, now all she felt was sadness. Sadness over how horribly her young life had been taken, betrayed by the man whom she loved, and sadness over how that same man now wanted to hurt the world.

Liz wanted to stop Absolom Spearz, not only to

keep the world from harm, but so that poor, sad Sally could finally rest.

The lab tech Hellboy had sent to get a map finally returned to the meeting. He unfolded it to its full size and laid it down in the center of the table. The ghost of Uncle Steve hovered over the map of New England, arms folded in deep concentration.

"The locations of the thefts that we're aware of are here, here, here and the medicine bag here," Kate Corrigan said, marking off the places with a blue highlighter.

Steve continued to study the map, a ghostly hand rubbing at his spectral chin. From this angle, Liz could see his resemblance to Tom Manning, the way they both furrowed their brows when they were deep in thought.

"What've we got, Steve, buddy?" Hellboy asked.

She could tell he was getting antsy. He didn't care for the sitting around and planning stuff. Just tell him where to go and what to hit, and hopefully everything would work out for the best.

"Don't rush me, guys," Steve said, as he adjusted his spectral glasses on his equally ghostly nose. "Remember, I was being sucked into that spirit battery the last time I got a gander at their map."

Sally was beside him, staring at the map as well.

"I just want to be sure," he said. "What do you think, doll face?" he asked. "Your memory any better than mine?"

Sally lifted her arm and pointed to an area on the map, the same area Steve appeared to be pondering.

"Yeah, me too," Steve said.

He looked up, his finger on a spot that at first glance looked to be all ocean, not far from Buzzard's Bay, but upon closer examination showed a chain of a dozen tiny islands.

"There were other areas, I'm sure," he explained. "But I seem to remember the largest section of push-pins being right around here."

Manning got up from his seat, checking out the location.

"What the hell could be out there?" Hellboy asked, craning his neck to see the map.

"Those are the Gosnolt Islands," Moe explained to Hellboy, as if that would mean something to him.

Liz knew all too well that Hellboy didn't do much homework, and his memory wasn't the best either. Not that she could criticize. She wasn't much better. Even so, Gosnolt did sound familiar, and it definitely had something to do with the BPRD.

"Yeah, and what's so special about the Gosnolt Islands?" Hellboy asked them.

"Are you sure, Steve?" Manning asked.

The ghost nodded. "Can't be one hundred percent, but that area was pretty heavily marked."

Hellboy sighed, throwing his hands into the air. "Would somebody please let me in on the big secret."

The Stooges looked too worried to answer.

"Not all the islands," Abe explained. "Just one of them."

And then Liz remembered. She'd seen the location written on many shipping labels, as items acquired on their various missions, too dangerous to be kept around, were shipped out to be stored someplace where they couldn't do any harm.

Gosnolt.

"The Depot," Liz suddenly said, surprised that she had spoken it aloud. The Stooges and Abe were slowly nodding, waiting for Hellboy to catch on.

"The Depot?" he echoed, looking to Manning and his ghostly uncle for some kind of clarification.

"The Depot," Manning said, and then she saw the look in Hellboy's eyes as it hit him.

"Aw, hell, the Depot."

It was freezing outside her home, the hint of yet another snowstorm present in the cold January air. *Looks to be another harsh New England winter*, Mary thought, as Absolom pushed her wheelchair down the partially snow-covered brick path.

"Are you warm enough, Mary?" Absolom asked her, and she turned in her seat to look up into the new face of the man she loved. She wasn't quite sure if she cared for his new appearance, but she loved him no matter what. *Look at what poor Silas is stuck with*, she thought, glancing at the dog that walked obediently alongside her wheelchair with the other members of her restored family.

"I'm fine now," she said, pulling the heavy quilt tighter around her. "Now that you've come back to me."

"To find you like this . . . our lord truly works in mysterious ways," Absolom said.

Mary rubbed her bulging stomach beneath the comforter. It throbbed with life—a vibrancy that she had not experienced since that fateful night when all had gone horribly wrong.

"Even when it seemed likely that you were dead," she said, watching from her chair as the structure at the end of the path came into view, "I never gave up hope that somehow, you'd find a way to come back to me."

She reached out from beneath her covers to stroke his hand lovingly.

"Is this where we're going?" he asked, propelling her closer to the gray building built of corrugated steel.

It had been ages since she was last out here. "It is," she told him. "Inside you'll see a true example of my faith."

"I never doubted your faith, my dear," he said, and she felt her heart flutter with his tender words.

They came to a stop in front of the black metal door. It was padlocked, but she had brought her key. Mary removed the key from her pocket and attempted to stand up from the chair.

"Some assistance please, Absolom, I'm not as young as I once was," she said, and she felt his gentle touch, supporting her as she stiffly rose.

Standing at the door, she grabbed hold of the cold, metal lock, slipping the key into the slot.

"Time is of the essence, sister," Absolom said as he placed his arm lovingly around her and pulled her close. "There is still much that must be accomplished if we are to meet the needs of our god, and if this . . . surprise you wish to show us doesn't aid us in our cause, we really should . . ."

She removed the lock, giving it to him to hold.

"You'll have to trust me when I say that this has everything to do with our cause," she said, and pulled open the door. It was dark inside, and a stale, musty smell wafted out to greet them.

"My husband enjoyed making sailboats," she said, carefully entering the darkened space. "In between dalliances with teenage boys. It was a hobby that he had since before we became involved. After we were married, he had this space constructed so that he could continue his second great passion."

Her hand fumbled at the wall inside the doorway, remembering where the light switch was the last time she was out here.

"But then I developed a passion of my own, you see," Mary said, flicking on a series of overhead lights, illuminating the large space.

It was exactly as she had left it.

Mary looked at Absolom, attempting to read the expression upon his face.

"Are you pleased?" she asked him tentatively, unsure how she would react if he wasn't.

"What is this?" he asked, his gaze darting about the expanse of the space. The others had now entered, and they were just as taken aback as he.

"After the barn was destroyed . . . everything that we had worked so hard to build ruined, I was crushed, swallowed by despair—but *he* inspired me," she said, running her hands over herself. "He made me realize that this was only a temporary problem—a bump in the road if you will. That we . . . *I* would have to start again in preparation for your eventual return."

Absolom left her side to walk among the great metal pieces, and the other Electricizers silently followed in awe.

"I knew nothing of building fabulous machines and mechanisms, and asked the savior how I could contribute to the cause, but as always he was silent to me."

Mary remembered the day like it was yesterday. She and her husband had been attending an event for one of the local charities that was taking place at the Museum of Fine Arts in Boston. She had been bored as usual, annoyed by the curious stares of people wondering about her *condition,* and proceeded to wander about the museum, losing herself among the great works of art.

The essence of the god inside her belly had fluttered happily as she came across the exhibit of metalwork done by a local artist. At first she had not understood, but as she studied the magnificent sculptures of iron and bronze, it came to her. The exhibit was called, interestingly enough, *Gods*, and at that moment Mary had known how she would contribute to the savior's eventual arrival.

"The sculptor's name was Berringer," she told Absolom, who was now standing in front of the large, disembodied head of iron. He stroked its featureless face. "I saw his work on display in Boston and knew that he would be perfect."

That night, despite the late hour, she had contacted the artist and immediately set up plans for him to work for her. *I want a sculpture,* she had told him. *Fifty feet high, the finest you have ever created—a creation befitting a god.* And the artist had done just as she had asked, taking up residence in one of the servants' quarters in her home, working out of the boat workshop, which Mary had had converted into an artist's studio.

"The way in which he approached his work," she said, "it was almost as if he understood the importance of what I'd asked of him—that he somehow knew that he was building the body of a god."

Absolom traveled from piece to piece, admiring Berringer's craftsmanship: the muscular torso, legs and arms of the unassembled armature.

"It's beautiful," he said to her, and she could have sworn that there were tears in his eyes.

She nodded, caught up in his emotions. "But never assembled," she said with a sad shake of her head. "It wasn't long after Berringer completed the work . . . I believe it was the head that was done last, that he took his own life."

Mary pointed to an area in the corner where a large black smelting furnace squatted, cold and unused for many a decade. "It was right over there—that beam," she explained. "That's where he did it—where he hanged himself."

She had been the one who found him, a ladder lying on its side beneath his dangling form. Mary wasn't sure exactly why Berringer had taken his life, but always believed that it was somehow his final gift to a powerful force that he knew would someday change the world.

Absolom came to her, taking her in his powerful arms, and he kissed her as she always imagined that someday he would. She had been anticipating this longer than the coming of Qemu'el.

"What we built before," he said, looking longingly into her eyes, "would have been more than sufficient. But this . . . this truly is a vessel befitting a god."

Absolom placed his hand upon her stomach, his head jerking back, his eyes rolling to the back of his head, as the divine being she carried spoke with him.

"But is *he* happy, Absolom?" she asked cautiously.

"Oh yes, he *is* happy," the high priest of the Band of Electricizers exclaimed, held in the grip of rapture, a euphoric grin spreading across his face.

"And so very eager to be born."

Tom Manning was at his desk, so caught up in the reams of paperwork necessary to begin the BPRD's next course of action that he didn't even notice the sudden drop in temperature until his hand and fingers grew numb.

Flinching, he looked up to see the ghost of his uncle floating around his office, looking at the framed photographs, certificates and commendations hanging on the walls. Manning was still a bit disconcerted by the spirit's appearance, for this wasn't the broken man he'd left in the care of the staff at the Mount Pleasant Rehabilitation Center. It was, instead, the eccentric uncle he remembered from those summer vacations that seemed so long ago.

"From the FBI to the BPRD," Uncle Steve said, moving from one framed piece to the next. "I'm really proud of you, Tommy."

Manning didn't know how to respond. *What do you say to somebody that you had institutionalized— someone you left to die alone?*

The guilt was like acid, bubbling just beneath the surface.

"I was keeping an eye on you," the ghost said, drifting closer. "Watching you climb the ranks." Steve smiled, allowing himself to drift into one of the chairs in front of Manning's desk. "Look at ya now! Big office, telling Hellboy what to do. Hellboy!" The ghost shook his head in disbelief. "Friggin' Hellboy, I can't get over it."

Manning tried to find his voice, his brain sparking and misfiring. He had never been very good at things like this.

"Always wanted to let you know how proud I was of you, but I doubt you would've heard me," Steve said, using a ghostly finger to push his slipping glasses back up onto his nose. "You know what I'm saying, Tommy?"

The shame was like a lead weight, growing larger—heavier in Tom's chest, the painful images of the last time he'd seen his uncle adding to its mass. If he didn't do something, he was positive that it would suffocate him.

"What's up, Tommy?" Steve asked from his seat. "Looks as though you might have something to say."

Manning had faced serial killers in their lairs, had shoot-outs with hardened criminals, dealt with supernatural threats that could very well have destroyed the world, but nothing compared to this.

"I . . ."

The first word was like a knife, cutting into the soft flesh of his belly.

"I never meant to hurt you," Manning blurted out, leaning back in his chair, feeling weak, finally having the opportunity to say what had been on his mind for twenty years. "I didn't know what to do . . . you were sick and I couldn't take care of you and . . ."

Uncle Steve nodded. "I was pretty out there," he agreed. "I was having a hard time remembering stuff. I knew something was wrong, but I wouldn't admit it."

With those words, Manning could feel the weight of his guilt start to subside; it was still painful, but it was a good pain, the kind that brought relief.

"When I saw you in the hospital I just didn't know what to do. You needed care that I couldn't give you . . . I did what I thought was right."

His uncle stared at him, the ghost's eyes seeming to look into his soul. "I know you did, Tommy. I understand all that, I really do—but what happened to us?"

The ghost leaned forward in the chair. "I thought we were pals—buddies. Where'd you go, Tommy? I missed you something fierce."

Uncle Steve grew still, staring off into space. Manning could practically see the past reflected in the surface of his ghostly eyeglasses.

"All those summers," Steve said, the slight hint of a smile creeping across his face. "Not sure if you knew how much those meant to me."

Manning remembered how important those summers had once been to him: the night before the drive up to Lynn from the South Shore, not being able to sleep, filled with the excitement over what the next two weeks would be like. He remembered all of Uncle

Steve's books and magazines, that musty smell of old paper and the mental list he would make of what he wanted to read first.

Manning smiled. Even now there was nothing he enjoyed more than spending a day off in a second-hand bookstore, perusing the stacks, the smells taking him back to those wonderful summers.

"I really didn't know what to do with myself once you stopped coming," Uncle Steve continued. "There was always next year, I used to say, but you didn't visit then, either. What happened, Tommy? What did I do to make you stop visiting me?"

Manning didn't want to hurt his uncle's feelings, but there really wasn't much wiggle room, and besides, this was all about coming clean—about giving up the guilt.

"I was growing up, Uncle Steve," he explained, as softly as he was able. "I had new friends, there were girls that—"

"Figures," Steve scoffed. "The broads always ruin a good thing." He held a hand up to his mouth conspiratorially. "But don't tell Sally I said that." The ghost chuckled.

"It wasn't just that," Manning continued. "It was summer vacation and the prospect of hanging around with you reading about haunted houses and alien abductions just didn't have the same appeal to a teenager."

"You must've thought your uncle Steve was a real

kook," the ghost said with a grin. "Didn't ya? C'mon, you can tell me."

Manning returned the smile. "And there was that."

Steve laughed, looking around the office. "Not so crazy now, am I, Mister Field Director for the Bureau for Paranormal Research and Defense?"

"I guess you weren't as crazy as I thought," Manning echoed, and his smile broadened. It felt surprisingly good.

"All my books and journals; I miss that stuff. Worst thing about being dead, I think."

Manning flashed back to the days after his uncle's passing, standing in the apartment that the old man had lived in the majority of his adult life, filled nearly to bursting with books, magazines and notebooks, and wondering what to do with it all.

"You know, I kept it all," Manning said.

"You're joking, right?" the ghost asked. "You kept all my stuff?"

Manning nodded. "It's all back at the house. I couldn't bring myself to throw it away. I went so far as to call a service to have it hauled off, but . . ." he shook his head. "I just couldn't bring myself to do it. It would've been like disappointing you all over again."

"You never disappointed me, Tommy," Uncle Steve told him. "Deep down I realized you had to have your own life. It was hard, but you never really disappointed me. I always knew you were gonna be something special."

There was still a piece of the guilt that had not been expunged, in Tom's chest, dug in deep, its roots leading straight to his heart. He had to be free of it, had to confess it all.

"You died alone," he said, feeling his eyes burn with tears of sadness, tears that he'd never allowed before. "I wasn't there . . . I should have been there."

The ghost of his uncle Steve reached across the top of his desk, placing his nearly transparent hand atop Manning's own. It was freezing cold yet strangely comforting.

"Let it go," his uncle said. "I was half out of my mind anyway, I probably wouldn't have known even if you were there."

Manning felt the last of his regret begin to dissolve, breaking up, the painful tightness in his chest, there since first reading the message left by his uncle, starting to loosen. He had yearned all these years for a forgiveness he did not think he deserved and was certain he would never receive. Yet here it was.

What a gift.

"And here I was thinking that you'd come to haunt me."

Uncle Steve scoffed. "Got better things to do with my time, Tommy Terrific."

Manning smiled. It was a nickname his uncle had used for him as a child now and again, something from the old *Captain Kangaroo* kids' show on TV.

The ghost drifted up and floated across the office.

"It's good we got this stuff out of the way, but I know you got important things to do," he said just before passing through the door. "Saving the world and all."

The specter of his uncle laughed, and Manning grinned. That laugh had always made him happy, been one of the things that he had looked forward to all through the school year. For a moment, just for a moment, he was back there again.

It was just like summer vacation.

CHAPTER 10

A bsolom saw the design in his mind, and began to build it upon the floor of Mary Hudnell's opulent bedroom.

He could feel his god's impatience radiating from inside the old woman as she lay upon the hospital bed, propped up with multiple pillows. Mary watched him, her breathing labored. He moved as fast as his mind and hands would allow.

The Electricizers had scoured the house for parts, bringing electrical appliances to him from wherever they could be found. Unable to carry the washing machine up the stairs, Arden and Wickham had dismantled it in the basement, carrying its motor up into the room. Parts from a grandfather clock, microwave oven, and a portable television from the guest room down the hall soon followed, and the vision of the device inside his brain, gradually became a reality.

"I found this in the attic!" Annabel exclaimed in her high, squeaky child's voice, as she stumbled into the bedroom, carrying an old windup phonograph.

Its large external horn resembled a tarnished metallic flower.

"Help her!" Absolom commanded, and Wickham and Arden rushed to the little girl's assistance.

"I remember when Father purchased that phonograph," Mary said wistfully from her bed. "The cold winter months we spent listening to music, dancing until my legs ached; seeing it brings back some of my fondest memories."

They placed the phonograph carefully down in front of their leader.

"And from this relic of the past, we shall bring forth the future—and new memories of a world transformed shall be forged."

"Bravo, Absolom," Mary cried, clapping her ancient hands together softly. "Bravo."

And the others joined in the applause, urging him on to finish his work. It wouldn't be long now, he imagined, carefully removing the horn from the phonograph. The finishing touches were all that remained, and his hands moved from one tool to the next, joining the scavenged pieces of old technology together to create something entirely new.

Their god wanted to address them all—his followers, his priests—and with this contrivance his voice would be heard. The screwdriver dropped from Absolom's hand. He was exhausted, both mentally and physically, from the act of creation. The communication machine was completed, and all he could do was stare at it, marveling at what his mind and hands had wrought. He had no idea how or why the machine would work, only that it would.

Absolom picked up the electrical cord and, without looking, held it out toward the closest disciple.

"Plug this into the nearest outlet," he said breathlessly, eager to test his work.

A crackling sigh was heard from the electronic voice box attached to the throat of Silas Udell's canine body.

"I . . . I can't," the dog said, a pathetic sadness pouring from the speaker in waves. "I have no hands."

"I'm sorry, Silas," Absolom said, holding the plug out to Wickham. "Geoffrey, if you would be so kind?"

Wickham approached, taking the cord from him and searching for an outlet.

"If I had hands, I could be of more use," Udell continued, his tail wagging nervously. "Could . . . could you build me hands?"

Absolom's eyes roamed about the communication machine, making certain that all the connections were in place before the power was switched on.

"You will not be in that form forever," he said, dismissing the dog's request. "There's no reason to invest time in the fabrication of hands for you if . . ."

"But what if I want to stay like this?"

"Stay like that?" Stunned, Absolom looked into the dark eyes of the animal. "You must be joking."

Udell shook his blocky head from side to side.

"Not at all," his voice crackled from the speaker in his throat. "I've never felt so free before—so in touch with myself—my senses so alive. For the first time I feel as though I truly know myself."

Absolom could not quite grasp what he was hearing. The man he remembered had not merely been a spiritual medium but a drunken womanizer, chased from at least three states by constabulary alerted by complaints of enraged husbands.

"All that I'm missing is the use of hands," the dog explained, lifting one of his paws. "These are next to useless, but if you could cobble together something with fingers—and opposable thumbs—I would forever be in your debt."

He continued staring at the dog, not sure exactly how to answer, when out of the corner of his eye he saw Mary writhing uncomfortably.

The god was anxious, eager to share with them his words of wisdom, and Absolom had made him wait.

"This is not the time or place for this," he told his canine disciple, picking up the machine and placing it upon the wheeled cart that had once held an EKG machine. He guided it closer to Mary's bed. "When things are as they should be, we'll talk."

"About hands?" the dog asked hopefully, tongue lolling pink and wet.

"About many things," he said, turning his full attention to the Madonna reclined upon the bed.

"I'm so sorry," he told her, reaching out to pat her

brow. "Your discomfort is a result of my distraction, and I beg your forgiveness."

"It . . . it feels as though . . . he's quite . . . excited," she grunted, hands gripping the sides of the bed in extreme discomfort.

"Impatient is more like it," Absolom said as he pulled the sheet and blanket down past her legs. "Eager to be heard."

He then politely asked her to expose the bare flesh of her stomach. Mary obliged, while he attached multiple sticky electrodes to the taut, papery skin of the old woman's abdomen. He glanced up to double-check if the machine had been plugged in before flipping the switch to activate it.

The Electricizers stood frozen—waiting.

The washing machine motor rumbled to life. A piercing wail, projected through the phonograph horn, filled the room. Absolom recoiled, his hands going to his ears. All of the Electricizers reacted the same except Udell, who had no hands and simply howled in discomfort.

The screeching sound gradually diminished to be replaced by a sound similar to that of a heartbeat. Absolom went to the machine, adjusting the controls.

"Can you hear me, my master?" he asked, leaning over to speak into the mouth of the horn.

The beating sound increased in pace, and then a voice began to speak, amplified by the horn. "I hear you," the voice hissed above the rhythmic thrumming.

Absolom felt as though he might cry, but managed to retain his composure.

"After so long, we are at last reunited," he said. "And can continue with our plans first set in motion over a hundred years ago."

The high-pitched whine returned and Absolom fidgeted with the controls, attempting to eliminate the annoying feedback.

"My patience grows short," their god growled. "Too long have I waited, prisoner within this slowly decaying bag of skin."

Absolom was taken aback by the harshness of Qemu'el's words, and chanced a look toward Mary. He saw that she was crying, the deity's words cutting her to the quick. He immediately spoke up, attempting to appease the agitated godling.

"And the plans for your imminent birth are proceeding . . ."

"Not. Fast. Enough." Qemu'el bellowed, causing the metal horn to vibrate violently. "There are forces in this world—forces with the power to challenge my return. Are you aware of this?"

The image of Hellboy and a horde of BPRD agents filled his mind, and Absolom Spearz shuddered with the thought.

"Yes, I'm aware, oh lord."

The Archon growled, voice rising from the phonograph horn. "I sense them out there—a possible impedi-ment to my return. We must move, and move quickly, before they can be made aware."

Absolom recalled how the acquisition of one of the objects of power had nearly been prevented, and shuddered. *How much does the BPRD know?* he wondered, deciding not to share his concerns with the angry god. There was no need to upset him fur-ther.

"And move we shall," he said. "The last of the objects of power needed for your birth have been located, and the fates have smiled upon us, for they are all in one location."

"This pleases me," the Archon rumbled. "And when will these relics be acquired? How much longer will I be forced to wait?"

"I will disperse a team at once," he explained calmly. "And while the objects are being obtained, the preparation for your arrival will begin here."

"Excellent," Qemu'el praised him. "And then it will begin, the end of all things."

A chill of foreboding crept up Absolom's spine as the god spoke the last of his words before going silent. *The end of all things,* Absolom thought, troubled until the god's words made sense to him. For any new be-ginning, there must first be an ending—an ending of all things.

That was it, of course.

What else could he have possibly meant?

* * *

Franklin Massie was feeling no pain. It was a dream come true, and he owed his good fortune, and health, to Absolom Spearz.

The funeral director sat behind the wheel of a hearse in the parking lot of Boston's City Morgue. He had been there for the last two hours—since receiving the phone call from Absolom, giving him instructions for his latest assignment. This was a big one, a huge responsibility, but it was the least he could do for all that had been done for him. Spearz had taken away his pain, made him a new man. Massie would have moved the world for him.

The man reached down, feeling the slight bulge of the apparatus that was attached to his chest. Staccato images flashed before him, causing his eyes to flicker in the darkness of the transport vehicle. He remembered the pain of old age, the arthritis that had caused his bones to creak and taken away his ability to move, to truly live.

Then he remembered the procedure he'd had to endure for this new life. There had been pain then as well, more pain than he would care to remember, but it had all been worth it.

Massie remembered the smell of blood, and the sounds of machinery as his body was prepared to accept Absolom Spearz's gift. He wasn't sure exactly, but he thought that he actually might have died upon the worktable in the cold, damp basement of the house not far from the entrance to Lynn Woods Reservation. He shivered with the memory of a cold saw blade biting into the trembling flesh of his chest, cutting through to the bone, before everything had gone black.

Massie pulled open the front of his white button-down shirt to admire the mechanism bolted there. He stroked the metal box with his fingertips, feeling the thrum of its power source from within.

What had Absolom said, after Massie had awakened to find the machine screwed to his chest and grafted to his nervous system?

It's powered by the nearly unlimited energy provided by the spirits of the dead, the man had answered. *They're all around us, you know, ripe for the picking.*

Franklin Massie had never believed in ghosts, but now he had no choice. They were what kept him alive. He laughed at the notion of the dead allowing him to feel this wonderful. After all the years of catering to them, they were at last doing something for him.

Who'd ever have believed it?

He pulled up the sleeve of his dark suit jacket to glance at his watch. Now was as good a time as any, he thought, stepping from the car out into the cold, early morning. It was after midnight, when there was the least chance for any interruption of his task. He had been here at this time before, and the place was dead quiet. Massie smirked at his unintentional pun, slamming the driver's side door of the hearse and approaching the brick building.

He rang the buzzer, wondering who would be on call tonight, and was pleased to see the disheveled form of Adam Sanders strolling down the corridor, paperback novel in hand. Massie could see the man squinting, trying to figure out who was buzzing, and he waved, peering in through the small window in the door.

"Hey, Mr. Massie," the morgue tech said as he pushed open the door to allow him access. "I didn't expect to see you tonight," he said, stifling a yawn.

"Busy night?" Massie asked with a sly smile.

"Got paperwork backed up my ass, but I can't find the energy to do it. Who are you here for?"

"I believe the name is Dollings," he said, reaching inside his suit coat pocket, pretending to search for a piece of paper where the name had been written.

"Dollings? The name's not ringing a bell, but let's go take a look out back."

They walked down the cool, cinder-block corridor toward the main storage room.

"Who's working security tonight?" Massie asked, knowing that the lab technicians were never in the building alone.

"Some guy named Davis," Sanders said, opening the door into the morgue room. "I think he went out to get cigarettes or something."

The mechanical box bolted to Massie's chest began

to vibrate, as if somehow aroused by the closeness of the dead. He gasped as he entered the room.

"Are you all right, Mr. Massie?" the technician asked, looking him over for signs of trouble, then the young man smiled. "Hey, where's your cane?"

Massie shook his head and smiled. "I don't need it anymore," he said, again experiencing the sheer joy of saying the words. Absolom had taken away the debilitating illness, and all Massie need do in return was provide Absolom with the raw materials he needed to make his vision of the world a reality.

"That's awesome," Sanders said, nodding his head in approval. "Some kind of new medication they put you on or what?"

The pulse of the box was growing stronger, and so was he. Franklin Massie wasn't sure if he'd ever felt so alive before, and he realized that the device was likely charging itself—collecting the spirit energies that lingered in the room. How else could he explain how absolutely amazing he was feeling?

"You might say that," he said, flushed from the rush of energy.

"Maybe I need some of whatever it is they put you on," Adam said, walking around his desk to pick up a clipboard. "So, what was the name of the pickup again?"

Massie could hear the device working, felt the movement of its internal mechanisms as it continued to feed. He wandered into the center of the morgue, tilting his head backward, basking in his growing strength.

Sanders was calling his name, asking him about the fictitious body that he had supposedly come to collect, when he realized that it was time to complete the task Absolom had asked of him.

"I've come for all of them," Massie explained, trying to ignore the intensity of the pleasure coursing through him.

Sanders didn't understand, slowly lowering his clipboard as Massie approached.

"What the hell is that supposed to mean?"

"All the poor souls stored in these drawers and freezers," the mortician said with a wave of his hand. "I'm taking them all with me."

Absolom needed drones to carry out his tasks, in preparation for the arrival of a new world. To make this a reality, bodies were needed, but there were limits as to how many corpses were available to him on any given day. He needed bulk, and what better place to obtain these raw materials than a city morgue.

"I don't understand," Sanders began.

Then Massie was upon him, crushing the man's fragile throat in his hands, feeling it collapse beneath his fingertips.

Stunned by his own display of preternatural strength, Massie watched as the technician's body flopped to the floor.

"But you will understand," he replied to the corpse

at his feet, feeling more alive at that moment than he had in his entire existence.

Soon, everybody will.

Hellboy sat at the back of the Chinook CH-47 transport helicopter, lost in thought, thinking about the plans of madmen.

Hadn't he been brought to the world for a similar purpose—as some kind of harbinger of a new age, a beast of the apocalypse that would reshape the world in its own horrible image? The similarities gnawed at him.

He stared down the length of the craft's fuselage, at the ten BPRD agents assigned to him as backup for the assignment on Gosnolt Island. A good group. He hoped they all made it back alive. Hellboy never minded risking his own butt, but he always resisted the idea of having backup. He didn't want anyone's death on his conscience.

He glanced at the large, phosphorescent dial of his wristwatch, attempting to distract himself from any more troubling thoughts. They had left Bradley Airport a little over thirty minutes ago, so they had at least another hour in the air before touching down on the tiny island that housed the Depot.

Hellboy sighed as he closed his eyes, leaning his head back against the seat, trying to relax. He listened to the powerful twin rotors of the helicopter, a kind of rumbling metronome easing him into a

fugue state somewhere between sleep and wakeful-
ness. He thought about Liz and Abe, off on their
own mission, wondering what they would find in
their reconnaissance of the house in Lynn. He wished
he could've been there with them, but the situation
at the Depot required a certain muscle. *They'll be
fine*, he told himself, drifting down into the nap
zone. *And besides, how many robot zombies can these
guys possibly have?*

Unbidden, his mind drifted back to the plans of
the Nazi madmen, and the similarities to what the
Electricizers were attempting. *Just what the world
needs*, he thought, *another me.*

A sudden chill in the air caused his flesh to prickle,
the coarse black hair on his arms rising to attention.
Hellboy pried himself from his nap, peeking out at his
surroundings through a slit in one eye.

Uncle Steve floated in the air before him, a hint of
a faint smile on his pale, ghostly face.

"Catching some z's?"

"Just resting my eyes," Hellboy responded gruffly,
sitting up straighter in his seat. He really wasn't in
much of a mood for small talk.

The ghost nodded in agreement, continuing to
drift in front of him.

"Do you need something?" Hellboy asked, hoping
to discourage any further conversation.

"Nope," Steve said with a shake of his head. "Just
noticed that you've been sort of quiet since the meet-

ing back at the BPRD—since Sally gave us the heads-up on what the Electricizers could be up to."

"Yeah, that," he said, unhooking a concussion grenade from his belt, tossing it in his hand. "Just got me thinking is all."

The ghost cocked his head.

"There are similarities to what the Electricizers are doing," Hellboy explained, even though he didn't want to, tossing the grenade from one hand to the other. "Y'know, similar to how I ended up here my-self."

Steve nodded. "Oh, I get it."

Hellboy shrugged. "Just me being a goof, I guess."

"Yep," Steve agreed. "But you know what the biggest difference between the two is?"

Hellboy stopped tossing the explosive, curious. "No, what?"

"Something really good ended up coming out of what the Nazis were trying," he said, shaking his nearly transparent head from side to side. "But this?" the ghost paused for effect.

"I don't see nothing positive coming out of this."

CHAPTER 11

Situated on an overgrown plot of land at the end of a rutted, winding, dirt road, the old farmhouse appeared perfectly harmless, except for the hearse parked by the side of the house, near the bulkhead.

"Looks like another delivery," Abe whispered. He was crouched behind a thick patch of overgrowth on the perimeter of the property, Liz at his side and Sally hovering between them. "Think we should go in for a closer look?"

Liz spoke softly into the headset she was wearing. "We're going in. I repeat: We're going in."

Abe's hand brushed reassuringly against the holster and sidearm he was carrying. He wasn't sure what good it would do if they were to come up against any of the robot zombies, as Hellboy called them, but it was enough to provide him with a certain sense of security. He moved forward cautiously and motioned for them to follow, Liz close behind, Sally floating just ahead, her hideously burned figure no less disturbing because she was a phantom.

Abe felt a pang of sympathy for the ghost as they neared the old house. It had been her home once, and now it was perverted, a nest of something entirely unnatural.

They crept up onto the porch and approached the front door. Finding it unlocked, Abe turned the knob and pushed it open. A wave of inviting warmth flowed out from the foyer to welcome them, a pleasant change from the bitter cold outside. Sally was the first to enter, drifting over the threshold into the entryway. Still the dutiful hostess, she motioned for them to enter. Abe wasn't quite sure why, but he found himself wiping his feet as he stepped into the home.

Liz carefully closed the door behind them as Abe surveyed their surroundings. It was silent, eerily so, and looked as though it hadn't been lived in for quite some time. Even so, he unsnapped his holster and removed the sidearm as they wandered from the foyer to the dining room.

Sally floated into the room and hovered over a spot in its center. She seemed to be staring, lost in a memory, perhaps.

"That's where it happened," Liz whispered, close to his ear.

The ghost seemed frozen there.

"Sally, we have to keep moving," he said quietly.

Slowly, she turned her burned features toward him, and he caught sight of ghostly tears flowing from the spirit's eyes. She acknowledged his words with a slight nod, took one last look about her, then floated toward him.

"Hey—over here," Liz called softly from the kitchen.

As Abe and Sally entered the room, she directed their attention to a door, slightly ajar, leading down into darkness.

"Down there?" Abe asked Sally.

The specter nodded again as Liz opened the door wider, a damp, moldy smell wafting up from below. Abe started down first, gun ready just in case. There was a sensation of intense cold at his back, and he knew that Sally was directly behind him.

The cellar was lit by a single bare bulb hanging from a thick, coiled wire in the center of the ceiling. Except for boxes of varying sizes scattered about the dirt floor, the room was empty.

"Lots of boxes," Liz said softly beside him. "But no product. Don't tell me we've missed them." She too was carrying her sidearm.

"No, there's something still here," Abe replied, realizing that Sally was no longer visible.

He moved around, away from the light, and found her floating in front of a wooden shelving unit. The shelves were empty except for a jar filled with screws and a rusty pair of pinking shears.

Abe stepped closer, examining the unit. Carefully he ran his hands along the rough surface of the wood, searching for what he was now almost certain he would find.

The trigger was made of metal, and as he pushed down upon it, a sharp click sounded, and the unit slid forward on a hinge to reveal another doorway hewn in the rock and a set of steps leading even deeper into the earth. A powerful reek wafted out from the secret doorway, and Abe turned his head away from the offensive odor.

"Not a happy smell," Liz said, her eyes watering.

Abe had to agree. He glanced at Sally, who pointed down the stairs, her dark eyes wide with fear. Steeling himself, he turned back to the doorway in the wall and started down. It was treacherous on the plank steps, and he carefully tested the strength of each with a tentative foot before following through with his whole weight. A soft glow suddenly illuminated the stairway from behind him, and Abe turned to see that Liz had partially ignited one of her hands, holding it above her head like a torch to light their way.

"Thanks," Abe said.

"Don't mention it."

The disgusting smell grew stronger the farther down they ventured, but Abe was distracted by the addition of a sound—a single voice muttering to itself, its statements punctuated with the occasional whine of a power tool.

Abe flipped the safety on his gun and stepped into the subterranean chamber, then froze. The room was huge, extending far beyond the square footage of the house constructed above it, and it appeared to be set up as a kind of workshop. Several workstations littered with tools and raw materials filled the vast chamber.

And then there was the source of the putrid odor that hung in the air like a shroud—the dead. There were corpses lying on stretchers and others piled on the floor like cordwood, cadavers of every conceivable size, age and condition.

Abe glanced at Liz. She wore a look of disgust he was sure rivaled his own.

The wail of a power drill caused them both to jump, and Abe moved slowly toward the sound, circling around a large ceiling support constructed from individual rocks and thick gray mortar. Cautiously, he peered beyond the pillar, gun raised, and was shocked by what he saw.

An old man, muttering under his breath, hefted the naked corpse of a corpulent woman from the floor with ease and dumped it onto a large wooden table. He immediately set to work, his rubber-gloved hands moving so fast that they practically blurred. Within seconds, the corpse's stomach had been sliced open, its insides removed and tossed into an overflowing basin on the floor beside the man. Clearly, this wasn't the first body to undergo this treatment, and as Abe looked to the shadowy areas behind the busy man, he saw exactly what the man was doing.

Corpses reinforced with metal and gears, clockwork zombies, stood at attention against one wall. They were motionless, as if waiting for the command to come to life.

The old man was building them.

Abe was about to let the man know that he was no longer alone, when Liz Sherman beat him to the punch.

"Now that's just wrong," she said, moving around the obstructing pillar, her gun aimed at the old man. "Stop what you're doing and put your hands in the air."

Abe followed her lead, backing up her threat with his own weapon.

But the old man didn't even look up. He continued his chore as if they weren't even there, installing what looked to be some kind of small motor inside the cavernous belly of the dead woman.

"Hey, Dr. Frankenstein, I'm talking to you," Liz snapped, sighting down the barrel of her weapon.

The old man reached for something on the table and Liz fired a shot into another stone pillar directly behind him. The gunshot was nearly deafening in the cramped space, but still the man didn't seem to notice, picking up an electric drill and beginning to bore a hole through the woman's forearm.

"Think he's deaf?" Abe asked Liz, still aiming his own gun.

"I don't know, but he's pissing me off."

The old-timer had picked up a strip of metal and began to attach it to the corpse's arm, using a long silver screw.

"I can't stand to watch this," Liz said, growing more agitated by the second. "Hey, buddy, knock it off!" she yelled, advancing on the old man.

At last he looked up from his work, a scowl upon his wrinkled face. There were spatters of dried blood on his cheek and glasses, but he didn't seem to care. "I'm not deaf, just extremely busy."

The top two buttons of his shirt had come undone and Abe could see a metallic object attached to the pale flesh of his chest.

"I have to finish all of these by tomorrow," he said, gesturing around the basement at the multiple bodies lying there. "Wouldn't want to give me a hand, would ya?" he asked, a smile upon his face and a demented twinkle in his eyes. "I could probably teach you quick enough. Be a good trade to know once things begin to change and all."

His smile quickly faded with their silence, and he looked carefully from one to the other.

"He said you'd be coming," the old man said. "What did you he call you again? Oh yeah, the killers of the dream."

"Are you Absolom Spearz?" Abe asked.

The old-timer chuckled, shaking his head. "Me? No way. I'm Franklin Massie, but thanks for the compliment. Absolom is a truly great man."

Liz scoffed. "He's great all right."

Massie shook his head again. "All he wants is to help the world to become a better place—to help humanity reach its full potential." He pulled open the white dress shirt to show them the strange apparatus that was attached to the center of his chest. "Pretty impressive, eh?" he said. "Runs on spirit energy. Best thing anybody's ever done for me. I haven't felt this good in years."

"We're going to stop him, you know," Liz said, continuing to stare down the barrel of her gun.

The excitement seemed to drain out of Massie at that point, and the old man began to button his shirt. "He said you wouldn't understand, and I guess he was right. Too bad, really."

The old man turned his attention back to his work.

"Where is he, Mr. Massie?" Abe asked. "Where is Absolom Spearz?"

The old man was silent, as if attempting to recall where it was he'd left off in his work.

"Where is he, Franklin?" Liz asked again, with more force this time.

"Gone," he said, not even bothering to look up. "He left a few hours ago. Came with some trucks and hauled all his machines away, leaving me with just enough to keep working on the drones—which I'll never get finished if you keep interrupting me." He sighed as he searched the tabletop for something, then located it, already placed inside the corpse's open stomach cavity.

"Ah, here it is," he said, holding up a remote control. He pointed the object over his shoulder. "He left you a message," Massie said, hitting a button on the remote, then dropping it and continuing his work.

A large television hanging on the wall near them came to life, illuminating the subbasement in an eerie white light. An ordinary-looking middle-aged man appeared on the screen.

"Is it working?" he asked someone off camera, and Abe heard the voice of what sounded like a child answer affirmatively.

"If you are witnessing this recorded message, then the time is growing near," the man, presumably Absolom Spearz, said, smiling gleefully. "The wheels are in motion, and soon nothing will be as it was."

Abe holstered his weapon, listening closely to the man's words.

"I urge you to stand down, agents of the BPRD, there is nothing that you . . . or your Hellboy can do to stop what was begun over one hundred years ago."

"I know it won't do any good, but would you mind if I shot out the screen?" Liz asked, her eyes locked on the grinning image of Spearz.

"Wait until he's finished," Abe said. "There might be a clue to his whereabouts in all this."

Spearz's expression grew grim. "But I doubt that you will listen," he said with a sigh, "even though your actions could very well jeopardize a glorious future for humanity." He shook his head in disappointment. "If only you could see that all of this is for your own greater good."

A voice in the background spoke to the man softly, distracting him for a moment, and then Spearz turned his attention back to the video camera. "I'm done here," he said. "But before I go, I wish to stress how sorry I am that this could not have ended peacefully."

He got up from his chair then and placed his face very close to the camera lens. "I really do abhor violence."

The camera was switched off, and the television screen went to static.

"Now can I shoot it?" Liz asked.

Abe was about to answer when he heard movement. He looked back toward Massie, who had continued to work, seeming to have lost interest in their presence. Then he saw them, emerging from the shadows.

The clockwork zombies had been activated and were coming toward them.

Abe looked at Liz.

"Looks like you're going to have to shoot something else first."

Tyler Arden cut the engine of the fishing boat, plunging them all into an eerie silence. Annabel watched from her seat as her lover pushed a button that released the anchor. The splash as it hit the water was quickly absorbed by the thick mist that surrounded Gosnolt Island.

The drones, in their long trench coats and hats,

sprang to their feet, anxious to perform their programmed functions.

"Prepare the boat," Tyler instructed.

They had brought along a smaller motorboat, and the drones went about the business of getting it ready to go ashore. Annabel thought that her lover seemed tense, agitated by the task that Absolom had assigned them. She found it all extremely exciting. It had been close to a hundred years since she'd had an opportunity to spend any time alone with the man she loved.

"Can you feel it, Tyler?" she asked, leaving her seat to go to his side. He was in the process of examining the map that Absolom had drawn for them.

"Excuse me?" he asked, seemingly irritated by her question.

"I asked if you could feel it," she said, hugging herself against the early-morning dampness. "Think of it, in just a matter of hours, a real live god will walk the Earth."

Tyler looked down at the map. "Not until we succeed in our assigned task," the boy grumbled.

Even though he appeared to be only eleven years of age, Tyler acted his true age, his older spirit coming through in his facial tics and mannerisms. Annabel had to smile. She found him adorable in this body. But then again, in her new body, she was actually much younger than he.

"Do you have any doubts?" she asked, reaching out to muss his hair.

"They stopped us once," Tyler said, combing his hair with his fingers. "What's to prevent it from happening a second time?"

Annabel laughed, a high-pitched, little-girl giggle. "Don't be foolish. Of course we'll succeed, we've been given a second chance. We have a god on our side, don't forget."

He didn't respond to her, folding up the map and placing it in his jacket pocket. "Are you ready?"

She retrieved the copper-coated steel divining rods from beside her seat.

"I'm ready," she said, trying hard to contain her excitement. She didn't want to disturb him any further.

Their leader had provided them with a general map of the island, but her talents with locating energy patterns—especially those emanating from items of supernatural power—made her the perfect choice for this assignment.

Tyler moved past her to the side of the craft, climbing over into the waiting motorboat. She'd felt a certain cold distance from the man that she loved since their return to mortal form. She'd blamed it on the intensity of their holy mission, but now she wasn't quite so sure.

Annabel gazed into the boat below. Tyler and the four drones sat there, waiting, none offering her any assistance.

Men, she grumbled beneath her breath, climbing

over the side and carefully lowering herself into the boat. *Even the reanimated corpses are all the same.*

"Thank you," she said sarcastically to Tyler as she carefully took her seat, trying not to rock the boat.

It was as if she hadn't said a word.

The boy turned to address one of the drones. "Cast off," he commanded, and it did as it was told, untying the knot that held the boat in place. Another started up the motor, and the boat began its journey through the fog toward the Gosnolt shore.

Her lover was silent, staring sternly ahead. Annabel remembered the first time they had met. Their introduction had been made by the spirits of two old women who had once lived in Annabel's Philadelphia home, sisters who had died husbandless and had not wanted her to share their sad fate. They had acted as spectral matchmakers, finding her what she thought to be the man of her dreams.

This man. She continued to stare at the new, young face that she was gradually starting to associate with the man she loved. He no longer looked the way he had, and neither did she. But the fates had been kind, providing them the opportunity to continue their love, even after the death of their original bodies. Their god had rewarded them for their faithfulness, and they owed him much, which was why they needed to succeed on this mission. These were the final objects needed to allow the most holy Qemu'el to cross over into this plane of reality, the last items of power that would allow him to manifest as a physical being and anoint the world with his glory.

"I wonder what kind of world we'll be married into?" she asked wistfully, as the boat cut across the dark waters. Far off in the distance, she could hear the sounds of waves breaking upon rocks.

Tyler shifted in his seat to look at her. "Married?"

Annabel nodded. "Of course. As soon as Qemu'el arrives, we'll be married. And I wonder what the world will be like for us—for our children."

Tyler laughed cruelly. "Have you looked in the mirror lately, Annabel?" he asked her. "You're a little girl—just a child. We can't be married."

It was as if he had physically struck her, although that would hurt less than the words he had just spoken to her. She could say nothing, staring at the body of the boy, but seeing the man whom she loved—and who she believed loved her.

"But I thought . . ." she began, and watched a spark of cruelty ignite in his eyes.

"You thought wrong. You're living in the past. Things aren't the same as they were, and they're going to change even more if we succeed."

With those final, jarring words, they emerged from the thick haze, the boat nearing a rocky and seemingly deserted section of beach.

Tyler leaped over the side of the craft into the knee-deep water, helping to guide the boat up onto the sand.

She was the last to disembark, still reeling from the shock of what he had said to her. Annabel wanted to cry, to curl herself into a tight ball, to will herself back to the darkness where she had dwelled after her death in Absolom Spearz's barn.

But she steeled herself, grabbing hold of her emotions. She had a task to perform. The fate of humanity was depending on her, whether her heart had been broken or not.

"Well?" Tyler asked her, a coldness in his tone, showing no sign that they had ever shared an emotional bond.

Yes, she had to agree, *things have most definitely changed.* Annabel turned her back on the boy, lifting the two divining rods, slowly turning, using the copper-coated steel rods to seek out any source of residual supernatural energies.

The rods moved toward each other dramatically, forming a cross as the girl pointed them toward a winding path through the woods.

"There," she said, starting to walk. "It's this way."

They followed her, the movement of the rods in her hands directing them to their goal. She wanted to ask Tyler what had happened to turn him against her, but Annabel kept herself strong, refusing to show any sign of weakness. If this was how he wanted it, she would never speak to him again.

The trek through the dark woods seemed to go on forever, and doubts in her abilities, mixed with a severe sense of rejection, filled her mind. *What if the rods fail?* she thought, beginning to climb a slight hill. What if she wasn't as talented at this as Absolom believed her to be? What if she led them to failure, and would it really matter now that . . .

But her thoughts quickly turned to excitement as she came over the hill to gaze down onto what appeared to be a town square. The rods crossed as if attuning to something of great power. What they had come for was down there, of this she was now certain. Annabel could feel the ambient energies traveling up the lengths of the metal in her hands, making her arms tingle.

She ran ahead, her tiny legs pumping madly as she rushed down the incline from the woods onto one of the deserted streets, following in the direction pointed out by the divining rods. Standing in the middle of the town square, Annabel turned slowly in a circle, the somewhat pleasing sensation in her arms growing more and more intense. The small downtown appeared completely abandoned, the storefronts boarded up tight as if they had been waiting for a powerful storm to blow through—a powerful storm that had never come.

The feeling in her arms was suddenly painful, and she cried out, dropping the metal rods to the street. Tyler and the drones stood behind her as she rubbed the pins and needles from her arms, staring at the location across the street that caused such a powerful reading.

"Is it there?" Tyler asked her, but she remained silent.

She picked up the rods from where she'd dropped them on the ground and walked toward the boarded-up store. It had been called McMaster's Department Store, once upon a time, and she remembered other stores very much like this one from her life in Philadelphia, before her untimely passing. Where once it had held products of all kinds to satisfy the wants and needs of consumers, it had now become a shell of its former self, containing something far more esoteric, and quite powerful.

"Inside," she said to nobody in particular. "What we're looking for is inside."

She stood before the front doors, trying to see through windows crusted with inches of thick dust and dirt. A padlock and thick chains denied them entrance, but not for long.

"Open it," she commanded one of the drones, and it lurched forward, reaching out with razor-sharp hands encased in metal. It took hold of the lock and easily tore it away.

As she reached for the door, however, Annabel was rudely pushed aside by Tyler Arden. "I'll go in first," he said, pulling a flashlight from his back pocket and shining it inside as he stood in the open doorway.

There was so much she wanted to say, but Annabel remained a lady and held her tongue.

"It's a mess in here," he said, moving the beam

about the inside of the filthy store. There were empty shelving units and mold-covered displays, but no sign of what they had come for.

"Are you certain it's here?" he asked her.

She chose to ignore his question, holding out the divining rods once again, pointing them within the store. Her arms felt as if they were on fire as she looked over her shoulder to the waiting drones.

"Inside," she directed them, and they obeyed, pushing past Tyler into the store.

"What do you think you're doing?" he demanded. He took hold of her arm and gave her a violent shake. "Absolom put me in charge of this mission—me— and I'm not about to see it jeopardized owing to matters of a fragile heart. I am in command of this situation, and you will report to me what I need to know. Do I make myself clear, girl?"

Annabel was furious, recalling anger so strong only once before. She remembered a time during a séance, before the dreams of god—before Absolom Spearz— when she had allowed herself to become possessed by the spirit of a man who had been murdered by his wife, the killing disguised as an accident.

It was just like that, only stronger.

She yanked her arm away, resisting the urge to plunge a divining rod into one of his bulging, angry eyes.

If asked before their deaths, she'd have believed that their love could have transcended any obstacle. She was obviously wrong.

"Where is it?" he snarled.

Still refusing to speak, she pointed to the back of the store, to a dust-covered sign over a door that read, APPLIANCES.

"Thank you," he said, moving away from her. "I'm glad to see you're finally acting sensible about all of this."

She watched him approach the door, reaching down to give the doorknob a shake. It too was locked.

"Open it," he instructed the drones, exasperation in his tone.

The automaton took hold of the knob in one of its hands, twisting it violently to one side, and then to the other. Annabel could hear the locking mechanism break from across the room.

As the drone pulled open the door, a thought occurred to her. If items of supernatural power were somehow stored here, it must have meant that somebody had put them here intentionally, and if that were the case, wouldn't such important objects be protected with more than just a locked door?

Annabel thought this just as the door came away from the frame, revealing a gigantic stone statue standing in the doorway. She gasped aloud as the rock thing moved, tilting its head to one side as it assessed them.

The drone closest to it moved to defend them, but the monolith was faster. It swatted the reanimated corpse aside as if it were nothing, sending it careening into a display for something called Moxie, broken beyond repair. The other three automatons attacked to protect their masters, but they too were made short work of, reduced to broken pieces strewn about the dusty store floor.

The stone giant looked at Annabel and Tyler, eyes blazing from the darkness within its chiseled face as it spoke. "Good morning," it said with a voice like two pieces of rough stone being rubbed together. "Is there something I can help you with?"

Geoffrey Wickham hated the sea. The motion of the fishing boat as it crossed the turbulent waters made the inside of his stomach lurch, an early-morning breakfast of sausage, eggs and toast threatening to erupt from him like Vesuvius.

He stood outside the main cabin, hoping the bracing ocean air would help to calm his internal turbulence, but the rise and fall of the horizon did more harm than good.

Wickham closed his eyes, attempting to distract himself from the motion of the seafaring craft. His hand immediately drifted to his left breast, and he began to massage the supple flesh there. He wasn't sure he would ever be used to existing in the body of a beautiful woman, and was even less sure that he really cared. He would still be able to enjoy the company of the opposite sex, even in his new form. And besides, it was good to be alive again—to be free of the seemingly endless deathlike existence within the storage batteries. The fact that the body that now housed his essence was female—healthy and extremely attractive—was just a gift from god as far as he was concerned.

And what future gifts were in store for them? he wondered. Once the god had made the transition to the world, would they be rewarded for their loyalty, for all of their efforts?

His stomach roiled violently, the contents of his belly suddenly on the move. Wickham threw himself across the deck of the boat and hung his head over the side as a torrent of vomit exploded from his mouth and into the sea.

A reward for my efforts, he thought, hanging on to the railing, attempting to recover. He wiped the foul-smelling spittle from the corner of his mouth, looking out over the water at the other three fishing boats that followed close behind, each containing parts from which the body of a god would be constructed.

He was pleased with how things seemed to be falling into place; finding Mary Hudnell alive—still containing the essence of their lord even after all this time—had been a blessing. The fact that the woman owned one of the largest fleets of fishing boats in the Northeast was just another blessing from their god.

Wickham sensed that he was no longer alone and turned from the ocean to see that Absolom and Mary had come up on deck.

Even in his new body, a charisma radiated from Absolom. Standing in his presence, one knew that this was the man who would change the world.

"Are you all right, Geoffrey?" Absolom asked, signaling that something was amiss by touching the lapel of his heavy, wool coat.

Wickham looked down at his own jacket to see the front had been spattered with vomit.

"A touch of seasickness, I'm afraid," he responded, ineffectually attempting to brush away the drying foulness. He wrinkled his nose at the sour stink coming from the stain.

Absolom helped the ancient woman, who was wrapped in a heavy down comforter, to a seat on deck. She had been growing progressively weaker as the hours passed, her already protruding belly seeming larger and larger. The god inside her knew that its time was growing close and had started to feed off the life energies of its host in anticipation.

Their leader knelt beside the chair, pulling open the comforter to expose the woman's stomach. Gently he laid a hand upon it, communing with the unborn god. His body shuddered, his eyes rolled to the back of his head, then he took his hand away.

"He's quite anxious," Absolom said, climbing to his feet with a chuckle. "But can you blame him?"

Wickham wholeheartedly agreed. "Yes, but even a god must have patience," he said.

"No need to concern yourself with that," Absolom told him, coming to stand by his side. "He simply wanted me to be certain that we had brought everything along that will be necessary."

It had been Wickham's job to inventory all the items that were to be transported to the birthing place. He had double- and triple-checked the list against the items as they had been loaded onto the fishing boats.

"It's all here," he said, going over the manifest again in his mind. "Everything except the last items of power." Wickham felt a twinge of panic as he remembered that the responsibility of acquiring these items had been assigned to the youngest of their band. "I certainly hope that . . ."

Absolom stared out over the ocean and at the boats that followed. "No worries," he said with the utmost confidence. "Nothing will stop us this time."

With those words of reassurance, a rabid barking filled the air. Silas Udell in his canine form scrabbled up from the hold onto the deck and raced for the front of the boat. He tossed his head back and howled.

"What's gotten into him?" Wickham asked.

"I think we're here," Absolom replied.

They watched as a large shape slowly materialized through the mist from the sea, a small island of grayish black, its surface spattered with years of bird droppings, rising from the sea. According to Absolom, it was a cold and barren place, void of any vegetation, of any life other than the occasional landing of seagulls.

It was called Egg Rock, and this was the place where a god would be born.

CHAPTER 12

The Chinook set down in the parking lot of the Roosevelt Elementary School on Gosnolt Island, its powerful double rotors kicking up a swirling cloud of dirt, dust and snow as it settled.

Hellboy emerged from the craft with Uncle Steve floating behind him like a child's balloon. He couldn't quite remember when it was he had last made a delivery to the Depot, although looking around, he knew it had been sometime ago.

Gosnolt had originally been established as a radar station by the Air Force during World War II. It had been a tiny island community set up for the officers and their families, but was decommissioned in the mid-sixties. It remained abandoned until 1974, when Trevor Bruttenholm found the perfect use for it. The storage vaults at the BPRD were becoming filled to the brim with all manner of ancient arcanum and artifact. Gosnolt had proved to be just what they needed to solve their storage problems—a place far away from prying eyes where they could quietly catalog their finds.

"Nice place," Steve said. "Quiet."

Hellboy grunted in agreement as four other BPRD field agents joined them on the makeshift landing field. He would have preferred to deal with this threat by himself, but Manning had insisted on a backup team—just in case. He had to admit they did assign him some good people, up-and-comers within the ranks of the Bureau. He'd worked with most of them at one time or another: Wendell Holmes, Chuck Delaney, Adam Feig; the only one not familiar to him was the lone woman on the team, Katherine Dexter.

"So what now?" Steve asked, rubbing his spectral hands together in excitement. "We head on over to this Depot and make sure that all the magical doodads are where they're supposed to be?"

Hellboy nodded. "Eventually, but first we gotta wait for somebody." He looked over toward the elementary school as two figures rounded the brick building, slowly moving toward them.

Agent Dexter lifted the machine gun hanging around her neck, and Hellboy reached over and pushed the barrel down.

"It's okay," he said. "It's just the Whipples."

"Who are they?" Steve asked. "Are they with the Bureau?"

The ghost was partially right. Hellboy watched the pair of heavily clothed people slowly crossing the playground. The two were holding gloved hands, wearing heavy winter jackets, their heads adorned with colorful ski caps. The only exposed parts of their bodies were their bespectacled eyes, peeking out from beneath heavy woolen scarves.

"Hellboy!" one of the figures bellowed, the sound of his voice muffled by the scarf, as he waved.

Baxter and Aubrey Whipple were two of the Bureau's most dedicated agents, a husband and wife team who had served the agency for well over thirty years. They continued to serve even after their retirement by taking up permanent residence on Gosnolt, dedicating the remainder of their lives to what they loved most.

Hellboy waved, strolling up to meet the old couple.

"So good to see you," Baxter said, slapping him on the arm. "You're getting so big. What are they feeding you back at the Bureau?" Then the old man laughed and removed one of his gloves. "I think I have something for you," he said as he dug into his trouser pockets and removed a silver dollar, which he placed into the palm of Hellboy's hand. "That's for you, my boy, don't spend it all at once."

"Baxter, you don't have to . . ."

"I know I don't have to, but I want to," the old man said. "How's your father?" he asked. "Haven't heard from him in a dog's age."

Hellboy felt a pang of sadness wash over him with the mention of his adoptive father, Professor Trevor Bruttenholm, who had passed away the year before.

He remembered visiting the Whipples with Brutten-holm as a young demon—Baxter had given him a silver dollar each time. But what really concerned Hellboy was the fact that Baxter Whipple had been a pallbearer at the funeral.

Aubrey took hold of her husband's arm and leaned in close to speak quietly in his ear. "Trevor's gone, Baxter," she said to him. "You remember; he left us last spring."

The old-timer's posture seemed to slump. "You're right," he said, putting his glove back on. "May God rest his soul."

She patted his arm affectionately, the twinkling blue eyes behind her glasses connecting with his. "He's been a bit forgetful of late," she said, directing her attention to Hellboy. "How have you been, dear?" She stepped toward him, standing on tiptoes and pulling down her scarf to give him a kiss on the cheek.

"I'm good, Aubrey. How are things here?"

"We're good," the woman said, tugging her scarf back over her mouth. "We received some lovely Nemidian scrolls last week. We're thoroughly enjoying them."

"I love the smell of scrolls," Baxter interjected. "Makes me think of fresh bread."

Things got suddenly quiet, until Hellboy changed the subject. "Have you noticed anything out of the ordinary lately?" he asked them. "Anything missing?"

Aubrey thought for a moment. "No, nothing that I

can think of. How about you, Baxter? Anything missing?"

"My left slipper," he spit. "Can't find the damn thing for the life of me. Took it off yesterday when I went to bed, and I couldn't find the damn thing this morning."

The old woman hooked her husband's arm in hers and pulled him closer. "Like I said, he's getting a little forgetful, but no, everything's accounted for as far as we know."

Baxter pointed to the ghostly visage of Steve standing silently beside him. "Who are you?" the old paranormal investigator asked.

"Steve Maitland," the ghost said, holding out his hand. "I'm Tom Manning's uncle—well I was."

"You're a ghost, aren't you?" Baxter questioned.

"Yes, sir."

"No sense in shaking hands then," the old man grumbled. "Nothing to hold on to really, so what's the point?"

"Guess you're right," Steve said with a shrug, and lowered his hand.

"Will you and your friends come up to the house for some breakfast?" Aubrey asked. "I've got some lovely sausages I can cook up, and a big pot of coffee already brewing."

"Maybe later," Hellboy humored her. "Why don't you two go and get out of the cold. I think we're going to go over to the Depot and check on some things first."

The old couple tottered off, heading for their home not far from the school. Hellboy gestured for the group to follow him and walked from the school playground onto the sidewalk that would take them to their destination.

"Seem like a nice couple," Steve said. "Getting up there in years, but nice."

"That's why we had to come here and check things out for ourselves," he said, bothered by how old the couple had seemed. "But those are two of the best researchers the Bureau's got."

Has it really been that long since I last saw them? he wondered. Time certainly had a way of sneaking by him.

They passed a row of boarded-up administrative buildings on their left, and were about to enter Gosnolt's small downtown when he noticed something odd.

"That ain't right," he growled, speeding up to reach McMaster's Department Store across the square.

"Hey, Hellboy, what's the rush?" Agent Holmes called to him. "They having a sale on delicates?"

He heard the other agents laugh at their comrade's joke, and he probably would've been laughing too if he didn't have the sneaking suspicion that things were about to get bad.

"Eyes open, guys. I think we got trouble," Hellboy said, drawing his weapon as he stopped to study the pile of stuff that had been stacked outside the front door of the store. Leather-bound grimoires and scrolls littered the sidewalk along with a variety of other ancient artifacts that had been collected by the Bureau and its operatives over the organization's years of existence.

"Is this it?" the ghost asked, his voice a whisper. "Is this the Depot?"

"Yeah," Hellboy answered.

"So let me guess, this stuff here—not supposed to be out on the curb."

"You got it."

Gun at the ready, Hellboy motioned for the others to follow and stepped through the open doorway into the store.

The place was a mess, but that was how it was supposed to appear. After acquiring the abandoned military installation from the government, Professor Bruttenholm had seen no reason to change any of the structures, deciding to keep everything exactly as it was. He had said it was a good cover if anybody decided to get nosy about what was kept on the island—nothing there but a bunch of old, abandoned buildings.

Hellboy knew otherwise.

There was a racket coming from the far end of the store, beyond the doorway with the yellowed appliances sign hanging above it. He raised a hand, motioning for the others to follow. Carefully, they made their way through the store, avoiding the obstacles of collapsed shelving units and dilapidated displays—and the bodies of the robot zombies.

"What the heck happened here?" Hellboy asked in a whisper, about to step over shattered remains, when he suddenly found himself face-to-face with a living statue carrying a wooden crate filled with what looked like crystal frogs.

Something that could have been surprise registered on the stone beast's face, and Hellboy reacted instinctively, aiming his weapon and firing three consecutive shots. The gunfire sounded like thunder in the confined space of the abandoned department store as the rock creature hurtled backward through the doorway, the crate of crystal frogs shattering as it dropped from its carrier's arms.

"Hope that was nothing important," Hellboy, already on the move into the room, heard Steve say from somewhere behind him.

The area called the Depot was the biggest room in the store. Some walls had been knocked down over the years to increase the size of the storage facility, and it appeared that they just might have to put on an addition if things kept going the way they were—*there was stuff everywhere*—but that was a worry for another time.

The great stone statue, carved to resemble some sort of armored warrior, surged at them, and the team reacted, their machine guns spraying their attacker but doing little to slow it down.

It was then that Hellboy remembered the last time

he had seen the Whipples—the last time he had paid a visit to Gosnolt and the Depot.

It had been to deliver this statue.

Six years before he had been called to Lebanon, to what had once, four thousand years ago, been the fertile Cedar Mountain forest located in the coastal mountains of Syria. It wasn't so much a forest now as a barren dryland with patchy areas of growth, a mere shadow of what had once grown there. They'd been having a bit of a problem after a series of earthquakes. It seemed that something nasty had been released; a demonic entity called Huwawa had possessed a stone statue carved in honor of the Sumerian god Enlil, and it was really getting a kick out of laying waste to the villages and terrifying the locals.

After a bit of a scuffle in a section of forest called Jabal el-Barouk where the cedars still managed to grow, Hellboy had defeated the entity and was about to finish it off for good, when it started to beg, swearing allegiance to the BPRD. Hellboy must have been feeling particularly soft that day, because he had remembered a conversation that he and his father had had earlier that month about the Depot's needing a better security system. He had suggested a good watchdog might be just the thing, and this demon Huwawa seemed to fit the bill nicely.

The demon had eagerly accepted his offer, swearing his loyalty to a new master in exchange for his continued existence within the stone body. There had been little problem getting the necessary clearances to import the statue to the United States, for Syrian officials were eager to be rid of the troublesome creature. As far as Hellboy knew, Huwawa had been doing just fine in his new line of employment as security guard for the Depot, but that was before today's shenanigans.

Huwawa moved much faster than it had a right to, pounding Holmes into paste with its boulder-sized fists before turning its attentions to Feig, Delaney and Dexter.

The BPRD agents didn't have a chance.

Hellboy cursed, firing his gun into the rock demon's ugly face. "Thought we had a deal, you two-faced son of a bitch!"

The gunfire did little damage to the stone, but it did distract the demon, who now turned its attentions to Hellboy.

"That was a bargain of the past, red one," Huwawa croaked, charging at him. "A new agreement has been forged this day!"

His gun empty, Hellboy threw the pistol with all his might, hitting the advancing demon on the top of its head before throwing himself at his attacker.

"What the hell was I thinking?" he asked himself as he brought his large right hand down on top of Huwawa's head like a sledgehammer. "That's why you never make a deal with the demonic; they'll always find a way to screw ya raw."

"Enlil is no more," Huwawa bellowed, recovering from the blow to the head with ease and socking Hellboy a good one on the jaw. "Fealty to my ancient master gone the way of the storm god's worshippers."

Hellboy's ears were ringing something awful from the blow and the floor seemed to pitch to one side as he tried to clear his head. The demon saw his opportunity and took it, wrapping his stone hands around Hellboy's throat, yanking him up from the ground and hurling his body across the room.

"And my allegiance to you and your masters?"

Hellboy collided with a shelving unit of burial urns, the fragile containers exploding as his hurtling body made contact. The air became choked with the remains of ancient people who had not walked the Earth in millennia.

The stone demon laughed.

"Like so much dust in the wind."

This guy was starting to really piss him off.

As near as Steve could figure, the living statue used to work for the BPRD, but had apparently double-crossed them by choosing to join up with the Electricizers.

The ghost hung in the air, stunned as he watched the powerful stone creature get the better of Hellboy. He had to do something to help, but he wasn't quite sure what.

"My new masters have promised me a place in their

young empire," Huwawa explained, crossing the room to continue the beating he was dishing out. "What did you and your masters promise me? The remainder of my eternal existence spent within this depressing structure, guarding the baubles and trinkets of civilizations long extinct."

Hellboy managed to get to his feet, coughing and waving his hands in front of his face as he tried to disperse the cloud of ash and dust that choked the air.

"Needless to say," Huwawa continued, bringing his arm back to deliver another blow. "I accepted the better offer."

The punch fell, but Hellboy had managed to get out of the way, moving in alongside the stone demon and driving his fist into the statue's face.

"Doesn't change the fact that you weaseled out on a deal," Hellboy said, grabbing hold of a wooden crate and smashing it over his opponent's head. Ancient maps spilled to the floor like confetti.

From the corner of his eye, Steve glimpsed movement. He looked across the room to see a little girl and boy, whom he immediately recognized from the farmhouse in Lynn, peering out from behind a stack of crates piled high in a corner.

Electricizers.

Steve didn't know what he should do, but did know that if he was going to do something, it had to be fast. He looked back at the fight in time to see another area of storage decimated in the struggle between the two behemoths.

The ghost drifted over to where the BPRD agents had been struck down, sensing life emanating from at least two of them. Hovering over the body of the agent named Delaney, Steve scoped out the operative's weapons belt and found what he thought could be useful to Hellboy.

He hated to do it, not having asked permission and all, but he didn't have a choice. Steve drifted down to the man's body, allowing his spectral essence to merge with that of the unconscious BPRD agent. It was kind of like stealing a car, getting behind the wheel to hotwire the ignition, only this time it was a brain being turned over instead of an engine.

Steve experienced a bit of a rush, being flesh again, feeling again, as he struggled to stand. He felt a razor-sharp pain streak down from the top of the skull to the lower neck, and knew it was likely that Agent Delaney had some kind of damage, probably a concussion, but it didn't seem as though the injuries were any worse than that. Ignoring the pain, he steadied himself, getting used to the sensation of mass, and crossed the storage room toward Hellboy and Huwawa, still locked in combat.

The stone sentry had once again gained the upper hand, sitting astride Hellboy and raining down continuous blows.

"Hey!" Steve yelled, a bit taken aback by the sensation of vibrating vocal cords.

Huwawa stopped in midpunch and turned its rock head slowly around to look at him.

"There will be time for you later, little human," the statue said. "Just as soon as I am done with the red-skinned spawn of Hell."

Steve ignored the demon, reaching for an item attached to his belt as he spoke to Hellboy. "Had enough of this?" he asked, and held up the grenade.

"More than enough," Hellboy replied.

Steve pulled the pin and rolled it across the floor toward him.

Huwawa watched as Hellboy snatched up the grenade from the floor.

"What is that?" the demon demanded.

"Payback for welchin' on a deal, you sorry son of a bitch," Hellboy barked, sitting up just enough to cram the grenade into the statue's rocky maw, using his powerful right hand to pound the explosive in good and tight.

The demon barely had time to react before its square head was obliterated in an explosion of rocky debris.

"That you, Steve?" Hellboy asked, pushing the now motionless—and headless—body of Huwawa from atop him and climbing to his feet.

"Yeah," the ghost replied with Agent Delaney's voice.

"Thanks for the grenade." Hellboy brushed the

rock dust from his trench coat. "Who knows how long that business would'a gone on for."

"Thought I should probably do something before you two ended up wrecking everything in the Depot."

Hellboy moved past Steve to approach the fallen agents.

"How are the others?" he asked, kneeling beside Agent Dexter. She seemed to be recovering; a nasty purple bruise was blossoming on her forehead. The woman moaned as she sat up, holding her head in her hands.

"This guy should be fine," Steve said, making reference to the body he currently inhabited.

Hellboy watched as Steve checked out the other two.

"Feig is good, but I'm afraid the same can't be said for Holmes."

"Damn it," Hellboy swore. Holmes had known the dangers of his assignment, but Hellboy always felt responsible, no matter what.

He removed his coat and draped it over Holmes's body, recalling the time he'd been on a flight with the good-spirited agent, on the way to an operation in Peru. Hellboy wondered if the poor bastard had ever gotten around to asking his childhood sweetheart to marry him.

Something scrambled from out of the shadows, darting from concealment behind a stack of crates, making their way toward a back exit at the far end of the room.

"It's the Electricizers!" Steve exclaimed.

"Hold it right there!" Hellboy screamed, reaching down to pick up a large hunk of Huwawa's head, and throwing it toward the door.

The piece of rock shattered as it hit the doorframe, and the two children froze. Slowly, they turned around.

"They're just a couple'a kids," Hellboy said, startled by the sight of the little girl and slightly older boy.

"On the outside, they're adorable," Steve explained. "But on the inside, we got a whole new can of beans."

The boy immediately threw his arms around the little girl. "Please don't hurt me and my sister," he said, his voice trembling with fear. "Our boat washed up onshore and our parents got hurt." The boy was crying now, hugging his sister close to him. "We were just looking for some help when we found this place. We thought there might be someone inside to help our mommy and daddy . . ."

The little girl suddenly pulled herself away from the boy, a cruel snarl twisted young features that shouldn't have understood the concept.

"Listen to you," she sneered. "What would our god think if he could hear you now?"

The older kid's eyes went wide with dismay. "You stupid bitch!" the boy screamed. "You've ruined everything."

The little girl just smiled smugly, as if that had been her plan all along.

Hellboy looked at Steve.

"Told you," the ghost shrugged, pulling a sidearm from the holster hanging from Delaney's side, and aiming it at the pair. "A whole new can of mean."

CHAPTER 13

The subbasement was filled with the buzzing and whirring of the mechanized corpses as they stalked toward Liz and Abe.

"Well, this isn't quite working out the way I expected," Liz said, firing her pistol ineffectually into the advancing force. She and Abe backed up, making their way toward the stairs.

Abe fired his gun as well. "Maybe if we can hit the spirit batteries we can . . ."

"Won't work!" Massie yelled from his workstation. He held up a curved piece of metal to show them. "New feature in the latest models," he explained. He rapped the metal with his knuckle. "Placed over the batteries to protect them. All these guys have them. Bullets won't really do a thing. Sorry." The old man went back to work again; it was like he'd already forgotten they were there.

Abe continued to fire his gun, aiming primarily at the zombies that were closest.

Liz glanced his way.

"What?" he asked, ejecting the empty clip from the weapon and slipping in a full one. "Can't blame a guy for trying."

The zombies were closer now, falling over themselves in an effort to reach them. *Thank God for confined spaces,* Liz thought. She knocked a stack of boxes filled with machine parts into the advancing legion's path, hoping to buy a little more time. She and Abe were almost to the stairs.

"We can't let them follow us," she said, watching as the automatons fought with each other to be the first over the obstruction.

"I was thinking the same thing," Abe said.

"This whole place and everything in it needs to be destroyed," Liz said, feeling that awful combination of fear and excitement she always did when about to unleash her power.

The zombie robots were practically on top of them, and there wasn't any more time for thinking.

"The place is old," she said, taking a deep breath of the fetid air. "Should go up like an oily rag."

"What about the old guy?" Abe asked.

Liz looked over the crowd to see the pale old-timer still diligently working. He was stuffing the large torso of the woman's corpse with wires. She could also see the boxlike object grafted to his chest, pulsing with an eerie inner light.

"It's too late for him," she replied. "I doubt that there's much difference between him and these guys.

Maybe a few days. Look at what the crazy bastards have done to him. No turning back for him now."

The fire was always there, like an eager dog anxious to be called.

"You ready?" she asked Abe, ascending the first step.

"Whenever you are."

For a moment, she closed her eyes on the sight of the reanimated corpses lurching toward them, fingers like knives reaching out to rend their flesh. She summoned the fire that was her curse, but also her salvation.

Liz extended her arms, feeling the air around her become superheated as she allowed the flame to flow from her body, engulfing the army of reanimated dead that was mere feet away. But she didn't stop there. She extended the hungry flame, allowing it to continue on through the subbasement, consuming everything that it could find in its voracious hunger.

On that bottom step she watched, mesmerized by the sight of a multitude of human shapes silently burning as they attempted to squelch the flames that covered their bodies. There was a series of small, muffled explosions from somewhere far back in the underground chamber, and Liz knew it was time to get out. She shook herself from her reverie and turned, ready to sprint up the stairs, when she noticed that Abe was nowhere to be found.

Odd, she thought, certain that he would have been

waiting for her to finish with her task, but then, out
of the corner of her eye she saw him. He was down
in the basement again, amid the flames.

"Abe, what the hell are you doing?" she yelled from
the steps over the increasing roar of fire.

The amphibious man didn't answer. He stumbled
through what little areas remained untouched by
flames, a large boxlike machine in his arms. She
rushed back down the stairs and into the conflagration to help him, wondering what could be so important that he would risk his very life to retrieve it.

There wasn't much time before it would all be
gone, destroyed by what she had loosed.

"What were you thinking?" she asked, grabbing
him by the arm.

Abe remained strangely silent. His scaly flesh
seemed parched and rough, dried in the heat.

Liz pushed him up the stairs and was prepared to
follow when she felt the sudden surge of warmth
behind her. She spun around to see one of the zombie
robots, its body burning, reaching for her. One of its
clawed hands closed around her arm, and she immediately felt the material from her shirt begin to burn,
scorching the skin beneath.

Liz hissed through her teeth, the pain intense.
Instinctively, she went for her gun, pulling it from the
holster, and pressing it up tight against the zombie's
blackened flesh. She pulled the trigger repeatedly,
emptying the clip into the monstrosity. Its body

lurched and bucked as the bullets careened around inside its carcass. There was a miniexplosion and a burst of green energy in the shape of a man erupted from the corpse to escape through the ceiling.

The zombie, its power source depleted, collapsed to the ground at the foot of the stairs, but its clawed hand still gripped her arm. Liz peeled back its fingers, then made her way up the stairs into the smoke-filled cellar, where she found Abe waiting. The look in his eyes was strangely vacant as he clutched the black box possessively to his chest.

"We have to get outside," she rasped, smoke filling her lungs.

They went up into the farmhouse kitchen. Smoke had found its way up into the main body of the house as well, and they navigated through an artificial fog that stank of wood and burning flesh.

Out in front of the farmhouse, Liz bent over, hands upon her knees, and greedily gulped the winter air. Catching her breath again, she turned her attention back to Abe, who stood silently watching as the smoke billowed out from the farmhouse windows. He was still clutching the black box.

"I wondered where you went," Liz said, as he turned to look at her. "It's you, isn't it, Sally?" she asked. "You've taken control of Abe, haven't you?"

Abe nodded. "There was no choice," she answered, using the voice of her teammate.

Liz picked up a handful of snow and began to rub

it on the exposed flesh of her friend. "He's going to be dehydrated from the fire," she explained, washing away some of the collected dirt and soot, as well as moistening his green-hued skin.

"Thank you," she answered. "I did not wish to harm him, but I didn't want the machine to be destroyed either. I believe it could prove to be very important."

"What is it?" Liz asked, watching as Sally dropped Abe to his knees, setting the machine gingerly down in front of him.

"It was a device that my husband made," she said as she flicked a switch at the front of the black box. It had only three sides, and Liz could see a series of tubes inside the box begin to glow with an eerie light. "One of his first."

"Looks like it still works," Liz said, kneeling beside her possessed friend. "What does it do?"

"He made it to communicate with the beyond," she explained, eyes riveted to the inner workings of the strange device.

"He built it to speak to his god."

It was nice and warm inside the house, the smell of greasy breakfast sausages making his stomach grumble hungrily.

"Look, Aubrey," Hellboy said, sitting in a chair at the kitchen table, along with agents Delaney, Feig and Dexter. Ghostly Uncle Steve floated in front of the sink. "We really have to get going."

He glanced at his watch, wondering how long they had before an ancient god of destruction was summoned to Earth.

The old woman, wearing a brightly colored apron with a flower print, continued to poke at the fat sausages sizzling in the large black frying pan.

"I know, dear," she said, and turned the flame down beneath the pan, wiping her hands on a towel beside the stove. "I don't know what's keeping him. I told him where I put it."

Aubrey toddled to the doorway between the kitchen and the dining room and yelled to her husband, who was somewhere else in the house. "Baxter, did you find it?"

There was a sound of something heavy being moved in the room above them, and Hellboy's eyes darted to the ceiling.

"He should be right down," the old woman said with a gentle smile, leaving the doorway to return to the stove.

Hellboy could now see through the kitchen doorway, through the dining room and into the parlor beyond. The two children they had found in the Depot were seated on the sofa, their hands bound behind their backs.

"You may have stopped us, demon, but you haven't stopped our master," the little boy screamed from the olive green sofa. The furniture was covered in clear plastic, like it was the 1950s all over again.

"You've prevented nothing—our god will still come and . . ."

"Why don't you just shut up," the little girl said with disgust. "It's over and done. We failed. That's it."

The boy turned on his companion. "If you hadn't opened your big mouth, we might have escaped. You're a traitor, Annabel Standish—a traitor to the Electricizers and to the holy mission we've worked so hard to achieve."

The girl child's face distorted with rage, words of anger spilling from her mouth. "A holy mission so sacred that you would cast me aside?" she exclaimed. Her voice cracked, and she began to cry. "You told me that you loved me—and I loved you in return. I thought we were going to spend the rest of our lives together."

"There were circumstances," he began, attempting to explain. "I didn't mean to hurt you, it was just that . . . things changed and . . ."

The girl turned her head away, refusing to look at him any longer. "Yes, they have. I suddenly have no interest in gods and the changing of the world. I'm very tired," the little girl said. "And I'd like this all to end now."

The boy struggled to his feet. "You stupid cow!" he screeched. "Do you realize what you've done?"

Hellboy left the kitchen and strode into the parlor. "That's about enough out of the both of you," he said, pushing the boy back down.

There was a squeak from the stairway nearby, and Baxter Whipple descended into the parlor, an old wooden chest in his arms. "What's all the ruckus?"

"Lovers' spat," Hellboy said, moving to help the man with his load. "Is this it?"

Baxter pulled a wooden folding table from out of the corner and set it up. "Yes, that's it." He patted the flat surface of the table with his hand. "Set it down here if you would be so kind."

Hellboy did as he was told, watching as the old man pulled a key ring from one of the deep pockets of his blue cardigan.

"Let's see if I remember which one it is," he muttered, reviewing each of the keys before deciding on one that didn't look any different from the others. "Here it is," he said, and slipped the key into the front of the wooden chest, turning it slowly until it unlocked.

Baxter flipped open the lid and a dusty aroma, like old clothes stored in an attic, wafted out from within. He reached inside, withdrawing something wrapped in yellowed cheesecloth. Carefully, he pulled the old cloth away to reveal an ancient-looking dagger, its blade nearly black from age.

"Isn't it lovely?" Baxter exclaimed. "Aubrey gave it to me on our twentieth wedding anniversary. It belonged to the Assyrian exorcist, Nykore Anyroda, and is the foremost instrument for the eviction of uninvited spiritual habitation ever forged."

Hellboy studied the ancient tool, simple in its design, an eight-inch blade with a crude carving of a screaming skull on its hilt. *And to think most married couples are satisfied with flowers,* he thought.

"I've loaned it out from time to time to the Bureau and some of its affiliates, and in all those times it's only failed once."

Hellboy looked from the ancient blade to Baxter. "Only once?"

The old man nodded. "Tried to use it on my mother-in-law, but it didn't do a thing," he said, raising a hand to his mouth and lowering his voice conspiratorially. "Come to find out she wasn't possessed at all, she was just a witch."

They both laughed.

"I heard that," Aubrey Whipple said, coming into the parlor.

Steve's ghost drifted behind her, as if carried in her wake, and he was smiling. Agents Delaney, Feig and Dexter soon followed, and each of them was holding a plate piled high with scrambled eggs and sausage.

"You know I'm only joking, darling," Baxter said, blowing a kiss to his wife, which she pretended to bat away.

The former BPRD agent turned back to Hellboy. "Perhaps a little breakfast before we proceed?"

Hellboy glanced at the bound pair still sitting on the couch. Their eyes had become wide, darting around the room fearfully. The ghosts possessing the kids must have suspected that their days were numbered.

"No," Hellboy said with a slight shake of his head. "I think we better do this now."

"Fine, fine," Baxter said, slightly agitated.

"Is there a problem?" Hellboy asked.

"No," the old man said, and he looked to his wife. "I'll take care of it."

Aubrey tottered over to them. "You'll do no such thing, you stupid old man," she said, taking the still-wrapped knife out of his hand. "Nykore's blade demands payment from its user," she explained, turning to Hellboy. "It drains a bit of life force from whoever wields it—so that it has the necessary power to complete the job."

"One of the reasons why Anyroda wasn't an exorcist for all that long," Baxter explained. "Eventually sucked him dry."

"This old coot," Aubrey said, gesturing toward her husband, "doesn't have life force to spare, I'm afraid."

"Any kind of special training needed to evict these creeps?" Hellboy asked, hooking a thumb at the two sitting on the couch.

Baxter stroked his chin in thought. "Not really," he said. "It's pretty self-explanatory."

Hellboy took the wrapped blade from Aubrey. "Then let's get cracking," he said, turning toward the couch.

"What are you going to do?" the little boy asked, a twinkle of fear showing in his eyes.

"Never mind," Hellboy barked. "What do I do?" he asked the old man.

"Take the blade from the cloth."

He could feel all their eyes upon him—the BPRD agents, the ghost, Aubrey and Baxter, the possessed children waiting on the plastic-covered sofa—as he gripped the blade by its hilt and lifted it out of its yellowed wrapping.

"Okay, now wh . . ." Hellboy began, but his voice was momentarily sucked away. He felt the blade familiarizing itself with his body, making itself at home.

"Whoa!" He swayed slightly on his feet.

"That's all right," Baxter said reassuringly. "This too shall pass."

Hellboy felt himself grow tired, not devastatingly so, but enough that he'd give his eyeteeth for a little snooze time.

"Now point yourself toward the subjects," the old man directed. Aubrey had gone out to the kitchen and returned with a plate of breakfast for her husband. Baxter had started to eat, as Hellboy pointed the blade at the boy and girl sitting upon the sofa.

Almost at once his mind was filled with the most fantastic images: exorcisms done throughout the blade's existence, thousands of demons and spectral entities ripped from where they didn't belong, forced to return from whence they had come, or to at least move on to the next plane of existence.

"Get away from me!" the boy screamed, standing up from the couch again, only to be pushed back down. "I'll tell you anything you want to know. Just please, let me stay in this body, I'm begging you. Please!"

"Listen to you," the little girl said to her companion. "To think that I once believed you to be wise and brave. Accept your fate. You don't know anything that could possibly be useful to them. Absolom purposely didn't tell us our destination from this point, for just this reason. He told the drones, but he didn't tell us."

The boy was crying, praying for help to a god that did not appear to be listening.

"It makes me sick to realize how wrong I was about you—about everything," the girl said.

"Now take the blade and . . ." Baxter began again, handing his empty breakfast plate to his wife.

"I know how to do it," Hellboy said, his head jammed full of examples.

The possessed child pleaded one last time as Hellboy brought the blade toward him. He touched the tip of the knife to the exposed flesh of the boy's arm, drawing a single drop of blood.

The child screamed, a strange howling sound composed of two separate voices that gradually became one. Hellboy watched as a writhing green energy squirmed out from one of the kid's ears, attempting to escape out into the atmosphere, only to disperse like smoke in a gentle breeze.

The little girl had been watching the entire time, and she looked at him fearfully. "Promise me that it won't hurt," she asked.

"I can't do that," Hellboy told her, starting to bring the knife blade closer.

The girl shrugged, following the blade's approach as it neared the exposed flesh of her arm. "At least you were honest with me. That's more than most."

The dagger drew blood, and she started to shriek as the ghost that had been the dominant entity was forcibly evicted from the little girl's body.

But before it was gone completely, onto whatever afterlife awaited it, the spirit gave something to Hellboy. She touched his mind, and he filed the information away, certain that it would come in handy later.

He turned his attention back to the kids. It was horrible to watch, children appearing to be in such pain, but it had been necessary. They slumped limply on the old-fashioned couch, as if worn-out from a hard day of playing.

Aubrey was the first to go to them, gently removing their bonds, and slowly they began to stir, awakening from their ordeal. Hellboy wondered if they would remember, or if their time not in control would seem like just a bad dream.

The girl was the first to come fully awake, and seeing them she started to cry.

"It's okay, child," Aubrey said, consoling her.

"We're here to help you. My name's Aubrey, what's yours?"

"Rebecca," said the small voice.

"Where's my mom and dad—I want my mom and dad," she asked, cuddled in Aubrey's arms. There was panic growing in her voice as she looked about the room filled with strangers.

Her brother was awake now, a dumbfounded expression on his handsome young features. He must have thought he was still asleep, in the middle of a very weird dream.

"What's your name?" Hellboy asked him.

The kid swallowed hard before answering. "Jack," he finally said.

"Hey, Jack, I want you to look after your sister," he said, pointing to the little girl with the Anyroda dagger. "Some bad stuff has happened to you and your folks, and we're going to try and fix it, okay?"

Jack nodded, mouth agape, sliding over on the couch to sit next to the crying little girl. He gingerly put his arm around her shoulder, all the while never taking his eyes off Hellboy.

"Excellent," Hellboy said, then turned toward Baxter.

The old man had retrieved the dagger's wrapping and was waiting for it to be returned to him. "Couldn't have done better myself," he said, extending the nest of yellowed material.

Hellboy went to lay the knife down, but found that he couldn't let it go. It felt stuck to his hand.

"What's wrong?" Baxter asked.

"It doesn't want to be put away yet," Hellboy answered, now feeling a tug on the blade as if from some powerful magnet. "It knows there are others out there—like them."

He looked back to the kids. Aubrey was comforting them both, asking if either would like to have some breakfast.

"And it wants to deal with them too."

An icy wind blew off the sea and ripped across the stark and rocky surface of Egg Rock, causing his eyes to water. Absolom scanned the horizon for a sign of the boat that would carry the youngest of his followers, as well as the final objects of power needed to complete the birthing ritual. He saw nothing but the gray Atlantic and a foreboding sky above it, thick with dark clouds that hinted of another winter storm to come. Normally from this vantage, he would have been able to see the coast that stretched north of Boston from Winthrop to Marblehead, but this morning the land was obscured by an eerie fog.

He turned away from the view and walked over the rocks to the center of the island. Once upon a time, a lighthouse and a home had stood here. He had seen this island countless times in his dreams, throughout his life, never realizing its purpose. Sometimes it had been adorned with a lighthouse tower, and others it had been as it was now, as cold and barren as when it first surged up from beneath the ocean waves during the birth throes of the world. Recently he had started to see how it would be, a glimpse into a future that was gradually on its way toward becoming the present.

In the place where a beacon of light had once stood, the body of a god was being erected. He watched his drones scramble about the scaffolding erected around the fifty-foot-tall figure of metal. Searing white sparks exploded from welding guns as limbs were attached.

Things are progressing quite nicely, Absolom thought, pulling up the sleeve on his heavy coat to check the time. *Now if only Tyler and Annabel would return . . .*

The sudden pain was as if a piece of his soul was being cut away.

Absolom fell to the rocky ground, unable to breathe as the excruciating pain cut through him again. All at once he understood the source of his misery. He heard Annabel and Tyler scream as their spirits were banished from the world of the living. Their voices echoed inside his skull.

He tried to scream his anguish, feeling a piece of himself slip away with them, but he could not find his voice—the darkness of unconsciousness threatened to claim him. And on the periphery of his failing vision, he saw the ominous form of his adversary, its skin the color of dried blood. In its hand was a dagger. *This ancient weapon—this is what was used to sever the ties of my acolytes to their new vessels.*

In his mind's eye he saw Hellboy raise his arm and point the tip of the blade at Absolom. *He's coming,* Absolom realized, panic coursing through his body like raw current. *He knows where we are.*

The high priest of the Band of Electricizers heard his name being called from somewhere off in the distance and felt something warm and wet upon his face. He awakened from his funk with a gasp, like a man breaking the surface from the depths of the sea.

Silas was worriedly licking his face. "Absolom, are you all right?" the dog asked, the question crackling from the speaker of the electronic voice box.

He pushed the dog away and scrambled to his feet. "I'm fine—but I'm afraid that the same cannot be said for Tyler and Annabel."

"What do you mean?" Silas asked, the hackles of fur around his neck bristling.

"They're gone," he replied, attempting to keep his own panic in check as the image of Hellboy flashed in his mind.

"What do you mean, 'gone'?" the dog begged. "How can they be gone—where did they go?"

Absolom glanced briefly toward the god's body, seeing that things still progressed, then turned his attentions to a makeshift shelter that had been erected to protect the more delicate machinery—and Mary as well—from the harsh elements.

"I have to speak with him," Absolom said, ignoring Silas's frantic questioning as he stalked toward the four-sided enclosure.

Wickham emerged, pulling aside one of the clear plastic sheets that made up the walls of the shelter. "He's asking for you," the attractive woman said, an unflattering look of panic in her beautiful blue eyes.

Absolom tried to pass, but Wickham blocked his path.

"What's happening?" he demanded, grabbing hold of Absolom's arm. "Is everything all right? Where are Tyler and Annabel? Have they returned? Tell me that they've returned."

Wickham had always been a nervous old man, prone to attacks of panic, and Absolom knew that would never change, no matter what body the man wore.

"Let go of my arm, Geoffrey," he warned. "And I would prefer if you waited outside. Qemu'el and I have some important things to discuss."

Wickham released his grip and slowly stepped out of the way. "It has to work this time," he said, desperation in his voice. "Tell me that it's going to work."

But Absolom said nothing. Turning his back on his disciple, he allowed the plastic curtain to fall closed behind him as he entered the shelter. It was warmer inside. A portable heater, also powered by the energy of the departed, hummed in the corner, filling the enclosure with a dry, artificial warmth.

"Is that you, Absolom Spearz?" asked Qemu'el.

Absolom circumvented the crowded set up, walking around the various machines to find Mary Hudnell's skeletal form lying upon a cot. Her heavy woolen nightgown had been pulled up over her bulbous stomach, exposing the veined, taut flesh. The apparatus that he had designed to allow the god to speak to them had been reattached, the voice of the future again coming through the horn of the ancient phonograph.

"It is I," he answered.

His god was silent, and for a moment Absolom feared that somehow his device had malfunctioned. But that wasn't the case at all.

"I felt something," the Archon at last said. "A disturbance in the ether. Are you aware of this?"

"I am aware," Absolom replied. "Two of my disciples—*our* disciples," he corrected, "have been vanquished by the enemy."

The only sound from the flower-shaped speaker was a faint hissing.

"And how will this affect my coming?" Qemu'el finally asked in an ancient voice filled with caution.

"I . . . I'm not sure," Absolom answered. "They were to bring the last of the items of power and . . ."

His god began to scream, the unearthly sound causing the communications device to tremble. Absolom blocked his ears from the chilling sound of a divine entity enraged, watching as Mary's body thrashed upon the cot, a victim of his deity's fury. If Qemu'el was not careful, he would damage his vessel, and put his survival at even greater risk.

"Please, my lord," Absolom begged, moving closer to Mary Hudnell's thrashing form. He reached out and placed the palms of his hands upon the flesh. "Calm yourself, before irreparable harm is done."

It was as if he'd placed his hands into molten lava, his head jerking, the spastic movement causing him to bite into his tongue, filling his mouth with the coppery taste of blood.

"Calm myself, you say!" the ancient being screamed. "Perhaps I have chosen unwisely! Perhaps another of the pitiful multitude who infest this planet would have appreciated the gifts that I have bestowed upon you more."

"Please," Absolom begged, trying to break the connection between himself and his angry savior, but it was as if his flesh and Mary's were one and the same. "I beg your mercy."

"I will not be disappointed again," Qemu'el growled, the sound of his angry voice like the deafening boom of creation. "You will find a way—you will utilize the gifts that I have so generously given to you, and you will find a way!"

Absolom was at last allowed to pull his hands away, and he fell backward against one of the many machines that crowded the enclosure. His body trembled as if every ligament, every muscle and tendon, had been strained to the maximum level of their elasticity. He wasn't sure if he could remain standing and began to slide to the floor, like a marionette whose strings had been cut.

A battery of spectral energy toppled from atop the machine and struck the metal corner of an adjoining device. The glass cracked, releasing an explosion of ghostly fire into the air. Absolom recoiled. The spirit that had been contained streaked up through the plastic ceiling and into the afterlife from which it had been detained. As he watched its escape, Absolom began to recognize the germ of an idea forming inside his head.

"Yes," he hissed, struggling to regain the strength in his arms and legs, pulling himself up from the ground. "Yes, it's possible—that could work."

"Tell me," Qemu'el demanded.

Absolom looked around for a piece of paper, found a notepad, and pulled a pencil from his pocket. The image inside his brain was taking form, and as it did, he sketched the design on the piece of paper.

"I believe I've concocted an alternative to the missing items of power," he said, his pencil pausing upon the paper momentarily, as he continued to formulate. "Yes, yes, I have," he said, his excitement starting to grow. "It will take some additional time but . . ."

"Begin at once," his god ordered.

"Yes," he agreed, a smile snaking across his face as he studied what he had just drawn. "The power of the spirits will give us the last of what is needed."

On wobbly legs, he made his way to the exit, pulling back the flap, to be hit by a blast of icy wind. Wickham and Udell were waiting outside for him, obviously eavesdropping on all that had occurred between him and their god.

"The dead," Absolom said to them, holding out the design for his latest invention. "The restless dead will give him life."

CHAPTER 14

A be Sapien's body felt strange—different.
Sally would never have possessed the fish
man without his permission, but she'd had no choice.
If she had not acted that very instant, the communication device would have been destroyed in the quickly
spreading fire.

But the amphibian had not escaped exposure to the
fire unscathed. That close to the withering heat of the
blaze, Abe Sapien had become dehydrated, his skin
parched and rough. Now she could feel its growing
need for water. The snow had helped, but he would
need to immerse himself shortly.

The ghost could feel the oddness of Abe's body, the
inhumanity of it. His hairless skin was slick and cool,
and his gills fluttered, eagerly awaiting the caress of
water. It was truly a unique sensation to be inside this
unusual form, but there was little time for her to
appreciate it.

"How's it coming?" Liz asked, kneeling on the
frozen lawn beside her.

Sally moved Abe's hands over the various knobs and dials, trying desperately to remember how it was operated.

"This was one of many devices Absolom constructed," she said through Abe. "He'd been hearing the call—the voice of the god—since he was just a little boy, and wanted to build something so that they could speak across realities."

Inside the box she found two rolled lengths of copper wire and remembered that this was how he had made the necessary connection.

"This was the machine that gave him his first taste of success," Sally continued, unrolling the wire and attaching two clips to each of Abe's ears. "Devices he built later were stronger, but with this machine, he was able to establish the first communication."

She looked at Liz Sherman through Abe Sapien's eyes. "Right now I am going to attempt something similar."

"Will it hurt Abe?" Although Sally had explained what she was doing, and whom she would be contacting, doubt was evident in the woman's eyes.

"I don't know," Sally said with a slight shake of his head. "I'll be as careful as I can."

Sally checked and double-checked the controls on the strange device. It seemed to be taking its power from the very air around them.

"Is there anything you'd like me to do?" Liz asked.

"You can pray," Sally said, bringing Abe's hand to the one switch that had yet to be touched.

And without any hesitation . . .

Sally's spiritual essence rippled with fear.

Still anchored to the physical world within the body of Abe Sapien, her mind rushed away from Abe's flesh, from the substance of her own spirit. She peered now into *elsewhere*. A place she had been before, when she was the sacrifice. A place darker than the deepest night.

A place where angels dreamed.

She sensed them there in the eldritch darkness, deep in the clutches of sleep. Gifted with this insight into their world, in their shadows, she could see into their dreams.

They dreamed of a time when they would awaken—when the Creator of all things would call upon them—and their purpose would be realized.

Sally recoiled with the vision as she saw all life on Earth wiped away by searing white light, leaving behind a world clean of blemishes, a planet as fresh and pure as the day it was first birthed in the cosmic upheaval called Creation.

But she could see into their unconscious minds and perceived that they understood it was not yet time for this, despite what Absolom and his followers believed and what Qemu'el—the wayward brother of the two sleeping angels—desired.

It was not yet time for the world to die.

She told them as much, reaching out with her own
puny mind, probing the ocean of darkness before her
for their attention. Sally cried out to them, begging
them to awaken and hear her pleas, but still they
slept; still they dreamed.

Please, she begged them. *Please, listen. Your dreams
will never be reality. Your brother will see to that. Selfish
thing, he's going to destroy it all, and you'll never have the
chance to perform the task for which you were created.*

Sally waited and listened, squinting into the undulating void of black, desperate to know if they had
heard. Frustrated, she lashed out at the somnolent
beings. *You're useless,* her mind shrieked. *And your
brother will prove it when he destroys the world all by
himself. Useless.*

She prepared to withdraw from the shadow realm
and return to the safe vessel that had allowed her to
make this journey. But as she began the process of
willing herself away, she felt a sudden change in the
atmosphere of the cold black void in which she
floated. She hesitated, waiting—just in case.

And she didn't have long to wait.

Before her, the darkness parted and two sets of
enormous eyes—eyes the size of small planets—
emerged from the beyond.

"I was correct, brother Duma," one of the Archons
spoke, its voice like the tuning of a million orchestras
all at once. "A wayward spirit—an insignificant
human spirit—has interrupted my slumber."

One of the eyes focused upon her, its pupil contracting to the size of a tiny moon.

It was as if her body was caught in some kind of powerful current, her spirit buffeted violently by the turbulent shadows.

"How dare it, Za'apiel," the ancient angel growled. "How dare it presume that it could do such a thing and not suffer the consequences of its foolish actions?"

"So true, brother Duma," Za'apiel, agreed. "And what of Qemu'el? How does the third of our trinity feel now that our sleep has been disturbed?"

There was silence in the void as the angels waited for their brother to reply.

"How can he still manage to sleep?"

It took all her strength to find her voice again, and Sally shrieked above the swirling maelstrom of black that buffeted her. "He's gone!" she cried out. "It's the reason why I've come . . . to let you know!"

"Let us know?" Duma questioned. "What is this loathsome gnat going on about? Where is Qemu'el?"

"He isn't here, brother," Za'apiel replied after a moment, and the currents of darkness calmed, and Sally's spirit found itself floating before the audience of eyes.

"Do you know where our brother is, little spirit?" the one called Za'apiel asked.

"Yes, yes, I know," she told them. "He's gone . . ."

"Gone where?" Duma bellowed. "Where could he have gone without us?"

Sally hesitated, waiting for the anxious Archon to

continue his rant, but the angel was silent, so she continued.

"To Earth," she explained. "He's gone to Earth—and I believe he has plans to destroy it."

The eyes were gone, and the void was quiet. Sally began to wonder if she had been left alone, when one of the Archons spoke.

"We have not been called," Za'apiel said. "It is not yet the time for it to be brought to end."

"But he is there," Sally confirmed. "Being worshipped as a god by followers who would sacrifice everything to bring him into the physical world—and allow him to walk the Earth."

"Blasphemy!" the two angels of destruction screamed in unison, and she sensed their movement; beings long dormant at last roused from their hibernation.

They were coming, swimming through the sea of shadow. She could sense them growing closer, but still she could not see them.

And then they were upon her, breaching the ocean of darkness, their screams of fury deafening as she became swept up in their passage, dragged in the wake of angry Archons.

Abe twitched and moaned, his arms dangling limply by his sides. Liz stared at the small beads of dark blood beneath the clips hanging from his ears. If something bad happened to him, she would never be able to forgive herself.

He groaned again, this time much louder, and she moved closer. His arms flopped; his body rocked from side to side. The machine had begun to hum, the glow from inside it seeming to get brighter.

"C'mon, Sally, hurry it up," Liz hissed.

Something was definitely up with the machine, and she debated whether or not to get Abe away from it. The machine was vibrating, its wooden black frame moving across the ground of its on accord.

She glanced at Abe and saw that his eyes were open, his mouth agape. His body suddenly grew rigid, as if an electrical current was being pumped through him.

This can't be good. Not good at all. Liz's mind raced.

She contemplated breaking the connection, pulling the copper wires from her friend's ears, but was afraid of what might happen. She couldn't risk hurting him—but wasn't she doing the very same thing by just kneeling and watching?

Liz felt the fire stir within her. It was eager to be released again, but she held it back, pushing it down, letting it know who was the boss.

Abe began to scream, and she came very close to joining him. She didn't know what to do. The light thrown from the machine was almost blinding now.

Finally, she couldn't bear the sound of her friend in pain any longer and wrapped her hands around the copper wires. She was about to rip their connections from the machine, when the machine exploded in a flash of searing white light, and she and Abe were tossed backward by a wave of unnatural energy.

Blossoms of white expanded in front of her eyes as she hauled herself up from the ground. Liz rubbed at her eyes, attempting to restore her vision as she went to her friend.

"Abe," she called, falling to her knees by his side.

He seemed okay, raising a hand to his smooth, green skull and giving his head the slightest of shakes.

"I'm all right," he said, blinking rapidly.

"Sally took control of you," Liz started to explain. "I wasn't really sure if I should let her, but she said that the machine could . . ."

"She did it," Abe said with an eager nod, as if suddenly remembering. "Sally talked to them."

The ghost of the horribly burned woman slowly materialized before them.

"And?" Liz looked from Abe to the charred, ghostly woman, hoping for an answer.

"They're coming," Abe whispered.

From the fear etched upon Abe's face, Liz wasn't sure that was a good thing.

"Say that again." Hellboy pressed the headset tighter against his ear. They were in the Chinook again, returning from Gosnolt, and it was difficult to hear Manning over the whine of the chopper's twin rotors.

"Was the mission a success?" Manning asked, raising his voice to be heard.

Hellboy glanced across the hold in the direction of the children. They were wrapped in heavy blankets, wearing BPRD ball caps, and were in the midst of a heated game of rock, paper, scissors with Agent Dexter.

"You could say so," Hellboy replied, glad to see that the kids didn't appear to have been adversely affected by their possession. "We're returning with two former Electricizers—minus the spooks of course. Baxter lent us a pretty neat tool for evicting the body-squatters. Worked like a charm."

"Excellent," Manning replied. "That could help in dealing with the rest of the family."

Hellboy could feel the presence of the Anyroda dagger in the pocket of his jacket. It felt warm, as if alive. It seemed to be content for now, but he knew that the closer they got to their destination, the hungrier it would grow—eager to perform the task for which it was created.

"That's the plan," Hellboy agreed. "We'll be dropping the kids off with our boys in Boston, and then we'll head to Egg Rock. It's a small island about a mile northeast of Nahant, Massachusetts. I think that's where our Electricizers are going to attempt their grand finale."

He could hear Manning passing the information to other agents at the Fairfield office.

"And you came by this information how?"

"A spook passed it on to me just before she vacated

the premises," he said, remembering the images that flooded his mind upon the completion of the spirit's exorcism, the fifty-foot-tall metal statue being the standout.

"We'll dispatch a team immediately."

"Negative. Why don't you hold off on that," Hellboy said. He glanced at the tarp-covered body of Agent Holmes. The case had been unpredictable, and it had cost the life of a good agent. He didn't want to take that risk again unless it was absolutely necessary. "We don't know exactly what we're going to be dealing with here. Have the guys on standby, and I'll let you know how the situation is looking as soon as we get there. Who knows, maybe it'll be something I can take care of myself."

Steve's ghost drifted over to him. "Ask how Sally's mission with Liz and Abe went." He sounded like he enjoyed saying the word "mission" quite a bit.

"How did the others do at the house in Lynn?" Hellboy asked over the commlink.

"They ran into a serious threat inside the farm-house, but it was neutralized," Manning replied.

"Neutralized?" Hellboy rolled the word over in his head. Liz encountered a serious threat, and it had been neutralized. "She burned it to the ground didn't she," Hellboy asked, looking at the ghost.

There was a long pause before Manning replied. "The house *was* destroyed by fire—"

"Knew it."

"But not before the team retrieved a machine that enabled the spirit of Sally Spearz to make contact with two spiritual entities of extraordinary power. They're related to the current crisis, but according to Agent Sherman's report, they may be turned to our purpose."

Hellboy felt a headache coming on. "Great. Spiritual entities of extraordinary power. Always best to have them on our side. Problem is, even if they're playing for the home team, these kinds of things tend to get really messy. Lots of death. Property damage. Should be a barrel of laughs. Just what kind of entities are we talking about here?"

"Liz said that their names are . . ." He pictured Manning shuffling through his notes. "Duma and Za'apiel."

"Never heard of 'em."

"Research has given us some cursory info. If the two Sally contacted really are Duma and Za'apiel, then the being that's being summoned by the Electricizers is called Qemu'el," Manning explained. "They're Archons."

"What the heck's an Archon?"

"They're world destroyers."

"Aren't they all?" Hellboy grumbled. "Archon is a much nicer term. 'World destroyer' lacks finesse. Got anything else that could be useful?"

"Supposedly they're a trinity, so the idea of only one being summoned has caused some problems with the siblings. At least that's what Liz is saying."

"Little friction in the family," Hellboy said. "Good to know. And that's the wedge we can use, maybe get their help in taking down baby brother."

He told the Director he'd communicate with operations as soon as he knew something more, then signed off with a casual, *catch ya later,* but Hellboy wasn't feeling all that sure about this one.

These clowns are actually on the verge of pulling this one off, he thought. They were summoning an Archon. *Why does it have to be destruction?* he wondered. *Why not the god of Buffalo wings or crazy dancing?* Like he would be so lucky.

"We've just received clearance from Logan to land, sir," the pilot informed him.

The Chinook landed with a slight bounce, and Hellboy got up from his seat to help the others. They were dropping off the kids, but as far as Hellboy was concerned the rest of the Gosnolt team was going as well.

"Keep the engine warm, boys, we ain't staying long," he told the pilots.

He opened the door to the craft to see that a van was indeed waiting for them. "All ashore who's going ashore." He waved them out the door as Agent Dexter approached, holding the hand of the little girl named Rebecca.

"We'll get the kids settled and be right back," she said.

Hellboy shook his head. "No dice," he told her.

"Stay with the kids." He looked to see that Agents Delaney and Feig were retrieving Holmes's body. "I'm doing this next part solo."

They tried to argue, but he wouldn't hear any of it, and besides, he was bigger. He waved good-bye to them as he pulled the door to the copter closed, turning the latch and locking it.

When Hellboy returned to his seat, the ghost hung shimmering in the shadowy interior of the chopper, waiting for him.

"It's just you and me, eh pal?" the specter asked, an excited grin upon his translucent features.

"Looks like it." Hellboy patted the wall between the hold and the cockpit of the craft, signaling to the crew that it was time to depart.

"You're the only one that I don't have to worry about getting killed."

It's worth the pain, Mary Hudnell tried to convince herself, as she reclined upon the cot that had been brought outside into the cold from the warmth of the enclosure. Her breath was coming in gasps, and her body was wracked with spasms.

They had inserted multiple needles into her pregnant belly, twelve-inch spears of metal connected to multiple strands of colored wire that trailed upon the ground like hundreds of thin-bodied tropical snakes. The wires were connected to all manner of machines, and the machines were in turn connected to a pyramid-shaped cabinet of copper and glass that contained the most unusual items.

Is that a Styrofoam cup? she wondered through her pain-addled delirium. She wished she had the strength to rise and examine the objects stored within the pyramid. Absolom had referred to them as objects of faith, explaining that each had absorbed the power of adulation, and that this power would be what their god would use to make its final transition.

Now the power from the collected items was being extracted, flowing down the wired connection, through the needles, and into her womb, where Qemu'el was gathering his strength to begin the journey to his new home.

The pain was unlike anything she had ever experienced, but she tried to look past it, imagining the good that she was doing for the world—the good that they *all* were doing for the world.

She watched her fellow Electricizers through a pain-induced haze as they maintained the many machines that had been built by the man she loved. Mary looked for Absolom, sure that she would receive a certain amount of strength from the sight of the great man. He stood by the vessel that would soon contain the essence of a god—that would soon *be* a god—and her heart took flight at the sight of him. The wind whipped across the barren island, his long, graying hair tousled by the blow. She would have preferred his old body, but this one would certainly do fine. It was so nice to have him here with her again.

Mary felt cold and wished that someone would at least give her a sweater to throw over her shoulders.

Monkeylike, Absolom scaled the scaffolding erected around the god-body, making sure that the cables that would conduct the quintessence of their most holy god into the human-shaped receptacle were properly secured. She gasped, fearing for his safety, as he spun around upon the interlocking metal rods, and gave a thumbs-up to Wickham, who waited below.

The woman—Mary wondered if she would ever get used to Geoffrey looking this way—stood behind a control panel, flicking a series of switches that caused the machinery close to her to hum to life.

The being within her squirmed, eagerly anticipating his birth. She felt him peering out through her eyes, watching as the final steps were taken to assure his coming. Mary Hudnell's spidery hands slowly went to her prominent belly, avoiding contact with the needles protruding from her flesh and the wires emanating from them. She didn't want to risk disturbing anything of importance. *Wouldn't that be a sin,* she thought. *To be so close, and then have my own carelessness cause us to fail again.*

She splayed her fingers across the hard, tight flesh, as she'd seen Absolom do on numerous occasions, and attempted to connect with the entity within. Since becoming impregnated with his essence, she'd always been aware of his existence—feeling him move inside her womb, experiencing his growth—but never had he spoken to her. Mary wanted him to know how much she truly loved him, what she had sacrificed over the long years in his name.

She wanted Qemu'el to know that she had done everything for her god. And suddenly, as the cold winds blew around her, and the hum of the unearthly machines filled her ears, Mary Hudnell experienced, however briefly, what it was like to be touched by the god.

The hate Qemu'el had for her was second only to the seething rage he felt for mankind and the world upon which it thrived. She was his prison, and he took no pity upon her in letting her know this—letting her *feel* this. She tried to explain the bond that she felt for him, the love that she carried, but the god just laughed, a horrible, horrible sound lacking all mirth. And then he showed her, showed the woman what he was going to do to the world, and Mary's vision become engorged with the sight of the world exploding in flames, mushroom clouds blossoming all across the planet, eradicating every living thing that walked, crawled or squirmed upon its surface, or swam in its oceans.

She felt his joy, as only a mother who had truly bonded with the unborn life within her womb could. But she was unable to share in his happiness.

You promised us Heaven, she thought, trying desperately to understand. *You said that you would bring us—all of us, all of humanity—that much closer to being one with the divine.*

And again her mind was filled with the most powerful of images.

The Earth burned molten hot from the countless explosions and nuclear fire. Rising from the destruction came a being of unearthly beauty, its body clad in armor burning white from the intensity of the heat. As it spread its arms, enormous wings unfurled from its back. The wings begin to flap, arousing the surface of the dead world; clouds of black ash stirred from the ground, the remains of all life upon the Earth floating up into the sky, carried upon the thermal updrafts, drifting higher, and higher.

On their way to Heaven.

The god then broke the connection to his mother, ejecting her forcibly from his vision of the future. Mary's eyes came open, seeing the world for what it was, remembering the sight of how it would soon be.

She could not allow this to happen.

Fitfully, she struggled upon the cot, her hands no longer concerned with disturbing anything of importance. She wrapped her hands around the wires, preparing to pull the needles from her body, and suddenly she felt a hand fall upon hers. It was cool, comforting, and she was awash with the feeling that everything would be just fine.

Mary looked up into the eyes of Absolom, the man

whom she loved, the man who had transcended death in order to fulfill his holy objective.

"It's time, Mary," he said, and she felt the cool bliss of his touch as he laid his hand upon her swollen stomach.

"Time to change the world."

The mechanical hands worked like a dream.

Silas Udell leaped up on his back legs, using his newly enhanced front paws to manipulate the controls upon the panel.

Absolom Spearz is a saint, the Electricizer within the body of a dog thought, experiencing a kind of euphoric joy as the segmented digits of his artificial hands performed their tasks as competently as if they were made of skin, muscle and bone.

In his canine form, he had been concerned about his ability to perform the appropriate task, his worry becoming even more pronounced when learning the fate of their brethren at the hands of the monster, Hellboy.

The hands had been a gift—something that the high priest had whipped up in a moment of divine inspiration. Silas could not comprehend his good luck as Absolom had slid the mechanisms, glovelike, over his paws. There had been some pain as he had drilled holes and stretched tendons to anchor the hands and ensure that they worked properly, but it was pain Silas would have experienced threefold to continue to have these gifts that had been bestowed upon him. Now he was complete, the happiest he could ever recall being in his troubled existence: all this, plus the fact that the savior was coming. Silas Udell seriously had to consider the question as to why he, of all people, had been so blessed.

All was in readiness. The power being siphoned from the objects of worship flowed smoothly out of the pyramid and into the stomach of the Madonna, feeding Qemu'el, giving him the strength to complete his ascendance . . . his transition from the ether to the physical world. Silas had the urge to bark—to toss his head back and howl his joy at what they were on the cusp of accomplishing—but he held his animal excitement in check, focusing instead on the task that he had been assigned.

Robot hand poised above the control panel switch, he waited for his signal. He turned to gaze at Absolom, who stood beside the Madonna's cot, hand upon her swollen belly.

Wagging his thick tail in anticipation, he let out a yelp of pure elation as his leader turned to him, nodding to signal that it was time.

With his new hand, the dog flipped the switch.

Absolom felt Mary's fear and sympathized with her as she trembled in anticipation. It wasn't every day that a hundred-year-old woman gave birth, never mind to a god. She was trying to tell him something, her mouth moving pitifully as she fought to speak. He laid his hand upon her brow and gave her his most loving smile, hoping to calm her. The time for words was gone, and there could be no turning back.

How he had longed for this moment. To have it at last within his grasp was almost overwhelming. Glancing over to the god-body, swaying ever so slightly in the winds coming off the Atlantic, he committed to memory the sight of it before it contained life. Now, it was little more than an elaborate armature—something that could be seen and admired as a work of art—but soon it would be so much more.

Absolom savored the moment, immersing himself in the time just before it was all about to change. A moment like this one would never come again.

With that thought fresh in his mind, he turned toward Silas and signaled for the next and final phase to begin.

Qemu'el fed.

In the darkness of limbo, the power of worship and devotion poured in around him, nourishing him—giving him the strength to pull open the breach a little wider.

Trapped between realities, his glorious essence existing on two planes, the god needed this sweet nectar of belief to allow him at last to complete his journey.

Yet he recalled the previous effort of his frail human servants, when his freedom seemed imminent only to be snatched away. Tormented by this memory, Qemu'el lashed out at his surroundings. Outside his darkness, he heard the piteous moans of the host body that had sustained him this last, tortuous century.

He would not be denied again.

Absolom Spearz had turned the key.

And now the door was swinging open.

Open wide.

The needles jutting from Mary's belly began to glow with an unearthly white light, like stars burning in the night sky. She writhed in agony on the table, and Absolom reached down, not to comfort, but to hold her in place. He couldn't allow her thrashing to dislodge any of the connections.

The flesh of her exposed stomach glowed as well, the taut skin of the protrusion pulsing with a queer light. Soon the god would at last be strong enough to leave the protection of the womb, flowing into the cables to finally merge his greatness with the body that had been built for him.

Mary convulsed, her skeletal frame pummeled by the preternatural forces that were attempting to escape her.

"That's it, my darling," he cooed, continuing to hold her in place, leaning down close so that she could hear him over the sounds of her screams. "You're doing fine."

Absolom looked into her wide, glassy eyes, remembering the first time that they had met so very long ago, and the spark of instant attraction that had passed between them. It had been nothing sexual. It had been something much deeper than that. He had known that this woman was going to play an important role in the future that he was attempting to forge.

How right he had been.

Mary arched her back violently, thrusting her stomach into the air and emitting a high-pitched, ululating scream of agony. He heard a sound very much like air rushing in to fill a vacuum, and then she fell limply upon the cot—her cries and wails suddenly silent.

Absolom released her. He noted with a furrow of his brow that the metal contacts jutting from the woman's abdomen no longer throbbed with an inner life. For a moment he was stunned by the eerie silence, broken only by the sounds of wind and surf. He looked toward the god-body, moved only by the ocean winds.

The unthinkable filled his mind. *Has something gone wrong? Has the god's essence somehow been released only to dissipate into the air?*

Absolom began to check all the contacts, making certain that all was as it should be. He could find nothing wrong and felt himself begin to panic.

"No, no, no!" he cried, sprinting from Mary's side to investigate the other machinery.

"Absolom?" Wickham called. "Where has he gone— where is the god?"

But he had no time for the old man's apprehension, pushing him—*her*—out of the way as he checked the god machines.

Diagrams and designs filled his head, each and every wire, screw, pump and gear. Everything was as it was supposed to be. He didn't understand. *What has gone wrong?*

Then he heard Silas begin to bark uncontrollably, the sound like a knife skewering his brain.

"Shut up!" Absolom screamed, coming out from behind one of the machines. He snatched up a stone, preparing to throw it at the baying animal, when he realized that the dog was reacting to something behind him.

Absolom slowly turned to see the god-body, no longer swaying from the caress of the ocean winds. It was moving on its own.

What has gone wrong? he asked himself.

Absolutely nothing.

CHAPTER 15

Qemu'el had successfully crossed over from the prison of darkness to the world of man.

But something wasn't right.

The massive metal structure that now contained his divine omnipotence was slow and sluggish to respond to his mental commands. The vessel screeched and whined with his every movement.

He could feel the energy derived from faith continuing to flow into his body. Thick cables attached to his arms, legs, neck and chest conducted the power that allowed him to transcend the pitiful existence bestowed upon him by the Creator and exist in the physical world.

Still, it was not enough.

The stolen power of worship allowed him to live, to move and to function like a thing alive, but that was all. More would be required if he were to accomplish his purpose—much more.

Through new eyes, made from glass, he gazed out over the ocean, sensing the life that thrived upon the land—beings that did not deserve the special gifts that had been given to them. He thought of this place, as it had once been, clean of life, pristine, pregnant with promise. It would be that way again, the Archon promised himself. A better world existed beyond this one and if not, that too would be destroyed, and another one after that if necessary.

Through Qemu'el's scornful destruction, the Creator would soon see the error of His ways. But in order for that to happen, the Archon must have a god-body befitting his magnificence and powerful enough to contain all of his wrath.

Qemu'el tossed back his metal head and screamed, his birth cry announcing to the world that he had arrived and that the end of their pitiful existence drew inexorably near.

A freezing rain started to fall.

He sensed the hated presence of human life and looked down to see his apostle kneeling in reverence.

"More," Qemu'el told his faithful servant in the electric voice of the massive metal god-body.

"I must have more."

Absolom staggered to his feet, held in a grip of awe by the sight before him. After all this time, he had succeeded.

"More," the giant metal man croaked, his thunderous voice causing Absolom to wince in discomfort. "I must have more."

He had been afraid of this. Without all of the items of power, there had not been enough residual energies to empower the god completely. But Absolom had a plan.

The high priest of the Band of Electricizers turned around to face his minions, finding them standing stock-still—their eyes riveted to the sight of the god.

"The batteries!" he roared.

The dog and the woman turned to him, and he could see that they were in shock. It was a day that would be long remembered, the day that mankind prepared to take its first step toward godhood.

"Now, my friends," he instructed. "The last of the spirit batteries. Attach them to the machines. The energies from the collected souls will provide Qemu'el with the power he requires."

Shaken from their awe, Wickham and Udell did as they were told.

The Archon stood watching, and Absolom slowly approached him to explain.

"The energy of the dead will provide you with what you crave, my lord," Absolom said, averting his eyes. "Through those connections," he explained, pointing out the thick electrical cables that trailed down from various places on the god's mechanical body. "The spiritual residue of the departed will be drained from the vast supply of storage cells, where it has been collected to power my various inventions."

The angel tilted his head back, looking up into the

steel gray sky, the snow now falling harder upon Egg Rock.

"This energy," the creature began. "It is all around us?"

"In its unrefined form, yes," Absolom said, moving closer to his deity, excited to be allowed to share something with him. "It is practically an inexhaustible source of power."

The angel looked around, as if somehow capable of seeing the energies flowing around them.

"Glorious," he growled.

The preparations on the machinery complete, Absolom went to the control panel, wanting to do the honors himself. He brushed the accumulated snow away, his hands hovering over the knob that would begin the flow, and gazed up into the hollow eyes of the god-body. Twin beacons of light burned in the darkness, looking down upon him.

"For you," he said, turning the knob. "It is all for you."

The machines hummed to life, the spirit batteries thrumming as the power of the dead flowed out from them and down the connections at the speed of light. Absolom smiled in ecstasy as the god's body went suddenly rigid, its hinged mouth agape as the energy poured into him.

"Yes," the mechanical deity screamed to the heavens. "Yesssssssssssssssssss!"

The body started to shift and change—the enormity of the power flowing through him allowing him the ability to reshape his iron visage into something more befitting a being that would change the world. With a shriek of bending metal, twin protrusions exploded from the divine entity's back, resembling the beginnings of skeletal metal wings. His iron skin was becoming more ornate. Ancient symbols that Absolom could not even begin to comprehend formed on the surface of Qemu'el's metallic flesh.

"Glory to you!" Absolom screamed.

Wickham and Udell had come to his side. Tears stained the woman's face as she gazed upon the sight of the god manifesting its true form, and the dog howled, head tossed back as if baying at the new moon.

Then there came an unfamiliar sound—something that disturbed the rhythmic pulse of the great machines that were feeding their savior the sustenance he required. Absolom stepped behind the control console, checking to make sure that everything was all right. But it wasn't. On the gauges he saw a flux in the amount of energy flowing out from the batteries into their lord and master.

"No, it can't be," he muttered, quickly going to the stockpile of containment batteries. But it was as he feared. The god's appetite was so voracious that the batteries were close to being completely drained.

He turned his attention back to the metal entity, watching as the savior reacted to the sudden end of its supply.

"More!" the Archon screamed, his metallic body on

the verge of being one of the most beautiful and yet frightening things that Absolom had ever seen.

He resembled some kind of great, mechanical angel—the wings—*yes, they are in fact wings*—that grew from his back had actually started to sprout angular feathers that looked as sharp as the deadliest of knife blades, but they were incomplete, large vacant patches, devoid of any adornment.

"Give me more so that you may all feel my love."

Absolom cautiously approached, pulling his coat tighter about his throat to protect his exposed flesh from the cold and falling snow. "There is no more, my lord."

"What did you say?" the creature boomed.

"But that does not mean that I can't—over time—provide you with more of the sustenance that you require in order to . . ." Absolom continued quickly.

The figure reared back, snapping some of the connecting cables with his sudden movement.

"You dare deny me?" he growled, disengaging from the remainder of the cables. "I require this power to live—to complete the task for which I have been born."

With an awkward, clanking first step, the metal god-body moved toward those who gathered in his glory, scattering them as he charged. "I will have it all," he cried, eyeing the pyramid-shaped enclosure that contained the items of worship. "Every iota shall be mine."

He brought his fist down upon the metal structure, and the glass exploded outward as the frame collapsed beneath his onslaught.

Absolom watched, stunned, as the god picked up each of the items and shoved them into its open maw, all of the objects tumbling down his metallic gullet and into the hollow recess of his belly.

"Please, my lord," Absolom tried to calm their savior. "Allow me to return to my workshop, and I'll—"

"Silence!" Qemu'el ordered, temporarily sated by his meal of reverence. "For a century, I have waited for this moment, imprisoned within that withering bag of flesh." He pointed to the body of Mary Hudnell, lying limp upon the cot, partially covered with a light blanket of snow.

"I will not be denied." He shook his metal head from side to side and, using the energy taken from his last meal, continued to reshape his body.

"What's he doing?" Wickham asked, wiping black lines of running mascara from his face.

"I don't know," Absolom said, watching as strange protrusions erupted from the entity's armor—bulbous tips at the ends of the tapered growths crackling with an energy all their own.

And then Absolom understood.

"Sweet mystery, I know what he's doing," the high priest said, held in the grip of wonder.

The sky above the god had grown as dark as slate, and the clouds whirled around the Archon's head in a counterclockwise rotation. Crackling bursts of energy erupted from the tips of the spiny appendages—lances of power reaching up into the swirling maelstrom, extracting what he required from the atmosphere.

"He's feeding," Absolom said, watching as vague, ghostly shapes were caught up within the whirlpool and dragged down to be absorbed into the ends of the hungry metal spines. "The death energies all around us—he's changed his body to absorb them, to gather the strength he still requires."

White-hot bolts of snaking energy hungrily sought out the batteries housed within the stomachs of the worker drones. The animated corpses exploded in a shower of charred flesh, metal, wires and wood as the spirit energies that drove them were ripped away.

"Run!" Absolom screamed to his disciples as their god suddenly turned his attention upon them.

"All for me," the voice thundered.

Bolts of jagged fury continued to erupt from his body, raining down upon the rocky ground of the small island.

Wickham was the first to be struck, a javelin of unearthly power entering his body through the spine, then drawn viciously back. The woman's body fell limp to the ground, and Absolom stifled a scream as he watched the ghostly form of his friend struggling on the jagged end of the energy spear as that tendril of godly power drew Wickham's spirit toward its gaping metal maw.

Silas barked uncontrollably, baring his fangs as multiple spears of crackling energy stabbed at the ground around him.

"Do as I say!" Absolom screamed, lashing out with his foot to kick the dog into action.

Silas yelped, loping away for cover, the metal of the animal's mechanical hands clattering across the island's rocky surface.

The angel of destruction bore down upon Absolom, but he stood his ground, looking up into the beatific face sculpted with the energy of the dead, doubt whirling through his mind.

Doubt about what he had wrought.

Hellboy looked out the window, watching as Swampscott, Massachusetts, passed below them. It was snowing pretty hard, and he had to wonder if the Electricizers might have had something to do with it, but then changed his mind. *It's freakin' winter in New England,* he thought. *What else would it be doing?*

They passed out over the water, and he knew it wouldn't be long before they arrived at Egg Rock. Hellboy experienced a moment of apprehension, weird butterflies in the pit of his stomach. He didn't get them often, but this was definitely one of those cases.

"So, what's the plan?" the ghost of Uncle Steve asked, as if able to read minds.

"Same old thing," Hellboy said, looking away from the view. "We go to the island, have a look around, and beat the crap out of anything that doesn't belong there." He shrugged. "It's worked for me in the past."

The ghost shook his head. "Not very scientific."

"Nope, most of the time it's not—and if it is, I'm usually not involved."

The ghost grinned.

"What? Why are you smiling?"

Uncle Steve looked around at the inside of the chopper. "Don't know really. Maybe it's just nice finally to be a part of something—not to be the odd man out. Before I passed away, I had a reputation for being a bit . . ." Steve searched for the word.

"Eccentric?" Hellboy offered.

"I was actually gonna go with 'crazy,' but 'eccentric' will do fine."

"Yeah, 'loco' was gonna be my first choice, but I thought better of it."

They shared a laugh.

Hellboy was just about to ask the ghost what Tom Manning was like as a kid, certain that the Director of Field Operations had been a creep, when the craft banked suddenly to one side, nearly spilling him from his seat.

"Something tells me we might be getting warm," he said, getting up and walking across the hold toward the cockpit.

"What've we got, boys?" He ducked his head as he peered through the doorway.

"Something came at us from the island—like some kind of weird lightning bolt," the copilot explained.

The visibility through the cockpit windshield was fair to poor, as the snowstorm swirled around the hovering Chinook, making it hard to figure out exactly what they were looking at. Hellboy leaned in closer, squinting to see through the swirling flakes.

"The storm's picking up, sir," the pilot said, struggling with the stick to keep the chopper steady. "I'm not sure how much longer we can remain fixed."

A strong gust of wind pummeled the craft and cleared the air in front of it. Hellboy caught a momentary glimpse of the small island below, catching sight of a mechanical giant. *You've got to be kidding me,* he thought. The thing was at least fifty feet tall, jagged metal wings making it seem larger, its body the color of rusted iron. A strange, whirlpool-like atmospheric disturbance swirled above it, pulsating with an unearthly light.

"There ya go," Hellboy commented. "Bet you didn't think we'd be seeing one of those today."

"No, sir, we didn't," the pilot grunted, fighting to keep the craft steady.

The temperature dropped in the cockpit, signaling Steve's arrival.

"Son of a bitch, they did it," the ghost muttered, as the storm howled outside the craft, and a sudden bolt

of crackling energy launched itself from the body of
the metal giant, cutting through the air on a collision
course with the Chinook.

The pilot swore loudly and banked the craft
sharply to the left. The helicopter dropped below the
strange lightning.

But it was as if the white-hot energy had a kind of
sentience, for it changed its course as well and
slammed into the side of the craft. The helicopter
rocked from side to side, the lights flickered and the
twin engines momentarily moaned, threatening to
stall. The pilots expertly fought the controls and
moved the chopper from harm's way.

Hellboy was about to ask if everybody was all right
when he heard a gasp. Steve had drifted back into the
hold, and Hellboy could see that the ghost was in distress.

"What's wrong?" he asked, watching as Steve studied his hand.

"Something's not right out there," the specter said.
Then the ghost's fingers started to stretch toward the
wall of the craft, as if something were trying to drag
him through to the outside. "It feels like it did when I
got sucked into the battery—only worse."

"Get us away from here!" Hellboy hollered to the
pilots.

"No, wait!" the ghost yelled. "It's too late for that.
It won't do a bit of good." His entire body was being
pulled now, his shape elongated, distorted. "It's out-

side. There, on the island—something that giant is doing."

"What can I do?" Hellboy asked.

"Sorry, pal, nothing to hit here, I'm afraid," Steve replied in surprisingly good spirits. The ghost had become even less defined, as part of his spiritual makeup was already being pulled out of the chopper.

"Tell Tommy I'm proud of him," Uncle Steve said, his voice becoming more distorted, harder to hear as he became less defined. "Tell him his uncle . . ."

But before he could finish, the ghost was gone.

"Sir, how shall we proceed?" the pilot called out from the cockpit behind him.

"I doubt we'll be able to get close enough to drop me off," Hellboy answered. Looking around the inside of the craft, his eyes landed on a stack of yellow supply bins secured in the corner of the hold.

"You guys wouldn't happen to have a manifest as to what you're carrying, would ya?" he asked, still eyeing the containers, an idea beginning to form inside his head.

There was a rustle behind him, and he turned to accept a clipboard from the copilot with a few printed pages of what the Chinook was carrying for ordnance.

"Thanks," he said, quickly scanning the list.

He found what he was looking for on the second page.

"Bingo."

* * *

The god was laughing as he fed. Spirits of the departed swirled around his head in a maelstrom of death energy.

Absolom could only stare, gazing up at the metal giant as his body continued to change, becoming more and more ornate. The surface of his copper-colored skin bubbled as if liquid, ancient sigils older than humanity rising to beautify the flesh of its new, powerful vessel.

"Now this," he roared, admiring the ornamentation of his arms and hands, "this is a body befitting a god."

This isn't how it was supposed to be—this isn't how a god is supposed to act. The wings upon the deity's back were enormous, and Qemu'el beat the impressive appendages at the air, whipping the storm into a new frenzy.

Absolom covered his eyes against the wind and snow, making his way toward the god, calling his name, but the Archon failed to notice. Determined to capture his attention, he looked around to find a stone, snatched it from the ground and hurled it as hard as he was able. The rock bounced off Qemu'el's chest plate with a clatter and, at last distracted, the angel looked down to find the source.

"What are you doing?" Absolom cried, emotions running wild. "I brought you here—*we* brought you here—to save the world."

Qemu'el tilted his large metal head as if considering the question. "And saved it will be, just as soon as all life upon it is wiped away. I'm saving you pathetic beasts from yourselves—it would be only a matter of time before your species accomplished this inevitable goal yourselves. As a result of your assistance, for which you have my gratitude, it will be decimated all the quicker."

"No," Absolom screamed, stamping his foot down upon the cold rock surface of the tiny island. "You were supposed to lift us—to bring us that much closer to perfection—to the Creator Himself."

Already starting to lose interest in his despondent follower, Qemu'el laughed, a horrible mocking sound.

"Consider yourself already blessed," the Archon growled, and returned his attention to the swirling energies he had called down to feed upon. "If it had been my decision, your entire species would have burned long before climbing down from the trees."

The words were like vicious blows, stunning Absolom nearly senseless. He stumbled away from the creature, who now reached up to the heavens, drawing enough strength from the ambient spirit energies to destroy the world.

I've been used—manipulated, he thought numbly, staggering across Egg Rock as if drunk. *I'm going to be responsible for the end of the world.*

Absolom's mind raced, searching for some answer to the quandary he faced. His inventions squatted silently, their awful purpose fulfilled, the wood and metal surfaces covered with snow. Was there anything he could do, or should he just accept his fate and that of the world?

At first he believed it to be only the wind, but then realized that someone was in fact calling his name. It was no more than a whispering croak, and he had to search for its source.

Mary Hudnell still lay upon the cot, her sagging stomach now resembling a deflated balloon. She remained attached to the various machines, the metal needles sticking up from the loose flesh of her abdomen. He approached the poor woman, listening for the sound of the voice again; it was insane, she couldn't possibly have survived. She appeared almost peaceful, lying upon the cot, partially covered in a powdery blanket of snow.

He reached out to touch the cold flesh of her face.

"It appears that I've made an enormous error, dearest Mary," he said. "And my Electricizers, as well as everybody upon this planet, will have to pay for it."

Mary's eyes came open, and he stumbled back with a gasp. "Impossible," he said, watching as she struggled to speak.

"There is . . . a way to stop him . . . to stop . . . Qemu'el," she croaked. Her body began to tremble.

Absolom was speechless. His terror rose as he stared at the woman—who had no right to be alive. Her stomach started to inflate, as if filling with life again.

"Help . . . them," she yelled. The ends of the nee-

dles had started to spark, some of the wire connections now broken.

"Help whom?" he asked in desperation. "Who am
I helping? What should I do?"

"They're coming," Mary wheezed. "Help them . . .
to come . . ."

"But I don't know what you mean," he stammered.
"How should I help?"

"Machines," she cried, her stomach nearly tripling
in size—the pale skin of her belly glowing hotly from
within, making it nearly transparent. "Make sure the
machines . . . work!"

Absolom ran to his inventions and inspected the
connections. They all seemed to be functioning, but
he worried over the power source. Most of the batteries had been nearly depleted.

"Turn them on!" Mary yelled from her bed, the
glow that emanated from her stomach nearly blinding.

"There isn't enough power," he called to her. "The
batteries are empty and . . ."

"Turn them on!" Mary Hudnell demanded frantically as her skeletal frame started to thrash upon the
cot—as it had done before when the creature had
been born into the world.

He did as he was told, certain it would be for
naught.

Absolom flipped the switch on the console and
moved to the others, doing the same. The cables that

had been used to transmit the energy essence of the god twitched like enormous snakes angrily writhing upon the ground.

"They're coming!" Mary screamed, bucking and heaving, bony hands holding on to the sides of the cot in a death grip.

She cried out one last time, one final pitiful wail, followed by a single blast of light as if the very sun had exploded.

Blossoms of color erupted before Absolom's eyes. Frantically, he blinked away the beautiful flowers in time to bear witness to the strangest of sights. The writhing cables were leaking enormous amounts of mysterious energy, energy that appeared to be collecting—forming an enormous ball of unearthly fire. The sphere continued to grow with a sound like the hum of a thousand angry insects.

Absolom glanced over to where Mary had been lying, only to find that she and the cot on which she had been lying had been completely incinerated, leaving only a small pile of ash on the smoldering ground.

The buzzing sound from the ball of energy grew louder, and his gaze was drawn back to it with wonder.

"What are you?"

As if hearing his question, it started to roll toward him. Bursts of steam erupted from beneath its passage as the snow vaporized on contact with the unknown energy source. He barely had time to leap out of its

way as it passed—the intensity of its heat strong
enough to singe his exposed flesh and make the fabric
of his coat smoke.

The energy sphere continued to roll, moving
toward the edge of the cliff, where it finally plum-
meted into the sea.

Absolom ran to the ledge and peered out. The
ocean below him bubbled and seethed, but the ball
was nowhere to be seen, the mystery of its origins and
purpose no closer to being revealed.

CHAPTER 16

Hellboy had never had much luck with gadgets, but at this point, he really didn't have any choice.

He slipped his arms through the shoulder harness of the flight pack, hefting its weight upon his back. This model seemed lighter than the ones he had used in the past. Hopefully, it was also a little more durable.

"Let me give you a hand with that," the copilot said, reaching out to help him secure the straps.

Hellboy had remembered that the flight packs were now supposed to be part of the standard equipment that all BPRD agents brought into the field. He was grateful that these guys had read the latest memos.

"Thanks. So, how do I look?" he asked, slowly spinning around.

"Like something out of Buck Rogers," the copilot responded with a hint of a smile.

Hellboy walked over to another storage container, flipping off the lid, and allowing it to clatter to the floor. "I'll probably be needing these too," he said, taking a bandolier of grenades from inside the yellow box and slipping it over his shoulder. "Wouldn't be caught dead in a jet pack without some explosives."

"I hear you, sir," the copilot said.

Turbulence again rocked the craft, and Hellboy grabbed hold of one of the supply cases to keep from tumbling over.

"What's the story, Captain?" he yelled to the pilot.

"Looks like we're about as close as we're going to get," he answered.

Hellboy caught a glimpse from one of the side windows of the faint impression of Egg Rock, just about visible through the snowstorm, bolts of energy arcing up into the sky from its surface.

"That's good enough," he said, walking toward the door.

"Oh yeah." He snapped his fingers and went back to the trench coat he'd left thrown over a seat. "Can't go without this," he said, going through the pockets and carefully removing the Anyroda dagger, still wrapped in its protective cloth. He slipped it through one of the loops on his gun holster and tugged on it to make sure it was secure. "That oughta do it."

He headed toward the door again, checking and double-checking his flight pack.

"We'll hang around, just in case," the copilot said, flipping the metal latch and sliding the door open.

"Naw." Hellboy raised his voice to be heard over the wind now rushing into the cabin. "You guys are probably getting low on fuel. Take off and head back to Boston. I'll deal with stuff here."

Squinting against the wind and snow, he looked for the shadow of the island. "There it is," he said, taking the ignition control switch into the palm of his hand.

"You take care of yourself, sir," the copilot said.

"I'll see what I can do," Hellboy promised, and jumped out of the chopper into the wintry void.

That was the part he hated the most. It was always the same. They'd give him a piece of the latest technology—something that, according to them, he wouldn't be able to live without—but it never quite worked the way it was supposed to. Usually the thing just exploded, and Hellboy ended up in flames.

As he fell from the sky, a parade of images flashed through his mind—all the contraptions they had ever given him to try out in the field. Yeah, some had worked like they were supposed to, but a lot of them . . . well, it was just better not to think about those.

Hellboy gripped the ignition switch tighter. The cold Atlantic was coming up pretty fast below him, and he figured that if the flight pack blew up, at least the fire would be put out quickly.

"Here goes nothing," he muttered, tucking his tail up away from the exhaust ports just before pushing down the switch with his thumb, and preparing for the worst.

Click.

There was a sudden roar as the double turbine engines kicked in, and Hellboy found his descent gradually slowing to a stop above the churning sea.

"Huh, how about that," he said, pleasantly surprised. "Things must be looking up."

On the island the mechanical creature spread its huge wings, its arms outstretched. Arcane energy swirled above it.

Then again . . .

Spirit energies flowed about him and Qemu'el basked in the power that would define him upon the world of man. He mused about their fear as they saw him, the last sight seared upon their eyes before the end.

"Glorious," he spoke aloud, his voice like the rumble of thunder. But his joy did not last for long as thoughts of his still-sleeping brethren intruded upon his pleasure.

They had been created to work as one—a destructive trinity to wipe away the mistakes of the Creator. He missed his brothers, but he knew they would not approve of what he had done and was about to do.

Qemu'el did not, however, have enough power to destroy humanity on his own. He could cause massive, widespread devastation and wanton death, but the angry Archon wanted more. Humanity deserved nothing less than to be annihilated, punishment for its petty greed, avarice, and cruelty to each other.

Without his brothers, he required another method of destruction. The humans would be put to use. They would assist him in their own demise. For countless millennia he had watched them from his limbo—observing as they evolved and their technologies developed, but never losing their animal ways, their killer instincts. How fascinated he had been with their inventions, especially their products of war. Now he would use their tools of annihilation against them—reaching out with his power to touch off multiple explosions, covering the globe in nuclear fire. When that was finished, all he would need to do was finish the job.

He had more than enough power of his own to complete that task.

Qemu'el closed his eyes, sated by the flow of strength into his new metal form, and saw in his mind's eye the Earth as it soon would be, barren, lifeless and cold—awaiting the touch of the Creator. And from the desolation an opportunity for perfection would emerge. His excitement wavered as he pondered his Creator's reaction.

I'll make the Creator see, Qemu'el thought. *I'll show the Lord of Lords that what I am doing is all for Him.*

Qemu'el was so caught up in his thoughts of the

future and how happy the Creator would be once He understood, that he did not take notice of the engine's roar and the threat that it carried.

Until it was too late.

Surprisingly, the flight pack worked like a dream.

Hellboy hovered in the air, thirty feet or so above the shore of the inhospitable-looking island. Held aloft by the jet pack's two, powerful engines, he wished for a pair of goggles as he watched the metal giant through the whipping snow.

The mechanical creature simply stood there, arms and wings stretched out to either side as a swirling vortex of some kind of supernatural energy churned above his head. A closer look at the energy source revealed it to be what Hellboy had suspected. Shapes were being drawn down from the unearthly whirlpool and into the metal giant; human shapes, which explained what had happened to Steve.

Spooks. Looks like the Colossus of Rhodes here is feeding on ghostly energies.

Above the roar of the wind and the turmoil of the ocean, Hellboy could just about hear the pitiful wails of spirits in distress as they were drawn down from the sky, to be absorbed within the strange spiny protrusions that stuck out from the giant's body.

Whatever he was doing, Hellboy decided that now was as good a time as any to put a stop to it.

Carefully, he removed a grenade from the bandolier

across his chest and began to drift toward the stationary being. He seemed distracted, as if daydreaming.

Good for him, bad for big metal guys with fragile-looking wings.

Hellboy flew in closer, getting an even better look at the guy. At first he thought he was seeing things, but then he realized that the giant's metal skin was actually changing, becoming less like metal and more like skin. It just went to show what a heaping helping of ghost-juice could do.

He took hold of the grenade pin in his teeth and yanked it away. Then he arched his body; dropping down—still unnoticed—toward the mechanical angel, and threw the grenade at one of the elaborate wings that still appeared to be in the process of forming. Best to keep the giant here on the island. Wouldn't want him flying away.

He heard the faint *ping* of the grenade as it hit the metal surface of the wing just before it exploded. Hellboy angled his body in such a way that he rode the concussion of the blast, the force of the explosion joining with the propulsion of the flight pack to hurl him out of harm's way.

Once clear of the danger, he spun around to see what kind of damage he had done. The big guy wasn't daydreaming anymore.

The mechanical creature screamed. A large, jagged hole had been blasted in the weave of metal feathers that made up one of his wings.

"Who dares?" he bellowed, examining the ragged hole in his appendage.

Why do they all say the same thing? Hellboy wondered. *It's like they all hire the same guy to write their material. Who dares? You cannot comprehend the power you are dealing with! Blah! Blah! Blah!*

He resisted the urge to yell something flip and instead concentrated on tossing another grenade in the behemoth's direction, this one aimed at his face. His voice was like really big nails being run down a really big blackboard, only louder. Shutting it up seemed like the right thing to do.

Hellboy again flew in closer, pulled the pin and lobbed his explosive present into the flapping maw. The powerful stink of ozone, like after a thunderstorm, wafted out from inside the metal giant, as he made his delivery.

Above the giant, he hovered, watching. There was a clap of muffled thunder, like somebody slamming closed a heavy metal door, and the metal creature lurched spastically; the side of the being's face now sported a smoldering hole.

This isn't going half-bad, Hellboy thought, somewhat surprised. Then he noticed that the spiny things sticking out from his armored body had begun to glow, and the spirit energy swirling around the creature seemed to be siphoned off even faster. Then he began to understand the mechanics of thing. The rip in his wing had started to close; the hole in his face was beginning to mend. He was using the spirit energies to fix himself.

The metal angel stared directly at him, his eyes burning like twin spotlights.

"You," he said, his voice like the rumble of a passing freight train.

"Who else?" Hellboy answered, not sure that he was even close enough for the thing to hear him.

He thought about hightailing it out of there, but he knew he couldn't. It wasn't his style, and besides, he didn't have a ride.

"I've sensed your presence in this world, demon," Qemu'el said. "I suspected that you and your friends would be a threat to my plans."

"What do you want, a cookie?"

Hellboy tried not to stay in one place too long. He zipped around the giant like a fly around a horse's ass, tossing grenades like flower petals. The explosives weren't doing as much damage now that the giant had noticed him. He kept swatting them away to explode harmlessly upon the rocky, snow-covered surface below them.

He watched Hellboy as the BPRD agent darted around; the creature's big metal head was swiveling from side to side. *This isn't going to work for much longer,* Hellboy thought, and he was right. The giant moved incredibly fast. He reached out to grab him. He angled his body to move out of his path but wasn't quick enough.

The metal entity snatched his tail. Desperately, Hellboy tried to twist from his grip, but to no avail. The motor on the jet pack whined furiously in protest, and he could feel the body of the flight harness heating up against his back.

"Now that I see you, I realize that perhaps we have much in common, monster," the angel said, the metal of his face contorting into a bizarre and disturbing smile. "Both summoned to perform a function—a function of destruction."

Hellboy didn't want to hear any more. He grabbed another grenade and wedged it into one of the joints of the metal monstrosity's hand. "Shut the hell up."

The grenade exploded, sending spinning pieces of shrapnel into the air, and Hellboy felt the Archon's grip upon his tail loosen. He pulled free and thumbed the jet pack's controls, driving himself straight up into the air.

But the mechanical being wasn't finished yet. Hellboy turned to see the beast, enormous wings now healed, leap up from the island in pursuit. Flying. *I can't let it leave the island,* he thought, turning around in midair to confront his pursuer. He removed another grenade from the bandolier, pulled the pin and prepared to throw it.

The creature screeched, lashing out, and Hellboy's world started to spin. The flight pack shuddered and groaned as he found himself spiraling downward. He tried to gain control of his descent, angling his body up toward the angel hanging in the snow-filled sky above him. The flight pack whined pitifully; black smoke poured from the motor, but he got it to respond, directing his ascent toward the creature's chest.

Blowing up the face, hand or wing really didn't seem to do any substantial damage. He wondered if maybe he was a little more vulnerable on the inside.

The swirling maelstrom seemed to be following the winged beast, and the spirit energies continued to flow into the giant, keeping him strong.

Let's see exactly how strong, Hellboy thought. He steered toward the Archon's head, the labored squeals of the machine upon his back a clue that his time was limited. The creature noticed his approach and tried to swat him away like an annoying insect.

Hellboy evaded the creature's swings, moving in close enough to land upon his neck. He sank the square fingers of his powerful right hand into the metallic flesh with a crunch and held on for dear life. With his other hand, Hellboy shut down the ailing flight pack, hoping that giving it a rest would buy him the luxury of a relatively painless escape, but he wasn't counting on it.

"Why do you fight me so, brother?" the angel's voice boomed, attempting to flick him away like a tick, but he held fast.

There were seven grenades left on his bandolier, enough for a pretty powerful explosion. He unhooked it. Pulling the pin on one of the remaining grenades, he struggled to maneuver himself into position. Deciding that he was as close as he was going to get, he brought the bandolier up over his head, and slammed it down.

The detonation of the single grenade caused the other six to explode. Hellboy was blown through the air, spinning out of control, eardrums thudding with the concussive force of the blast. He managed to stay conscious all the way down, his finger frantically hitting the ignition switch on the flight pack. Finally, the motor sputtered and the engines turned over.

Just before Hellboy hit the ground.

Absolom watched as the red-skinned figure fell from the sky.

Scrabbling across the rocky surface, the ground now slick with snow, he hoped that there was something he could do. Not long after the mysterious sphere of fire disappeared into the ocean, he had heard the sound of explosions and had seen that something—someone—was attacking the god.

He had known at once who it was.

Hellboy.

The red-skinned figure hit the island in a near-deafening explosion of fire. As Absolom approached, he saw that the figure lay crumpled upon the ground, his back burning. Carefully he moved closer, not sure if he was still alive.

"Son of a bitch," the red-skinned creature growled, rising up on all fours.

Absolom stepped toward him, scooping up handfuls of snow and throwing them onto his still-burning back.

Hellboy's hand shot out and grabbed hold of his arm.

"Who the hell are you?" he asked, his eyes glowing an eerie yellow.

Absolom didn't know whether or not to reveal his identity, but decided that he had nothing to lose. They would all likely be dead in a matter of hours anyway.

"I am Absolom Spearz," he said, and immediately the grip on his arm tightened.

Hellboy climbed to his feet, the remains of some kind of machine sloughing from his still-smoldering back to clatter onto the ground.

"You're the creep who started this whole mess," he said, and fumbled at his belt, as if looking for something that was no longer there.

"Aw, crap," Hellboy grunted, releasing Absolom's arm. "Must've lost it in the fight."

He was about to ask what it was that had been lost, when an ear-piercing wail filled the air. Both he and Hellboy stopped dead in their tracks, looking in the direction of the mournful cries. The beast had fallen backward to the island after the explosion and now he was slowly pulling himself to his feet. Swaying as he stood, the giant stumbled in their direction, his undamaged hand pressed firmly to his chest.

"What have you done?" he roared, removing his hand momentarily, revealing a large hole that had been blown in his center. As the hand came away, Absolom took note of objects falling from the open gash, spilling upon the island, some rolling down into the sea.

The items of faith.

"What have you insolent worms done?"

Absolom watched as Hellboy brushed himself off and started toward the furious creature.

"I never expected it to turn out like this," he called after the agent of the BPRD.

Hellboy stopped, reacting as if struck with a rock from behind. He spun around, a look of anger on his craggy face. "If I had a buck for every time I heard somebody say that. When are you jokers gonna learn? Voices whispering sweet nothings from the ether equals bad news."

He turned around again. "Now if you'll excuse me, I've got to clean up the mess you've made—and then I'll deal with you and your ghostly pals."

Absolom watched him go off to battle, quite possibly even to his death, remembering the beauty of the voice from beyond that had promised to take the world by the hand and lead it toward paradise. He'd only wanted the best for the world—to take away its suffering, to make them all better.

Then from the corner of his eye, he thought he saw movement, and turned to see a lone female figure moving through the storm. It was the woman, the wife of his own host body, Bethany Thomas, who had once housed the spirit of his friend and comrade— Geoffrey Wickham. She was moving over the rocky surface of the island, as if drawn to its edge.

Absolom followed. There was a part of him that wanted to apologize. He wanted her to realize that what he had done was not out of malice toward her and her family. They had simply been tools for the machinations of his much bigger—*more foolish*—plans.

She looked toward him briefly, her expression wan and vacant, her cheeks damp, snow clinging to her hair.

"I'm so sorry," he began, but the woman had already turned away.

She was looking out over the edge of the cliff, looking down at the sea.

And then he saw it—what had captured her attention.

The ocean had begun to boil—to bubble and churn. Something was coming.

Coming up from below.

Qemu'el dropped to his knees, looking for the objects that had fallen out of his body. The spirit storm that had been whirling above him was now dramatically diminished.

As Hellboy approached, he noticed some of the items scattered on the rocks and picked them up, throwing them as far away from the Archon as he could. He didn't want Qemu'el getting them back into his belly anytime soon.

One of his hooves connected with a loose stone, causing a bit of ruckus as it rolled down a slight incline. *So much for stealthy and catlike.*

The creature looked up, what appeared to be a child's doll and some old, leather-bound books filling the palm of its large hand.

"You," he said, a tremor of intense anger in his metallic voice. He quickly shoved the objects he was holding into the jagged hole the explosives had blown in his chest. Unlike his other injuries, this one had not started to mend.

Hellboy noticed a Styrofoam cup at his feet and bent down to pick it up. "Do you know who drank from this cup?" he asked, holding it out to his adversary, wondering if an ancient angel of destruction had the first clue as to who the King really was.

"That's mine!" the metal creature shrieked, his massive metal bulk scrabbling across the rocky surface toward him like a runaway train.

Nothing worse than a desperate angel, Hellboy thought, as the creature plowed into him, sending him flying through the air. It was a good thing that the island had so many nice, rocky surfaces to break his fall.

He landed on his back, doing a kind of somersault. His circus roll stopped only when he hit a collection of machines. *The gizmos used to open the door that brought Mr. Cranky Pants to Earth,* he thought.

Shaking his head to clear the ringing, Hellboy climbed to his feet just in time to see Qemu'el gliding through the air in his general direction. Strange crackling energy leaked from the jagged opening that had been blasted in his chest. *That can't be good.*

Out of grenades, and doubtful that gunfire would have much of an effect, Hellboy looked for something he could use as a weapon.

The Archon landed in a crouch before him.

"I could not find all of my objects," he said, eyeing Hellboy with a curious tilt of his metal head. "But it does not matter. There is more than enough strength stored within this glorious form to commence my plans. But you . . ."

The Archon reached for him again, and Hellboy lunged for the nearest something he could find.

"You are an annoyance that must be dealt with before anything can commence. Who knows how much mischief you can cause underfoot?"

"You know me and the mischief," Hellboy grunted, hefting one of the machines off the ground and hurling it into Qemu'el's face. "Can barely get anything done without me fooling around."

The metal console bounced off Qemu'el's forehead with a loud clatter, barely slowing him down. Before he knew it, he was in the monster's hands again, being hauled into the sky.

Hellboy waited for his opportunity, feigning helplessness as the metal creature brought him closer.

"Such a troublesome little thing," he said, bringing Hellboy closer . . . closer . . .

Close enough.

Hellboy leaned forward in the giant's metal grip.

"You don't know the half of it, buddy," he growled, lashing out with his right hand, the rocklike fist connecting with the creature's face.

It was like hitting the side of a bell. A dull ring reverberated through the air. The angel was stunned, stumbling slightly to one side, his grip loosening just enough.

Hellboy grabbed hold of Qemu'el's thumb, wrenching it away from his body, practically tearing it from the being's hand.

He slipped from the thing's grasp and dropped to the ground.

The snow was falling more heavily; wind and visibility were even worse than before. Hellboy doubted that the cavalry would be arriving anytime soon. *What I wouldn't give for one surface-to-air missile right around now,* he thought, breaking into a run, trying to get some distance between him and the angry angel. *Blow this animated hunk of metal back to the junkyard.*

At first he thought he was hearing things, the

sound of a barking dog, completely out of place upon this barren hunk of rock, but that's exactly what it was. And through the whipping snow he saw it, a black dog, barking to beat the band, and it seemed as though it was trying to get his attention.

He sprinted away, the hair on the back of his neck bristling in anticipation over what the metal giant might try to do to him next. Hellboy chanced a quick glance over his shoulder to see that Qemu'el had actually stopped his pursuit and was kneeling down to retrieve some more of the objects that had fallen from his body.

Whatever, as long as it buys me some time, Hellboy thought, coming to a stop in front of the dog.

The mutt wagged its tail happily as he approached, immediately conjuring childhood memories of his old pal, Mac. But then he noticed that the dog's front legs ended not with paws but with a pair of mechanical hands.

"What the hell happened to you?" he asked the animal, never expecting the dog to answer.

"My name is Silas Udell, I'm one of the Electricizers," he answered through the electronic voice box bolted to his throat. "We were supposed to be bringing a loving god to Earth—to usher in a new age. We never expected this."

Hellboy was momentarily stunned, but vaguely recalled that Steve had said something about the family and a dog that was behaving strangely. *Any port in a storm,* he thought, eyeing the possessed animal suspiciously.

The dog reached down with its artificial hands and picked up an object wrapped in soaking cheesecloth. "I was watching you fight the monster," the animal said, lifting it toward him. "And you dropped this. Thought it might be of importance."

Baxter's dagger, Hellboy realized, taking the proffered item from the dog. "Thanks, I was looking for it."

The sound was sudden, like the roaring approach of a tidal wave, and he had barely gotten the dagger in his hand when Qemu'el was upon him.

The metal giant emerged from the storm, one of his fists pounding the ground mere inches from where Hellboy and the animal were standing. It didn't look good for the dog. Hellboy lost sight of the animal as he flew through the air, along with jagged pieces of island rock.

Hellboy managed to hold on to the dagger, ripping away the cloth to expose the ancient blade of exorcism. He wasn't sure what it could do for him, but beggars couldn't be choosers. His mind raced with the possibilities. If the dagger could drive a single spook from one body, how about a whole bunch of spooks trapped inside one giant? It was worth a shot, he thought, as he spun around to see the winged angel bearing down on him again.

Hellboy braced himself, running the blade across his left palm, feeding the Anyroda.

The angel snatched him from the ground, shaking him like a petulant child angered by one of his toys. Hellboy's arms flopped at his side, but he held on to the blade. The Archon stopped abruptly, taking notice of what was clutched in Hellboy's hand.

"What is this?" Qemu'el asked, tilting his head in a curious manner, his large headlight eyes boring into the agent. "That weapon—I sense within it enormous power."

Hellboy noticed that as the being spoke these words, his other hand had gone to the still-unhealed hole in his chest, fluttering around the wound.

"Power that I will need if I am to cleanse the world," he said dreamily.

Hellboy had an idea, a crazy one at best, but it was the best he could come up with at the moment.

"You want it?" he asked, waving the dagger around to get the creature's attention. "You can have it, my gift to you." Hellboy held it out at arm's length.

"This is a trick," Qemu'el growled, squeezing him tighter.

Hellboy felt as though his head might just pop from his body if he didn't play this right.

"Fine," he wheezed, having a difficult time breathing. "I'll just fling it in the ocean then." He made a move to do so, and Qemu'el reacted.

"Wait!" he screamed. "It must be mine."

The grip upon him lessened, and the Archon slowly—cautiously—brought him closer. One thing he could say about this particular ancient being, he wasn't exactly the brightest bulb in the box.

"Why would you give this to me?" Qemu'el asked suspiciously. "You are my enemy—the one that wishes to see me fail."

Hellboy shrugged. "You yourself said that we were kindred spirits. Maybe I've come to realize that you're right."

The angel of destruction thought about it for a moment, and Hellboy guessed it must have made sense.

Too much sense. He hated that the Archon could believe it, and how reasonable it would've seemed to just about anyone else. Anyone who didn't have to live it.

"Feed it to me," the creature commanded, then opened its cavernous maw, that horribly odd smell wafting out.

Hellboy wriggled around in the angel's grip, making a good show of it. "I'm afraid I'll miss," he told him. "Loosen your grip so I can get it in."

The Archon did as he suggested, allowing him just a little more freedom.

"That's better," Hellboy said, making the motion to toss the knife.

Instead, he sprang from Qemu'el's palm, hurling himself at the angel's surprised face. Hellboy plunged the dagger into the center of one of the angel's circular eyes, the metal being shrieking in surprise and pain.

"Treacherous maggot!" the giant wailed, his arms and metal wings flailing.

Hellboy found himself airborne and wishing he had a jet pack. He landed on his side, rolling across the hard, unyielding surface, every ounce of breath he had knocked from his lungs.

Through a haze of injury and swirling snow, he saw Qemu'el attempting to remove the dagger from his eye. He couldn't be sure, but it looked as though the dagger might be working—the enchanted weapon actually allowing the trapped spirit entities to escape. Sparks flew from the stabbed eye, and strangely hued flames sprang up there.

"You traitorous blight upon the land!" Qemu'el exclaimed, his metal hands tearing at his face, but it didn't seem to be doing the creature much good.

Must've stuck it in good and deep, Hellboy thought, attempting to shrug off the shrieks of pain from his own body as he strained to stand.

Then over the sound of his grunts and moans of discomfort, he heard something else, a strange rushing sound. He was just about to chalk it up to head trauma when he saw Spearz come running up from the edge of the island, dragging a woman behind him.

"Get away from here," Hellboy screamed at the pair, glancing over his shoulder at the metal giant, who was still struggling to remove the Anyroda dagger from his eyeball. Spirits now leaked from the giant's damaged socket like smoke trailing from the end of a cigarette.

But Spearz didn't listen, coming closer and yelling at the top of his lungs.

"Something's coming!" he shrieked, pointing off in the distance.

Shielding his eyes from the pelting flakes of snow, Hellboy looked out across the island to the ocean beyond it. The water looked to be boiling, movement beneath making the water froth and churn.

"What now?" he muttered beneath his breath, fresh out of ideas on how to deal with this rapidly degenerating situation.

Then it rose up out of the ocean, a thing as tall as the metal giant. It was in the shape of a man, its body huge and powerful, but the surface of its glistening flesh seemed to writhe and undulate. Clouds of shrieking seagulls flew circles around its oddly shaped head.

Hellboy moved closer, just to be sure—just to see that what he had begun to suspect was indeed true. "You gotta be friggin' kidding me," he said, his mouth agape.

The new giant was made up of ocean life—countless fish and other marine animals coming together to form its massive body: dolphin, haddock, skate, octopus, starfish and horseshoe crab. There were sharks, and even a right whale that composed the majority of its undulating torso.

Hellboy stared in awe. Every time he'd thought he'd seen it all, something more bizarre would come along to prove him wrong.

He wasn't sure if there was anything to top this, and really didn't care to see it if there was.

There was only so much a guy could take.

The angel of destruction felt his newfound strength gradually waning. Frantically he clawed at his face, trying to dislodge the offending blade protruding from his eye. The spirit energies were leaving him, escaping from his body where they had been contained, reducing his power source.

The god swatted at his face yet again, and suddenly the pain was gone. He scanned the snow-covered ground at his feet, searching for the offending dagger, then found it.

Such a dangerous tool, he thought, still drawn to the supernatural energies inherent in the black metal of the knife, energies that could surely restore him to the level of power required to achieve his purpose.

Folding the metal wings upon his broad back, the god squatted, eyeing the tiny item lying in the accumulating snow. Carefully he reached for it, his large, segmented metal fingers surprisingly dexterous as he picked up the dagger. Upon touching the black metal blade, Qemu'el could see the knife's history, see how it had been worshipped throughout the ages as a tool that could vanquish evil on some grand, cosmic scale.

The Archon chuckled, studying the tiny object that could have very easily thwarted his designs. *Would the ancient race that forged this knife view me as evil, or see me in the light of savior?* he wondered.

In the distance he heard a commotion and attempted through his one good eye to see beyond the whipping snow.

What is the red-skinned abomination up to now?

The angel opened his hinged metal jaws and dropped the dagger down into his gullet, where it joined the remaining items of power. Qemu'el immediately felt his strength increase. The Archon gazed down at the hole through his chest, watching with two good eyes again as his metal skin flowed like water, the wound healing over as his power was again on the rise.

The angel then reached out with his mind, dancing around the weapons of mass destruction that would soon bring cleansing fire to the world. He had admired them from his stygian prison, coming to know each and every one of the atomic devices intimately.

Nothing can stop me now, Qemu'el thought. He would show the Almighty the perfection of his creation, and how he was able to achieve this most sacred task alone, and he would be looked upon with adoring eyes.

The angel of destruction smiled, gazing up to the heavy clouds, swollen with storm, and beyond to Heaven.

"Are you watching, oh Lord?" Qemu'el asked, ready to commence.

But before beginning, Qemu'el gazed down to see his red-skinned bane come running out of the swirling storm, followed by two who had been his disciples upon the Earth. He tensed, preparing for their onslaught.

"You are too late, worms!" he proclaimed, his new-found strength crackling around him. "In a moment's time, it will all be brought to a close, paving the way for the next age, and all that exists upon this blighted planet will be but a sliver of memory, so easily forgotten by me, and eventually the Creator."

But something was not right. They did not attack him, they did not attempt to thwart what there was no hope of averting. Something was amiss.

Qemu'el swiveled his head briefly, watching perplexed as they continued to flee past him. He turned back in time to see a gigantic shape emerge from the mist and storm, its body glistening colorfully in the muted light that shone down from the cloud-filled skies.

Every inch of its body was moving—its entirety composed of individual life—and from this writhing mass, Qemu'el sensed something strangely familiar.

"What are you?" he asked.

"Do you not know us, brother?" the creature asked, its voice like the squeals and shrieks of millions of life-forms attempting to communicate all at once.

And Qemu'el knew what had happened. His brothers had awakened and found him missing.

"We are your end."

Hellboy turned to see that Spearz and the woman had started to lag behind. The surface of the island was slippery with snow, and the two held on to each other as they tried to keep up.

"C'mon, move it!" he yelled, knowing that Captain Fishsticks's charging the giant, winged metal guy wasn't going to amount to anything but big-time trouble. He stopped to grab hold of them, pulling them along, and found himself mesmerized by the sight in the distance.

At first it looked like the pair of giants were about to have a nice little chat, as if they knew each other, but that all changed when Qemu'el spread his metal wings, crouched and sprang into the air, attempting to escape.

Fishsticks moved like a blur—pretty amazing for something that big—its body almost fluid as it reached up to grab hold of the fleeing angel's ankles, pulling him back to down to Earth.

Qemu'el landed with a horrific crash that Hellboy could feel through the solid ground of Egg Rock.

"You might want to think about running like hell," a familiar voice said nearby, and Hellboy jumped, looking around to see the ghostly shape of Manning's uncle Steve, the scorched specter of Sally floating nearby. He hadn't felt their approach as he normally would have, probably because of the storm.

He looked back to see that the entity from the sea had thrown itself atop the thrashing Qemu'el, fists made up of a variety of marine life, raining powerful blows down upon the body of the metal giant.

The ocean creature engulfed Qemu'el, its living body flowing over the struggling entity, covering him completely.

Hellboy turned back to the ghosts, but they were gone.

"Oh, crap," he said, starting to run.

There came a clap of thunder that shook the sky, then a tremendous flash of searing white light followed by a brief second of eerie silence. The quiet broke with a torrent of noise that sounded an awful lot like Niagara Falls.

Hellboy managed to clear away the spots dancing before his eyes just in time to see the wall of water, teeming with aquatic life, rushing across Egg Rock toward him. He braced for the inevitable.

Should've listened to the spooks, he thought, just before being hit by the tidal wave as it rushed to flow back into the sea.

Absolom Spearz hugged the woman tightly to him, his back pressed against the small outcropping of stone. The ocean waters rushed over them, trying to rip them away from the land and drag them both into the sea.

A moment after the water came it receded, washing away most of the accumulated snow and leaving behind hundreds of thrashing fish and crabs and other sea life in its wake.

The woman shook in his arms, her clothing, as well as his own, sopping wet. In a moment of compassion, he pulled her closer to him in an awkward attempt to warm her body with his own. For a moment she allowed herself to be held, before her body stiffened, and she pulled herself away.

Bethany Thomas stared at him with eyes that swam with a mixture of emotions; he saw fear there, as well as confusion and anger. She had been through much these past weeks.

Absolom felt a pang of something that could very well have been love for the woman, some residual aspect of emotion leaking from the true owner of the body he wore. It felt wrong for him to be experiencing it, for it did not belong to him.

"You're not my husband," she said through trembling lips that had started to turn a soft blue.

He climbed to his feet, leaving her sitting on the ground, and surveyed their surroundings. The landscape was littered with dying fish of all shapes and sizes, as well as other forms of ocean life he barely recognized, but the god he had summoned, as well as the behemoth that had emerged from the sea, were nowhere to be found. The storm was practically finished, residual flakes drifting gently from a gradually lightening sky.

Absolom held out his hand, catching a single flake of snow upon his outstretched palm before it melted away. He would miss being alive, he thought, closing his hand into a fist and turning to the trembling woman.

"No, I'm not," he said to her. "And it's time that I gave him back to you."

With those words, Absolom Spearz let go of his mortal host, withdrawing his ghostly essence and allowing its rightful owner to assert himself.

The man screamed out for his family, responding to his frightful last recollection. Stanley Thomas fell to his knees, trembling first from the trauma of what had happened to him, and finally from the cold.

"Stan?" Bethany whispered, crawling across wet stone and the remains of dying fish to take her husband into her arms.

The spirit of Absolom Spearz watched them for a moment, envying them for the life they had. Absolom wondered about the others—his Electricizers—curious if they still haunted this world or had gone on to the afterlife.

The visage of a horribly burned woman materialized in front of him, and he found himself recoiling from the gruesome sight. Slowly he came to recognize the spirit as kindred, another restless entity, but there was something more about this one.

Something familiar.

The woman drifted closer to him, her eyes never

leaving his, and slowly, ever so slowly, she reached a charred hand out to him, to touch his face, and it was then that Absolom knew.

"Sally," he said, the fetid memories of the guilt he carried over her sacrifice bubbling to the surface as she allowed her ghostly essence to mingle with his own.

He felt her love of him, as well as the pain and rage she had experienced upon her death. Absolom's ghostly form shuddered, threatening to dissipate and drift away upon the ocean breeze, but she held him together, refusing to let him go.

Another spectral image had materialized, not too far from where they stood, a normal-looking soul, except for the expression of sadness he wore.

Sally looked away from Absolom to gaze at the man, and something seemed to pass between them.

"Go ahead, girl," the other ghost said, shoving his transparent hands into his pockets. "I'll catch up to you later."

Sally turned her blackened features back to her husband, and he knew then that his time upon the plane of the living had come to an end.

"I . . . I'm afraid," he whispered, as she pulled his head toward hers.

Though they were both merely phantoms now, he felt the roughness of her charred and blackened lips as they pressed against his, their ethereal bodies mingling as they at last responded to the pull of the world beyond this one and slipped into the ether.

Together.

* * *

Hellboy's cloven hooves clattered across the rocky surface as he pushed upon the deadweight, grunting with exertion.

Steve's ghost watched the BPRD agent struggle to push the whale back toward the water. He wished he could help, but he had no substance, no flesh. His spirit was melancholy.

"Is it still even alive?" the ghost asked, gazing around the island, which was littered with flopping sea life.

Hellboy looked over his shoulder. "I think it's just stunned," he said. "If I can get it back into the water, it should be all right."

He placed his back against the whale and pushed again. Its bulk slid across the rocky ground. They came to a slight incline, where the whale caught on an outcrop of rock.

It didn't look like the whale was going anywhere, when it suddenly started to thrash excitedly, as though it sensed the nearness of the ocean. The movement jarred it loose from the rocks. Hellboy continued to push, grunting with exertion as the animal began to slide down the incline at the island's edge.

Finally, the whale was back in the water, and with the continued help of Hellboy, was soon swimming away.

"Don't forget to write," Hellboy called after it with a wave.

Steve clapped, his spectral hands making no noise as they came together.

Hellboy paused to bow as he came out of the water.

"That pretty much does it for me today," he said, placing his hands at the small of his back and stretching. "I'm beat."

He straightened and looked around. "Where's Sally?"

"Left with her husband," Steve said.

"Voluntarily?" Hellboy asked, seeming surprised.

The ghost nodded. "Think the boy knew that he screwed up big-time, decided to get while the getting was good."

"Excellent," Hellboy said, looking around at the ground. "Don't have a clue what ended up happening with the Anyroda Dagger," he muttered. "Baxter's gonna be really pissed."

They heard the sound of an approaching helicopter, and both searched the sky to see the Chinook coming toward them over the misty horizon.

"Here comes the cleanup crew," Hellboy said. He started to walk around, checking the bodies of the fish, throwing the ones that were still alive back into the sea.

The chopper was almost there, and Steve had made up his mind.

"Think I'm gonna get going," the ghost said.

Hellboy looked up, a dead octopus draped over his hands. "Get going where?"

"Y'know," Steve said. He pointed up into the sky. "I'm kinda curious to find out what's next."

"Don't you want to say good-bye to Tom?"

He shook his head. "Naw, think I've caused enough problems for him, still being around and all. He's probably had more than enough of me. It sure was a blast though," he said with a smile.

"Anything you want me to tell him?" Hellboy asked.

Uncle Steve shoved his hands deep into his pockets. "Yeah, tell him that I'm proud of him."

"Will do," Hellboy replied, dropping the octopus and wiping his hands on his shorts. "You take care."

With a wave, the ghost turned away. Then it came to him, one final thought for his nephew.

"Oh, yeah," he said, turning back to Hellboy. "Tell him don't take any wooden nickels."

"Wooden nickels. Got it."

With those final words, Steve moved on, letting himself slip from the world he had known since birth, the world that he had refused to leave in death. A place that he certainly would miss.

Like a balloon, he felt himself drifting, and for a moment he feared where the winds of change would take him. But that was only for a moment, for he knew that something different—a whole new mystery, was waiting for him.

There was nothing better than a good mystery.

The Chinook had returned refueled, along with the usual cast of characters and a BPRD response team.

Hellboy watched as members of the team assisted the formerly possessed couple back to the chopper. They looked like they were in pretty good shape, despite what they'd gone through. A little while ago he'd heard a *thank God* from them, and they hugged each other. He guessed they'd probably learned that their kids were all right and waiting for them back onshore.

The family was pretty much intact, except for the dog. They had found its broken body underneath some rocks where the final battle had taken place, the ghost that had been possessing it having flown the coop. He recalled the talking animal with the mechanical hands and stifled a chill. That thing had given him the creeps.

He glanced over to see Manning finishing up a conversation with Liz and Abe. They had given him a brief rundown as to what they had gone through in Lynn, and he was eager to hear all the details over beer and pizza back at his place, but first they had to wrap things up here. There were pieces of giant metal Archon strewn all over the island, and then of course there were all the dead fish. Hellboy wondered if there was as much cleaning up on cases that didn't involve him. It was something he was going to have ask about one of these days.

Manning approached him, hands shoved deeply into the pockets of his heavy winter coat. The sun was going down, and it was getting colder on Egg Rock.

"Good job today," he said, coming to stand beside him.

"Thanks," Hellboy answered.

The two were silent, but Hellboy knew that Manning was dying to ask.

"Looking for Steve?"

"Yes," Manning answered. "I was looking around and didn't see . . ."

"He's gone," Hellboy said. "Said that it was time for him to leave, that he'd caused you enough problems."

Hellboy watched the disappointment on Manning's face.

"Also said that he was proud of you," he added.

Manning nodded, the beginnings of a smile cracking his usual all-business demeanor.

"I've gotta go and ask Abe a favor," Hellboy said, excusing himself, but then remembered that he hadn't given Manning the full message.

"Oh yeah, your uncle said to tell you one more thing."

"Don't take any wooden nickels," Tom Manning said with a grin.

Hellboy didn't know if it was only a reaction to the cold, but there were tears in Manning's eyes. Maybe the guy was human after all.

EPILOGUE

It had snowed again, a nor'easter dropping a good seven inches of the white stuff on the Massachusetts coast before finally coming to an end. The weathermen were talking about another one possibly coming in that weekend.

It's shaping up to be one of those winters, Hellboy thought as he made his way across Don Kramer's snow-covered backyard in Plymouth, Massachusetts.

His arms were full, and he bent with the weight. The tarpaulin-wrapped object that he carried weighed at least five hundred pounds. Hellboy trudged through the fresh accumulation to the far end of the yard, careful not to lose his footing.

"Is that it?" Kramer called, and he turned to see the man standing on the deck, bundled in a coat that appeared to be two sizes too big. He looked like hell, his beard having grown out. Hellboy thought he'd lost quite a bit of weight.

"I've been waiting out here for hours," the man said. "What took you so long?"

Hellboy could have smacked him but decided to cut the guy some slack. It was obvious that he'd been under some strain since the disappearance of the stone. He could only begin to imagine what it would be like having to live with angry Graken Spriggin.

"Got slowed down on account of the snow," he said, at last reaching the far back of the yard. "You might want to stay up on that porch until we know they're satisfied."

With a grunt he set the tarp-covered stone down at his feet. "You know how they can get."

Hellboy stood there in knee-high snow and, using what he could see of the trees and bushes, tried to recall where the Graken's stone had rested.

Not finding the stone initially, he'd remembered that some of the metal giant's stomach contents had fallen into the ocean around the island, and he had asked Abe to help with the retrieval process. It hadn't taken all that long to locate, and with the help of the Chinook, they had hauled it up from the sea.

"I told them you were coming," he heard Kramer yell from the porch, just as the snow around him suddenly seemed to come to life with movement.

Once again the Graken were dressed for war in their soda can armor, junk-drawer weapons ready to draw blood in battle, but this time there was a difference.

Hellboy said nothing as they emerged from their hiding places beneath the snow, and strangely enough,

neither did they. The Graken moved slowly, as if tired.
The few of the pint-sized creatures who managed to
glance his way somehow looked older.

The army took formation on either side as the
snow-covered bushes in front of him rustled and
shook. The snow that had collected there cascaded
down to be added to the accumulation below. King
Seamus's rabbit steed emerged from a tunnel in the
snow beneath the bushes, the old king slumped dan-
gerously to one side in his saddle. Hellboy was afraid
he just might tumble off.

But the king held on, bringing his ride to a stop
before him. Two Graken soldiers left their ranks to
come to the king, helping him to dismount.

The two soldiers returned to their ranks, leaving
the king standing alone. Hellboy noticed that the old
Spriggin was wearing armor as well, his fashioned
from an Old Milwaukee beer can, and there was a
sword dangling at Seamus's side that, if he wasn't mis-
taken, had at one time been the big hand from an old
Grandfather clock.

"Are you guys all right?" he asked the king.

"Silence!" the old Graken's voice boomed. Well, as
much as a guy who was six inches tall could boom.

"Here we go again," Hellboy muttered, not sure if
he had the patience today for the Graken's malarkey.

"The lifeblood of our kind has been stolen away,"
King Seamus went on. "And we stand on the brink
of war."

More like the brink of a nap, he thought, crossing his arms and waiting for the old-timer to finish. He hoped it was soon; his feet were getting cold.

"But a promise was sworn atop the head of the blessed woodchuck."

He knew *it was a woodchuck.*

"And the fearsome legions of the Graken Spriggin held their righteous thirst for battle in check, allowing the one who had vowed to return to them what had been stolen to fulfill his sacred oath."

It became eerily silent in the yard, the snow doing that weird thing where it seemed to take away all the sound.

"And did you?" King Seamus then asked, a look of intense anticipation on his dark, weathered features. "Was the sacred oath fulfilled?"

He thought about busting them a bit, telling them that he didn't find their special rock, but he did get them all their very own lawn gnome, then decided against it. These guys were looking a bit rough, and he was sure that it was tied to the missing Sheela-Na Gig.

"It was," Hellboy said, and he glanced down at the large, tarp-covered object at his feet.

A collective sigh went up through the gathered Graken, and King Seamus started to cry.

The tiny king raised his arms above his head, and a strange lilting song filled the quiet void of the yard. It spread among the other Graken, and in a matter of seconds they were all singing as one.

A sudden wind kicked up, whipping about the top layers of the snow, and he watched with surprise as a miniature twister slowly began to take form, the magical vortex clearing away the inches of snow from the area of ground where he believed the Graken's special stone had rested.

The naked earth exposed, the Spriggin folk stepped back, giving him room to come forward.

"There," King Seamus said, pointing to the lifeless winter ground. "Return our blessed mum to the bed whence she was taken."

Hellboy picked up the stone and brought it to the waiting Graken. Carefully he lowered the great rock down into the impression, trying to place it precisely as it had been.

"Let us see her," Seamus said excitedly, the other Graken eagerly gathering at the sides of their king. "Uncover her loving face."

Hellboy did as he was told, ripping the tarpaulin away to expose the stone beneath.

"She's been through a lot," Hellboy said, reaching down to pat the sacred rock. "But I got her back to you. Just like I promised."

Seamus remained silent, gingerly going to the stone and laying a tiny hand upon it. He then pressed the side of his face to the smooth surface, and closed his eyes.

He remained like that for what seemed like hours. Hellboy found himself getting a little antsy, pulling up the sleeve of his coat to look at his watch.

"Would you look at the time?" he said. "I've got at least a two-hour drive back to . . ."

King Seamus opened his eyes, removing his face from Sheela-Na Gig.

"She's weak," he said sternly. "Some of her magic was stolen by forces that cared not for her well-being."

Hellboy nodded. "Yeah, sorry about that. There was nothing I could do—but at least you got her back, right? That's gotta count for something."

The old Graken king looked back to the stone. There was love in his eyes. "Yes, yes it does," he said, reaching out to adoringly stroke the surface of the rock. "And with our love and care she will grow strong again."

Hellboy smiled. "That's the spirit. So the war's been averted?"

"There will be no war," King Seamus said, turning to his gathered people to address them. "There will be no war!"

A wave of cheers went up through the crowd of Graken Spriggin, each of them now rushing forward to lay hands upon the holy object.

Seeing this as a perfect opportunity, Hellboy slowly began to move away, preparing to leave, and to allow the Graken Spriggin the opportunity to get reacquainted with their blessed mother.

"Hold," called a voice behind him, and he turned to see King Seamus riding upon his rabbit mount toward him. *Weird,* he thought. *Even the bunny looks healthier.*

"What can I do for you?" Hellboy asked, as the brindle-colored rabbit came to a stop, kicking up a small icy cloud, as the king pulled upon its reins.

"On the night you were born into this world, a terrible tremble was felt by Seelie Court," King Seamus began, his brogue especially thick. "And with your birth we of the old folk feared the end, that you were the harbinger of new times—dark times—and we were afeared."

Hellboy couldn't help but think of the Electricizers and their plans again, and how familiar it all was.

"Perhaps we have much in common, monster," Hellboy heard the words of the Archon Qemu'el rattling around inside his head. *"Both summoned to Earth to perform a function—a function of destruction."*

He found himself staring at the Graken Spriggin crowding around the stone at the back of the yard. "Just keep your noses clean and there'll be nothing to be afraid of," he said, with all the appropriate bluster.

He had rejected his dark destiny, but it still haunted him, circling like some hungry shark. Hellboy wished he could forget, to put it out of his head completely, but it was always there.

He turned to leave again, feeling the need to get back to the Bureau as soon as he could manage.

"But now, instead of fear, I feel only the joy of gratitude toward ye," King Seamus continued.

Hellboy looked down at the king, sitting astride his rabbit.

"A bringer of darkness that has instead returned the light to our lives," Seamus continued. "'Tis a wondrous thing that has happened."

The king removed his crown of animal teeth, and lowered his head. "And I bow to you in gratitude, and in reverence for all ye have done."

Then the King placed his crown back atop his head and steered his steed toward his people. They cheered as he approached, and Hellboy saw that some had started to dance around the great stone, the beginning of a celebration that he was sure would go on well into the night.

Hellboy left the festivities to the Graken, walking through the snow, suddenly feeling *lighter* than he had in days. *Maybe tonight'll be good for pizza, beer and a little Caltiki,* he thought, wondering if he could con Abe and Liz into joining him.

As he passed the porch on his way to the driveway, Don Kramer came out through the sliding door from inside the house, still wearing the coat that looked huge on him.

"Is . . . is everything all right?" Kramer asked, looking past Hellboy to see what was happening at the back of his yard.

He thought about the man's question, really chewing it over before answering. "Y'know, surprisingly enough," he said, continuing on to where he had parked the van, "Everything's just fine."

Hellboy glanced back one final time.

"Don't take any wooden nickels."

ABOUT THE AUTHOR

THOMAS E. SNIEGOSKI is the author of the ground-breaking quartet of teen fantasy novels entitled *The Fallen*, which is being turned into a trilogy of movies for the ABC Family Channel. His other novels include *Force Majeure*, *Buffy the Vampire Slayer/Angel: Monster Island*, tying in to the two popular television series, and *Angel: The Soul Trade*.

With Christopher Golden, he is the coauthor of the dark fantasy series *The Menagerie* as well as the young readers fantasy series *OutCast*, recently optioned by Universal Pictures. Sniegoski and Golden also wrote the graphic novel *BPRD: Hollow Earth*, a spinoff from the fan favorite comic book series *Hellboy*.

As a comic book writer, his work includes *Stupid, Stupid Rat Tails*, a prequel miniseries to international hit, *Bone*. Sniegoski collaborated with *Bone* creator Jeff Smith on the prequel, making him the only writer Smith has ever asked to work on those characters. He has also written tales featuring such characters as *Batman*, *Daredevil*, *Wolverine*, and the *Punisher*.

Sniegoski was born and raised in Massachusetts, where he still lives with his wife LeeAnne and their Labrador retriever, Mulder. He graduated from Northeastern University. He has just completed the two books in his *Sleeper Conspiracy,* a new series for Penguin Razorbill, and is currently hard at work on the first novel in a new supernatural mystery series called *A Kiss Before the Apocalypse.* Please visit him at *www.sniegoski.com.*

Don't miss these other exciting
Hellboy adventures!

Unnatural Selection
by Tim Lebbon

On Earth as it is in Hell
by Brian Hodge

The Bones of Giants
by Christopher Golden,
illustrated by Mike Mignola

The Lost Army
by Christopher Golden,
illustrated by Mike Mignola

HLBY.01